Praise For Alan Spencer

"*B-Movie Reels* by Alan Spencer takes the reader on a wild ride with even wilder monsters. Fans of B-movie horror flicks will eat this book up."
—The Writer's Journey

"A fun, campy, cheesy book with a high body count. If you like 60s and 70s style low budget horror films, you'll enjoy this fun homage to the genre."
—Famous Monsters of Filmland on *B-Movie Reels*

"*B-Movie Reels* proves Spencer to be a master of the pen (or word processing program) worthy of a look by any horror fan. Read this book now!!! (4.85/5)"
—Rage Circus

"This had all I could hope for in a horrific read; blood, gore, scares, suspense, and most importantly, depth of character."
—The World of Horror.com on *Ashes in Her Eyes*

Look for these titles by Alan Spencer

Now Available:

B-Movie Reels
B-Movie Attack
Psycho Therapy
Protect All Monsters
B-Movie War

The Doorway

Alan Spencer

SAMHAIN PUBLISHING

Spencer

Samhain Publishing, Ltd.
11821 Mason Montgomery Road, 4B
Cincinnati, OH 45249
www.samhainpublishing.com

The Doorway
Copyright © 2015 by Alan Spencer
Print ISBN: 978-1-61922-981-5
Digital ISBN: 978-1-61922-593-0

Editing by Don D'Auria
Cover by Kelly Martin

First Samhain Publishing, Ltd. electronic publication: August 2015
First Samhain Publishing, Ltd. print publication: August 2015

Dedication

For my wife, Megan, who saw me through a serious rough patch. Because of her, I didn't go insane. Instead, I wrote this book.

Chapter One

Morty Saggs accomplished what he always set out to do every Friday night after work. He hit Side Pockets for beer and billiards. Morty was riding a nice buzz with his coworkers from the United States Postal Service when the time hit midnight. Lighter in the wallet and even lighter in the head, Morty finally called it quits. The bar was only two blocks from his house, so he walked home on foot. What happened when Morty arrived at his house would play on repeat for the next days to come. That's how long his life would stop, because Morty would have no life, only this coming moment, and the impossible questions to answer.

He lived in the quiet town of Meadow Falls, Virginia. It was October 15th. The residential area was full of houses where people knew their neighbors. If someone was breaking into a house, a neighbor would call the police. If kids were being followed by a stranger, the little one could run to any house on the block and find safety. It was one of those neighborhoods where people wanted to grow old and retire. It soon wouldn't matter the type of neighborhood Morty lived in. Nobody would be able to help him.

Standing outside his house on the front lawn, Morty noticed the porch and kitchen lights were left on. Strange, because they should've been off at this hour. Making the house dark was his wife's passive aggressive way of saying he was out too late drinking. Glenda should've been asleep by now. Maybe she was waiting up for him, Morty supposed. That was unusual, though, because Morty could come home as late as two in the morning, and Glenda didn't wait up. He thought harder and decided Glenda might've had too much wine and gossip with her friends and passed out in bed and forgot about the lights. That had to be it. It wasn't anything complicated. Why else would the lights still be on?

Entering the house, Morty turned off the porch light and was about to turn off the kitchen's when he announced, "Sorry I'm late, honey."

No reply.

That wasn't a surprise.

The wine, he kept telling himself. Glenda was a hibernating bear.

Morty stripped out of his jeans. His heavy belt buckle thunked against the floor. He quietly edged down the hall, snuck into the bathroom, brushed his teeth, splashed water into his face and took a piss. Even if Morty was "retirement ready" and "old as the hills", as his post office counterparts dubbed him, Morty could still down the beer like those half his junior. Four more years, and Morty could retire. He imagined the RV that was parked out in the backyard right now, and Glenda and him taking that cross country tour of the United States they talked about doing one day. They would sell the house and the things they didn't need and travel from RV park to RV park. The American dream.

Wearing only boxer shorts, Morty walked to the upstairs bedroom. Morty relaxed on his side of the bed and reached out to spoon his wife when he realized the bed was unoccupied.

"Glenda?" Morty swept his hands up and down the bed. "Honey?"

Did she go over to Hannah's house? Old hens probably got it in their heads to do something out by the lake. Get enough wine into those two, and they can gab their faces off all night.

Morty laughed under his breath thinking about his wife chatting at a hundred miles an hour to her best friend Hannah. He got up, went down the stairs, and returned to the hallway where his jeans were spread out on the ground. Glenda would scold him about not throwing his pants in the laundry hamper. *You can go out and drink and be stupid, but it is too much to ask to put the laundry where it belongs?*

If Glenda left him a text, Morty had missed it. He was too busy getting lubricated at Side Pockets to notice texts. Retrieving his cell phone from his pants pocket, he found there were no missed messages. Morty thought about the kitchen fridge. There could be a note for him there. He flipped on a few more lights. On the fridge were the usual magnet souvenirs of the places they'd been like Las Vegas, The Alamo, Niagara Falls and Branson, Missouri, but there was no note about Glenda's whereabouts.

He peered outside through the front window. Glenda's car was still here. That didn't mean Glenda wasn't at Hannah's house.

Glenda forgot to tell you she's going out.

You've done it before without meaning it.

Morty's eyes were wide open. He was no longer on his way to falling asleep under the heavy blanket of alcohol. Something wasn't right. That gut feeling nagged him. He imagined various scenarios. Glenda on the basement floor having had a stroke, or a heart attack, or suffering a bad fall. Glenda's skin being sheet-white. Glenda dead.

"Glenda!"

Maybe it was his drunken state that was elevating his emotions. It didn't stop him from doing what he thought was best. Morty headed down the basement stairs. He almost took a header until he stopped himself by grabbing the handrail he installed two years ago after suffering a fall and breaking his left wrist.

Morty was in his boxer shorts, but he was burning hot. He flipped on the light. The crawlspace was designed as a homemade rumpus room. A door connected this room to the laundry room. The laundry room led to their backyard. On the porch, a grill sat under an awning where family gatherings were hosted. The Saggs had their family reunion in that backyard last year. Morty's sixtieth birthday party was the last event under that awning, pulled off flawlessly by his loving wife.

How many times had the name "Glenda" left his lips? He kept saying the name louder and more insistently. Morty returned upstairs and dialed Glenda's cell phone. She didn't leave the house without it. She was all about having what she needed in an emergency. She wasn't the type to go off somewhere without telling him.

Morty dialed the phone. It went off in the kitchen. Glenda's cell phone was on the table. Wherever she had gone, she didn't take it with her.

Glenda was at Hannah's. She had to be.

Call Hannah.

In the back of his mind, Morty wondered if he was overreacting.

You drank way too much tonight. It's messing with your thinking.

Morty wanted this matter resolved in a hurry nonetheless. He rushed into the room they designated as a computer/office room. He opened the drawer of the desk and fished out the book of phone numbers of everybody they knew. Hannah Albertson was the second name he located. Morty dialed her number. He didn't care if it was late. This was his wife, and until he knew where Glenda was at, he'd turn over every stone and call every person.

Nothing bad has happened. Calm down. What if she's over at Hannah's house, and Glenda forgot to leave you a note or call you? It happens. People forget. You're going to make yourself look like an asshole.

Morty had trouble going along with that idea, even now, because Glenda always communicated everything to him. She had had a father who suffered from Alzhemier's. The man just up and walked out of the house and was found three days later emaciated and near death. From then on, Glenda always wanted to know where Morty was between

Point A and Point B. The three-day panic involving her father was hell, and Glenda refused to live through that hell again.

The phone was ringing. On the fifth ring, a sleep-heavy voice answered.

It was Hannah.

"Hello?"

"It's Morty. I'm sorry to wake you. Is Glenda there?"

"Why would she be over here? We came over to your house, remember? We were done at about ten-thirty. We can't stay up like you, Morty. Mr. All-Nighter."

Morty wasn't in a joking mood. "So you're saying she's not over there? That Glenda didn't leave the house tonight? For anything? Anything at all?"

"No, Morty. She was at your house when I left. Morty, you're scaring me. Is there something wrong? Morty? *Morty?*"

He didn't hear Hannah anymore. Everything around him was cancelled out by the odd smell of burnt wood and rubber, and something he else he couldn't quite put his finger on. Something, wrong. Morty hadn't smelled it earlier. He would've, because it was so distinct and unpleasant. It was heavy and uncomfortable. It made him think if he kept breathing it in, he could get sick.

Morty put the phone back on the receiver, cutting off Hannah's words. He was drawn to the smell. Every part of him was compelled to seek out the odd tang.

What the hell is that smell?

The search led him to the upstairs bedroom. The stench was eye-watering and gag-inducing. Morty coughed against it, his throat wanting to close, every part of his body shielding itself from something that was potentially poisonous and so wrong.

When he flipped on the bedroom light, Morty was startled so hard he backpedaled against the wall and unleashed a shout.

"*God!*"

Morty had no chance to get a grip. He faced the bedroom doorway without moving an inch. Under his breath, he was muttering the words fast, "*It shouldn't be there. It shouldn't be there. It shouldn't be there.*"

Jagged lines traced the bedroom's doorway. The tracing was the color and texture of charcoal. How long had it been there? Why did it smell so awful?

"*...Glenda...Glenda, where are you...?*"

Morty sank into the floor, bursting into tears.

He couldn't take his eyes off the strange charred marks around the doorway.

Chapter Two

Morty didn't hear the police enter the house, nor had he heard their knocks at the front door. The cops ended up letting themselves inside. Morty hadn't moved an inch since spotting the odd markings around the bedroom doorway. He was brought back to life by the tall officer who was startled by the homeowner crouched on the ground with wide eyes and a horrified expression.

"Sir, are you okay? Mr. Saggs?"

Morty pointed at the wall. "The doorway. Do you see it?"

It was the officer's turn to wear an outrageous expression. "It's just a doorway, sir. I'm not sure what I'm supposed to be seeing. Could you please put some clothing on so we can ask you about the concerned call we received from a Hannah Albertson?"

The charcoal tracings around the doorway were gone. Morty blinked his eyes in disbelief. The black marks had simply vanished. The smell was missing too. Morty realized he was standing in his boxer shorts with two police officers in the room. What use would it be to argue what he'd seen when it wasn't there anymore? He'd only make himself look crazy, if he hadn't already.

What mattered now was finding out the whereabouts of Glenda.

The officers let him put on pants and a shirt. When Morty entered the living room, the police officers were ready to ask him questions about his wife. Hannah had already told them a lot about the situation.

So you came home from where?

When was the last time you saw your wife, Mr. Saggs?

What time did you leave the house tonight?

When did you return?

You have no idea where Glenda could be?

Any chance she'd be out somewhere and you don't know it?

Did you two get into any arguments of any kind, or anything that could've made your wife want to leave the house? Anything at all, even if minor, we need to know, Mr. Saggs. I know this is difficult.

Morty answered the questions the best he could while grappling with what he'd seen in the bedroom. The black tracing around the doorway. Why did it disappear when the police arrived? Had he imagined it? Was he losing his damn mind?

By the time the officers asked their questions, and re-asked a few of them, one of the officers, an Officer Greene, offered Morty a business card.

"Since Glenda's only been unaccounted for such a short period of time, we can't start a search just yet. It still could be a misunderstanding. These kinds of things happen. We're going to double check the property to make sure there's no signs of foul play. Call the number on this card if anything happens, especially if your wife turns up. In the meantime, just sit tight, Mr. Saggs."

Officer Greene went on to say other things designed to be comforting. *These things happen. It's only a matter of time. She'll turn up. And if you think of anything else we should know, don't hesitate to call.*

When the cops were finished and had left the house after finding no signs of a break-in or foul play, Morty could only do one thing. He called his daughter. Cheyenne answered on the fifth ring. She sounded a lot like Hannah, being disturbed from a deep sleep. Cheyenne was a five-hour drive from their house. It was almost three-thirty at night. Morty didn't consider the hour when dialing.

"Dad, is that you?"

Morty failed to tone down the sense of urgency.

"Yes, it's me. Please be honest with me. This is very important. Has your mother been in contact with you recently?"

"Dad, what's wrong? You sound upset."

"Just tell me if she's called you. Has she told you anything in confidence? Like she's upset with me, or anything. Please. Don't hold back anything. This is very important."

"I haven't talked to Mom since two weeks ago. We were planning on coming over with the kids. Dad, why are you calling me at this hour and asking about Mom? Has something happened to her?"

Morty was breathing hard. "I, your mom, I can't find her. She just, I came home tonight, and she wasn't there. I went out like I do with the boys from work, and she stayed home, and when I came home, your mom wasn't there. I don't know how else to explain it. I'm so worried. I think something might've happened to her. I've got a bad feeling. I hope it's nothing. I didn't make her mad. We haven't been fighting. Everything's good between us. So if you know anything that might explain her disappearing like this, I really need to know it. Even if it's hard for me to hear."

Morty had trouble breathing. He clutched his chest with his free hand and concentrated on taking breaths.

"No, nothing. Dad, I swear, nothing's going on as far as I know. I promise."

Cheyenne asked what the police had to say. He told her the police thought it was too soon to form a search party. It could be anything. It could be nothing. Cheyenne told her the police's advice was sound and promised she'd be over first thing in the morning. After telling Morty she loved him, and that everything would be okay, she ended the conversation.

Sitting on his hands and letting time burn agonizingly slow until he did hear or didn't hear anything from Glenda wasn't enough for Morty. It was still pitch black outside. Glenda could be out there. Something could've happened to her. Somebody might've taken her somewhere. She could be in danger, and he was sitting in this house doing nothing. Damn his imagination! His mind wouldn't stop spinning awful scenarios involving Glenda.

Morty put on his shoes and jogged up and down the block with a flashlight. He combed through everybody's yards for anything strange or out of place. The cops didn't look this hard. Why didn't they look that hard? They would scour the land for their own wives and kids.

Coming up with nothing, Morty ran back to the house and got into his car. He canvassed the neighborhood, peering into dark lawns, parked cars, and houses with only their front porch lights on. Everybody in Meadow Falls, Virginia, was asleep, as they should be. Morty envied those who got to sleep through the night peacefully.

Where could she be? She's not upset at you. Maybe she's thinking somewhere alone. Where would she go at this hour?

There was only one place Glenda would go to think. It was unlikely at this hour, but maybe, just maybe…

Morty drove to Hillsdale Lake. It was a fifteen-minute drive, and by the time he reached the lake, he remembered Glenda's car was still at home. She couldn't have driven here.

Maybe someone drove her here.

That's not right. Her friends were with her.

Yeah, until ten-thirty. Then everybody went home. That doesn't make it impossible for somebody to take her here.

What am I really doing? I have no clue what I'm doing.

Driving around the edge of the lake itself, he knew this was a mistake. He was panicked. He should calm down. It was only a matter of hours Glenda had been gone. Morty had watched too many of those unsolved mystery shows.

Morty gave a start when he saw a red flicker in the distance. A light of some kind. He rushed out of the car and ran on foot towards the unidentified light.

"Glenda! Please let that be you! Glenda!"

"Shit! Run!"

He caught three teenagers, two guys and a girl, stub out a cigarette, and then take off running. Morty smelled marijuana.

Morty was shouting like a maniac. "Have you seen a woman? She's about sixty years old. Black and gray hair. About five foot tall. Her name's Glenda? Please, have you seen my wife? Hey! Come back and answer my questions!"

The three left Morty in the dust. They were long gone.

Seriously. What am I doing here?

Morty caught his breath from running so hard and then he got back into his car and drove home.

Chapter Three

Morty smoked because he couldn't sleep. It was something to do to keep him occupied. He watched the sun turn the night into purple, red, then orange. Morty should've been tired, but he was shaking. He knew he'd crash at some point later that day. What did somebody do in this position? Did they lose their minds with worry?

He ran through the previous day, how him and Glenda were both facing a full weekend off of work. Glenda was a nurse who worked in the ICU. She had three days off in a row. It was her weekend to pick out where they went out to eat on Saturday night. They talked about normal couple stuff the other day. The kind of things two people who'd been together for several decades talked about.

What if he didn't ever find out what happened to Glenda? She would be one of those people who disappeared one night, and the mystery would only deepen as the days, weeks and months ticked by. How could he live not knowing what happened to her?

Morty didn't pray. He wasn't religious. But the way he prayed recently, it was more like begging and hoping God might hear him. He prayed out loud that this was only some stupid misunderstanding. Morty wouldn't be mad. He'd hug his wife, hold her close, and maybe he wouldn't ever let go of her ever again. It would be his turn to be the overbearing partner. *Call me when you.../check in when you.../let me know when you.../don't forget to let me know if you end up doing.../if you stay out late, please...*

Nothing was bad between them. He told himself that for the hundredth time. They loved each other. Nothing was wrong. They weren't fighting. Furthering his argument, none of Glenda's things were packed. Her jewelry, family heirlooms, even her purse (her purse!) were all in the house. That solved the mystery. Glenda didn't leave him, or go off somewhere to escape her husband.

That was a small consolation.

Glenda was still unaccounted for.

It was worse that her possessions were still here. Maybe it would be better if her things were packed. Morty pictured every dresser drawer empty of her things. Her side of the closet being cleared out, leaving his simple button-up shirts and T-shirts and pants. It would mean she left on her own accord. She was safe. She could be won over. Glenda could return home.

Someone forced her out of the house. He knew it. That gut feeling. Nothing was right in this house.

And the smell suddenly returned.

The doorway.

Smells he couldn't identify caused the house to reek. Morty tried to hold his breath against it. There was no use trying. The smell was so intense everything in the house stank, including his own skin.

Morty was afraid to enter the bedroom. He was compelled because he didn't understand what was happening. It was clear the two cops hadn't seen the doorway and the charcoal tracings.

He stood in front of the doorway in challenge. Morty's body quivered. His heart was on speed. What was he supposed to do now? The black tracings around the doorway, who, or what, put them there?

Stress. It had to be stress. People acted different when under extreme duress. Morty was imagining the doorway and the smells. That had to be it. His imagination was at work.

Morty stepped up slowly to the doorway. He touched one of the vertical lines. It crumbled, coming apart like greasy chalk. New smells were kicked up, ones he could only describe as burnt wood, maybe burnt meat. When he crushed the piece of black between two fingers, he uncovered an insect's exoskeleton.

"What *is* this?"

It disgusted him, causing him to run into the bathroom and wash and scrub his hands under such hot water his skin turned bright pink.

Somebody's messing with me.

I'm going crazy.

Morty was on the verge of breaking down into tears, when a surge of white-hot anger burned in him.

One thing I do know, those markings are gone!

Morty stomped into the kitchen, reached under the sink for a plastic bucket and filled it with liquid dish soap and water. He grabbed a Brill-O pad, and if it tore the wallpaper, Morty didn't care. He didn't want those nasty markings on his walls.

Returning to the bedroom, Morty was scrubbing the walls wearing yellow dish gloves. He wouldn't touch that infernal black shit ever again! He furiously dipped the Brill-O pad into the soapy, burning hot water. Morty rubbed the rough side against the wall. He was gritting his teeth, sweat was rolling into his eyes and he was cursing, muttering things unconsciously, and feeling his skin burn red. Flicking bubbles and splashes of water onto the wood floors, he was making fast progress. The outline of the door was almost erased completely. The soapy water in the bucket was a nasty gray and black, the color of tar and fresh asphalt, and just as hot, or was he imagining the black owned a heat?

The doorbell was going off. How many times had it rung before he heard it? Pounding against the front door could be heard between the doorbell rings.

"Dad? Dad, are you home? Dad? *Dad!*"

The floor surrounding him was soaked in sudsy water. His pants were covered in bubbles and soaked through wet. Parts of the wallpaper were scratched up to the bare grain. Only water and soap dripped down. There was no black. No mess. Only soap water. Morty was sobbing as the doorbell kept ringing and his daughter called out for her father, who was possibly losing his mind.

Chapter Four

What a mess Cheyenne had walked into, Morty thought while taking a shower. Cheyenne told him she would clean up the mess in the bedroom. She asked what he was doing, and all he could do was cry and say, "*I don't know. I just don't know.*" Morty could only apologize. Cheyenne said don't worry about it. No need to explain. He'd had a bad night. And Morty knew he wasn't much to look at, with his teary eyes and body covered in soapy water, trying to tell her why he was covered in soapy water and only crying harder because he couldn't tell her because the reason was insane. He didn't dare tell her about the markings around the doorway. Morty could've slipped headfirst into that torturous world of self-pity and helpless desperation if it weren't for his beautiful daughter.

Thank God for Cheyenne, he kept thinking. *She'll see me through this bad situation.*

Cleaned up and dressed, Morty met his daughter in the kitchen. She had made him breakfast. It was a nice spread of eggs, bacon, toast and coffee. Morty knew she was doing something just to be doing something. He understood that. What else could they do? They both picked at the food, drank coffee and hashed out the situation. Looking at his daughter, who was already in her thirties, had two little girls (Cindy and Jessica) and was enjoying a career as a tax auditor, he knew she was just as much of a mess about Glenda as he was, because in reality, things weren't looking good. They could lie, inject false hope into their conversations, but something was seriously wrong here. Glenda should be home. She shouldn't be somewhere else. Glenda was in danger.

Cheyenne asked this question after rehashing Morty's conversation last night with the police: "Then what should we do next? What do people do in these situations?"

"I never thought I'd go through something like this," Morty said. "It's hard to answer that question. Your mother's always been a straight arrow. I've been the bad one. The guy who goes out and drinks and stays out too late when he should be home with his wife, making sure nothing bad happens to her."

"Dad, no." Cheyenne moved across the table and hugged him. "You've done nothing wrong. You can't live life like bad things are going to happen constantly. People go out on Friday nights. There's nothing wrong with that. Don't blame yourself, Dad. I'm your daughter. I grew up with you, and I know you, Dad. You were great to Mom. I have a lot of friends who can say a lot of bad shit about their parents, but you two were great. I'm a lucky girl to have a father like you. We're going to figure this out together. Everything is going to be okay."

"What about your kids? And your husband? I bet he's worried sick."

"I've taken care of everything. Dane is out of town on business, and the kids are being watched by Dane's mother. They'll be okay. I'm here, Dad. So what's our next move?"

The next move was checking in with the police. Nothing had turned up, they told Morty over the phone, and he was told to keep waiting. A detective was being assigned the case, and the investigation into the disappearance of Glenda Saggs would be underway very soon.

The investigation into the disappearance of Glenda Saggs.

The sound of it hit Morty the wrong way.

The food he ate, what little, wasn't staying down.

"Excuse me, Cheyenne."

He rushed to the bathroom and puked up the breakfast. The process left his midsection in pain. Morty rested his head against the rim of the toilet, closed his eyes and tried to collect himself.

You have to be strong for Glenda. Do everything you can to find her. Break down later, fall apart later, blame yourself when all else fails later, but not now. Glenda needs you right now.

Another thought bothered Morty. The way the police assigned a detective so quickly to the case. It was less than twenty-four hours, and they were already treating this like a murder. Things were happening so fast, and Morty questioned if he had it in him to take everything on.

Cheyenne tapped on the bathroom door.

"Dad, you okay in there?"

Morty got up off the floor, rinsed out his mouth with tap water, and looked at his haggard face. He had graying hair on both sides of his head with no hair on top. A bird's nest, as they called it. His eyes were heavy, every feature sagging a little from lack of sleep and hard emotions. If he didn't find his wife soon, Morty hated to think how he'd look in the future.

"Yeah, honey. I'll be okay."

After he came out of the bathroom, the phone rang. Morty rushed to the phone, hoping it was Glenda.

It wasn't Glenda.

It was a man named Detective Larson. He asked Morty if he wanted to come down to the station for a talk. Morty said he did. Cheyenne drove him, the two of them eying every house, stretch of highway and building with extra scrutiny. Morty imagined seeing Glenda laid out on a patch of grass, or being pulled into a car as she screamed and attempted to escape the clutches of some evil criminal or pervert, or worse, her body sprawled out in a vacant lot.

People die when they disappear.

You have to be prepared.

You have to be realistic.

"…Dad?"

Morty snapped out of it. "Yes, honey."

"Who was the last person to see Glenda last night?"

"Three of her friends came over to the house to play board games and drink wine."

"So between you leaving for the bar, and Glenda having friends come over, she's unaccounted for."

"That's what it looks like."

"And no signs of a break-in, or a struggle inside, or anything suspicious?"

They'd been through this before, but Morty didn't mind going through it again. What else were they going to talk about?

"That's what confuses me. Glenda didn't up and leave. I don't see *how* with the car and her belongings still here. And it doesn't look like anybody got into the house. I don't know, Cheyenne. I wish I did. I'd give anything to know where your mom is."

"I know you would, Dad."

Father and daughter were quiet for the rest of the way down to the police station.

Chapter Five

Hannah, Glenda's best friend, was standing outside Detective Larson's office. She had talked to the detective ten minutes before Morty's arrival. Hannah worked with Glenda, both women being nurses in the ICU. They were inseparable since they were friends in grade school. Hannah told Morty and Cheyenne how she kept calling the station demanding they take action, and Morty thanked her for it.

"I feel like I'm falling apart. I'm worthless." Morty fell into a bout of tears. "I looked for her in the neighborhood last night. I searched people's yards. I even drove out to Hillsdale Lake shouting her name. I swear I'm going crazy. It doesn't feel right without Glenda in the house. I'm so busy feeling sorry for myself I should be doing more."

Hannah grabbed Morty by both arms.

"No, Morty. You're upset, and you have every right to be. I kept calling the station last night, and they wanted to shrug me off and tell me to wait. I'm not waiting another second. Glenda was happy last night. She even said she was looking forward to her big lug of a husband barreling through the door. I talked to that Detective Larson asshole in there, and he had the audacity to question you, Morty. I've known Glenda practically my whole life. Everything was good between you guys. How dare he even whisper an accusation your way."

"He thinks maybe I had something to do with it?"

"Okay, maybe he didn't directly say you could've done something. The detective just asked a ton of questions about your relationship with Glenda. He was implying things, and I didn't like it."

Cheyenne stepped in and gave Hannah a hug. "Thank you for helping, Hannah." Cheyenne and Hannah knew each other well. When Cheyenne was growing up, Hannah often babysat her. "The police are only doing what they can to put everything together. They know Dad didn't do anything. It's only procedure."

"Yeah, I suppose. I still don't like how he kept asking questions about you, Morty.

The guy rubs me the wrong way."

Morty tried to calm Hannah even though he enjoyed her command of the situation.

"But it makes sense, thinking like a detective. Between you and the girls leaving the house and me showing up last night, Glenda vanished. Why not question me? If it gets Glenda home again, accuse me of anything. As long as I get her back, none of that matters."

"Just don't let that detective bully you around. If he gets to grilling you too hard, ask for a lawyer. These detectives only want to solve their cases and move on. They don't love Glenda like we do.

"Speaking of, would you help me drive around town putting out flyers, Cheyenne? I ordered the print shop in town to make a bundle. We'll go around town posting them. I have to keep doing something, or I'll go out of my mind. After that, I want to go door-to-door and ask everybody in the neighborhood if they saw anything last night. We have to do this as fast as possible. The more time passes, the more details people forget."

Cheyenne agreed. Dad said he'd call them after he was done talking to the detective and meet up somewhere. The three of them agreed today would be dedicated to Glenda.

Detective Larson stepped out of his office. The man was in his early fifties, his face peppered gray and black from not shaving. He had a sizeable gut but his hard face said he was far from lazy.

The detective shook Morty's hand. "Good morning, Mr. Saggs. I'm Detective Larson."

Cheyenne and Hannah left him and the detective alone. Morty entered the detective's office. It was a cramped room with steel filing cabinets, a computer covered in sticky notes and pages and files stacked on his desk.

"Have a seat, Mr. Saggs. This is going to be easy today. I only want to run through a few things."

The detective asked about the details about last night up to and after Glenda's disappearance. The expected questions: *Was she upset about anything? Would she leave for any reason? Did you guys have any arguments?*

Morty gave him the answers.

"Hannah pretty much gave me the same details," the detective said when Morty was finished talking. "It appears Glenda had no reason to leave. Everything was good in her life. So her disappearance is confusing. I'm sure this must be hard for you."

"It has been, Detective. I never thought I'd be in this situation."

"Nobody does."

The detective opened a file, read it over and suddenly remembered something he wanted to say.

"Oh yes, I read the report from last night written by one of the officers on the scene. They said nothing was out of place, *except for you*."

"Except for me?"

Morty didn't like the way he said "except for you".

Hannah's warning was ringing true.

This detective could turn out to be a serious asshole.

If this joker grills you too hard, mention getting a lawyer.

Morty had nothing to hide, but the way the detective was looking at him with question marks in his eyes, he felt anything but reassured.

"I'm sorry, Morty. I'm making you feel uncomfortable. I meant to say one of the officers said you were in an especially distressed state. Care to explain why that may be?"

"It's simple really. My wife is missing. She wasn't home when I came home. Glenda never does this. Ever. I was frantic. I lost control over myself. What else can I say?"

The detective eyed Morty for ten agonizingly long seconds.

"Any husband would feel that way. In the report, it states you didn't answer the summons at your door. The officers had to come in, and when they did, they heard you making strange noises. Like you were scared of something. 'Terrified' was the word used in the report. You were up against the wall pointing at a door. Care to share what was going on in your mind? Honestly, that's my only concern. Your state of mind that night, Morty, raises questions. I'm sure you can clear things up for me. Please don't take this the wrong way."

Detective Larson didn't like Morty's shift of expression, because Morty was angry.

"Now hold on, Mr. Saggs. I'm not accusing you of anything. Everything I know will help me in this investigation. Anything, and I mean anything at all, that stands out in reports, I have to follow up on. It's my job. I'm only doing this to find your wife. Answering the question will only allow me to move on to something more pertinent to the case. Please, Morty, what was on your mind when the officers came onto the scene?"

Morty wasn't sure if being honest was the best option. He'd make himself sound crazy. Suspicious too. The detective was giving him the inquisitive eyes again. The detective could cut him open with that stare if it meant facts would spill out of him. But if he lied and said nothing was going on in his head that night, it might mean the detective spending too much time on Morty as opposed to concentrating on other things that might actually help find Glenda, like the man had suggested.

So Morty told the truth, though everything in him told him it was a bad idea.

"It's going to sound crazy."

"Then sound crazy. Just say what you know. That's all I ask. Let me make sense of it. It's my job. That's why they pay me."

Morty sensed the shift in Detective Larson's demeanor.

"When I couldn't find Glenda, and I was alone in the house, I smelled something awful."

That tidbit made Larson sit up straighter behind his desk.

"You *smelled* something?"

"It was like the smell of burning. I go into my bedroom, and there's a black outline around the doorway. It was like a charcoal outline. When the cops get there, it vanished. That's why I didn't say anything. I'm going to admit it. I think I might've imagined it."

"Or maybe not." Detective Larson jotted a few things down on the notepad tucked in his breast pocket. "So the charcoal outline around the doorway isn't on the wall now?"

"No, it's not."

"But you believe it was last night. Was there anything else around the doorway, or on the wall itself? Anything else, like, forgive me, satanic symbols, or something that would resemble cult activity?"

"Oh no, Detective. Forget it. I shouldn't have mentioned it. I imagined it. It's nothing like you say."

"You should mention everything, Morty. Please, anything else you might know? Seriously. It's very important I hear it, no matter how strange."

"Well, the only other thing is that the outline smelled awful."

"And you're sure nobody was in the house with you last night?"

"Pretty sure, but then again, I was really worked up. I can't say for sure."

Detective Larson was in his head for several minutes while writing things down. "Okay, Morty, that's all I need for now. I'll get back with you very soon."

The detective got up and shook Morty's hands.

"You have a wonderful daughter, and Hannah, she kept calling our office last night checking in. They're good people, Morty. We're going to find your wife. Don't worry."

Morty left the office, and before he reached the car, a young woman wearing a blue dress and overcoat flagged him down. She was a reporter. Her name was Janet Ranscombe. He had read a few of her articles in the local paper. Morty wanted to tell her to go take a hike until she mentioned talking to Hannah and Cheyenne just twenty minutes ago. Janet was quick to mention that the more media coverage there was on the case, the better off they were in regards to finding Glenda.

Morty really liked that idea.

It made sense to him in the moment.

He would later regret it.

Morty touched on how Glenda was a dedicated nurse, a loving wife, a mother and just a good person, and that made the fact she was missing all the more concerning. Janet asked more details about last night, specifically if there was anything suspicious to take into consideration. He was tired from last night, and Morty didn't mean for the detail to slip out.

"Someone painted around your bedroom door?"

"No, I mean, it's, I'm not sure what was around the doorway. I might've imagined it. Never mind. Please, I'm under a lot of stress right now."

Janet didn't hear the "I might've imagined it" part. She was onto something, and she was really cooking.

"Tracings around the bedroom doorway, huh? So somebody was in the house, possibly? Sounds like foul play to me. Maybe somebody from the neighborhood. What do you think, Mr. Saggs?"

Morty couldn't reply. He'd said too much. He had said the wrong things on top of that. He shouldn't be talking to anybody even if Hannah or Cheyenne already did. They were strong women filled with determination, and he was on the brink of a collapse. Without Glenda, who was he? The reporter wouldn't understand that. And mentioning the doorway! He really fucked up.

"I have to go, I'm sorry."

Janet was hurling questions at him while in pursuit.

Morty ignored her, piling into his car and driving as fast as he could home.

Chapter Six

Morty had trouble breathing on the way home. His chest was full of pain. His breaths were shallow. It felt like someone was pressing against the bones of his sternum and compacting his lungs. Was he having a heart attack? A panic attack? Some kind of attack?

He breathed and breathed to steady his body and thoughts. So what if he told some dumb reporter about the doorway? He could deny it if anybody asked. Then again, he told Detective Larson about it being altered. He couldn't deny it.

Worry overcame him. He was pouring sweat, so worried about the doorway and the state of his sanity.

I'm going to end this nonsense right now. If I do this, I won't have to think about it anymore!

Morty pulled up into his house, stormed into his bedroom and stared hard at the doorway. It was just a doorway. Nothing more, nothing less. He wasn't crazy.

You see, it's nothing.

God, what does Cheyenne think of me? I looked like a crazy person when she came into the house this morning.

She doesn't think anything.

Nobody thinks anything.

This is about Glenda, not me.

Morty decided the best thing to do was call Cheyenne's cell and stay busy. Keep himself occupied so his mind wouldn't turn up the volume on the things that made no sense. He called and met Hannah and Cheyenne at Hammond Park. Cheyenne, Morty and Hannah split up, each taking a heavy stack of printed flyers. Seeing recent pictures of his wife and the word MISSING above her gave Morty a start. This was really happening. Glenda could be found dead. She might *never* be found at all. The weight of it was impossible to overcome, so Morty threw himself into the effort of putting up flyers and asking locals and friends, shop owners and literally anyone he crossed paths with if they'd seen Glenda Saggs, and would they please take a flyer and call the police if they knew anything?

How many flyers had he handed out? Hundreds? Hannah was the one who created the flyer, purchased the copies and was adamant about keeping the search going. Carol Myers and Brenda Jacoby, the other two women who drank wine and played board games at Morty's house last night, joined in the effort. Each was very disturbed that Glenda's whereabouts were unknown. After canvassing the neighborhood, they ate a late lunch. It was already three in the afternoon.

The four ladies, including Morty's daughter, kept spinning the scenarios as they waited for the food at Mac's Diner, a popular local eatery with hamburgers, shakes, and their famous chili fries.

Glenda was home at ten-thirty last night. Glenda was happy. Glenda didn't act strange, nor had she acted strange in the previous days, or weeks, before that night. Morty returned home at a little after midnight, and Glenda was gone, so that meant somewhere between ten-thirty and midnight, something had happened to Glenda. Glenda didn't leave on her own accord, because her purse, keys and car remained on the property.

Morty chimed in whenever he could, repeating facts, repeating times and repeating the question: where could Glenda be? What else could he do, or anyone, without any real evidence or leads to Glenda's whereabouts?

They talked more. Morty nibbled on his food. He couldn't force much down. Every small bite upset his stomach. He wasn't hungry. He wondered if he could ever eat again.

After leaving the diner, there didn't seem to be much else they could do, so they returned home. Hannah and her two friends returned to their homes, and that left Cheyenne and Morty alone.

It was four-thirty in the afternoon now. Cheyenne was calling her husband and giving him updates on what was happening.

I'm not sure when I'll be home/how are the kids?/Morty's hanging in there/it's hard on all of us/no telling where Mom is/it's a mystery right now/I'll tell Dad you said hello and to hang in there.

Off the phone, Cheyenne had that exhausted look on her face. She woke up in the middle of the night and drove into town to help her father. Morty loved his child in this moment. She was everything a parent wanted out of a kid. Responsible. Hard-working. And loving. So loving.

Morty ran his hand through her long black hair.

"Why don't you lay down and take a nap?"

"You need some rest too, Dad."

There was a knock at the door. Morty feared it was Detective Larson with bad news, or that Janet Ranscombe reporter with more questions or another attempt to make him look and feel like a fool.

Could you tell more about the doorway tracings? Paint a picture for me, would you? You really are crazy, Mr. Saggs. Clearly you murdered your wife, so let's go ahead and get that confession out of the way. Just let me hit the record button on my tape recorder.

The person at the door was Bruce Spaniel. Bruce was Morty's best friend ever since high school. They called him "The Spaniel". They both played high school football. Morty was the quarterback, and Bruce was his best wide receiver. Bruce used to be tall and lean in high school, but now he had a huge gut and a bald head. He was stern-looking to those who didn't know him, but Bruce was one of the most fun-loving, joking-around kind of people Morty had ever met.

"I heard about Glenda. I want to help in anyway I can."

"I'm not sure if there's a lot anyone can do but to keep looking for her."

Morty told his daughter he'd be outside talking to Bruce. Morty led his friend into the backyard and onto the back deck that faced the RV. They smoked cigarettes together, and Morty explained what exactly had happened last night with Glenda. There wasn't much to tell except "my wife is gone and I don't know where she went".

"I hope nothing bad has happened to her. I'm full of all kinds of terrible feelings. Something's not right. I know it. I'm not sure what I'd do without Glenda."

"You can't talk like that," Bruce said. "You say you didn't fight, and that she wasn't mad at you. You know women, pal. They get worked up over something, and you wouldn't have a clue. Something might've been riding her mind you didn't even know about. Who knows?"

"If it's that easy, it'd be a load off of my mind. Seriously. But I swear there wasn't anything wrong. I miss her, Bruce. I'll go crazy without her. I don't like to be alone. I hate not knowing what's going on. I know I haven't been the best husband in the history of husbands."

"What do you mean?" Bruce blew a jet of smoke from the corner of his mouth. "That's not true. Everybody has their bad spells and rough patches, but you're not a bad husband. You are good to Glenda. Valarie and I have gone through some shit too, especially when she lost her job and we went into debt. Oh my God, you have no idea how bad it can get. That's probably why we divorced. Money puts two people against each other like no other. But you two are rock solid."

Rock solid, Morty thought. That wasn't always the case. Not early on in their marriage at least. Morty couldn't help but let it all out. He hadn't told this to Bruce, or anyone, ever.

"God, I remember back in high school when we played for the Grizzly Bears. Every girl would lift up their skirts at us. Those were the fucking days. But that's what I enjoyed about Glenda so much. She didn't play into that popular quarterback bullshit. Glenda didn't care who you were. She was only impressed by the things that counted.

"It's funny, because I wouldn't have met my wife if it wasn't for that game against Fort Osage high school. Remember that one, man? I was going to throw a Hail Mary into the end zone, but one of the defenders bashed into my left side. My throw went wide, and I mean wide! The football sailed into the stands, and it hit Glenda right in the nose. You could hear the breaking of her nose from downfield. I think the whole county felt that hit. I basically punched Glenda in the face with a football.

"I stalked the hallways the following week to apologize to her. She had that giant bandage on her nose, and around her nose was all purple and swollen. I was so sorry, and she said it was okay in the way that you knew it was most definitely not okay. Glenda became my obsession. I had to win her over at any cost. I wasn't getting anywhere. She wanted nothing to do with me.

"Then it occurred to me, I worked at that Kroger grocery store. Her father was the manager. I don't know why I did this, but I apologized to her dad about the football to his daughter's face. Funny thing, he's a very religious guy. Super Christian. Fire and brimstone and damnation and all that stupid shit. But he loved football! I was this guy's hero. So I do what every father loves, and I ask his permission to take out his daughter to the prom. And I'm the only guy he'll let take his daughter to the prom, because he's so religious and protective of his daughter. I mean *really* overprotective to the point it's borderline psychotic. He'd cut your nuts off if he found out you'd even touched his daughter the wrong way. So it's either Glenda goes with me, or it's no prom for her at all, right?

"I don't know why I thought Glenda was super religious like her father. That's why I was shocked when before the dance, she offers me pot. Glenda's already got friends who can hook us up with booze after the prom. She's very much one of those wild childs pent up by their God-fearing parents. So after I apologize a million times about her nose, we realize how much we get along. We get drunk after prom, and one thing led to another, we have sex in my truck. The thing is I was stupid. I didn't use a condom. I didn't even know what pulling out was, or how to do it, and Glenda gets pregnant.

"Holy shit, her dad wanted my head on a platter. Our parents meet up in our living room after Glenda's pregnancy was made known. My mom offers them cookies and tea, and they talk things out like rational people. Can you imagine how awkward that was? Me, an eighteen-year-old sitting in my room as these people are talking about me and my future?

"The final outcome of the conversation is what my parents and Glenda's parents both decided. I was to get my high school diploma and then work full-time. I was to marry Glenda, support her and let Glenda go to nursing school. I heard Glenda's dad really dig into my parents. The guy was a mean old son of a bitch. I hate talking ill of the dead, but he's a fucking piece of work. According to that asshole, I wasn't going to deny his precious daughter a single thing out of life just because I couldn't keep my hands off of her on prom night. So I was to finish the few weeks of high school I had left and start working fulltime.

"I watched Glenda go to college, do well, become a nurse, and I started harboring this resentment towards her. I hated my job. I really hated it. I was trapped in that goddamn factory. I loved her, and I loved Cheyenne. Don't ever get me wrong on those two things. But I started to think about my future, and my life. I suddenly couldn't sleep at night. I would go out at night and drive around. Just around, I wasn't going anywhere. Glenda thought I was going out drinking and cheating on her. I didn't blame Glenda for thinking that. It looked suspicious. What else would a woman think when their husband sneaks out at night, right?"

He hadn't told Bruce this before, and the man was very curious about his story. Bruce wore a strange expression. Something was constantly on the tip of his tongue.

Whatever it was, Bruce wasn't saying.

"So what *were* you doing at night? Where did you go? Don't tell me you got into trouble."

Morty eyed the RV and couldn't help but tear up.

"I drove around town and tried to figure out what I was missing out on. It's like everybody conspired against me when Glenda got pregnant. Life stopped being about me and started being about everybody else. I did this for months, trying to come up with the answers. Then I come home real late one night, and there's a note on the refrigerator that says: *If this isn't what you want, then you need to tell me. I love you, but I'm not doing this anymore, Morty.* I did love her, and being at the house alone, like I was last night, it filled me with terror. A worse terror than working a job I fucking hated for the rest of my life. Being without her, I just can't imagine it. I won't. I refuse. My life is so much better with Glenda in it. So I figured out my shit real fucking quick. I quit my job, found a new job at the post office and the rest of my life has been great. Swear to God. So we do have a strong marriage, you're right, but it wasn't without its pitfalls. So I really don't get why Glenda would up and leave. After everything we've been through."

Morty was out of stamina to talk.

Bruce removed that odd expression.

Whatever was on his mind, it was gone.

"I never knew you went through that, Morty. You could've told me way back when, you know that? I would've listened."

"Sorry, man. It was very personal, what I was going through."

"No worries. I get it." Bruce flicked an ash off of his cigarette. "So what's going on now with the search?"

Morty talked about the flyers, spreading the word in the neighborhood, and how the police were going to take the next step in performing a wider search soon.

There wasn't much else Bruce could say.

Morty didn't have much of anything else either.

Bruce wished Morty the best, and if there was anything he needed to just ask. His friend went home. Morty walked back inside the house.

Cheyenne was sound asleep on the couch. Morty put a blanket over her and let her rest. He needed to sleep too. They were both exhausted. He laid in bed, closed his eyes, and hoped his missing wife would turn up soon.

Chapter Seven

It wasn't the God-awful smell or the strange red color of the room that forced Morty out of a deep sleep. It was the chills raking his body. Every muscle ached and throbbed, as did his head. The sheets were soaked in feverish perspiration. Morty was curled up on his side shivering so hard his shoulder blades were in pain. His throat was sore from a cold? The flu? Or some other sickness he didn't know about, maybe? Whatever was attacking his immune system, it kept him paralyzed on the bed facing the bedroom doorway.

Morty couldn't look away from it.

It was like a force compelled him.

What the fuck do you want from me? Goddamn you! What have you done with my wife? Am I going insane? Tell me, am I going crazy?

Morty thought he said those words out loud, but they only echoed in his mind. The charcoal tracings around the doorway burned. The charcoal black became a bright cinder-red. A heat emanated from the outline of the door.

Tell me what you want with me or else leave me alone? Did you take her away? Do you have Glenda? Give her back to me! Give her back, or, or, or I'll kill you!

God help me, I'll—

Show yourself so I can—

Tell me what this doorway means, and I will—

The room was thick with the smell of burning things. He could've been inside of a giant toaster oven. Glenda had overcooked a Thanksgiving turkey one year, and the bird was crispy black and inedible. The damn thing was nearly on fire. The gray smoke was something you could choke on. What was coming from the outline of the doorway was so much worse.

The doorway had crippled him. It had injected a sickness into his weary bones. Weighed down with these afflictions, Morty couldn't shout for help.

Cheyenne, run! Call the police, and get away from here fast! It's dangerous. The doorway.

It's evil!

Morty was coughing up smoke. His insides were being cooked by an intense heat. He could feel fluids boil inside his stomach.

Run, Cheyenne, run!

"—*she's dead, she's dead, she's dead, she's dead, she's dead, she's dead...OH GOD SHE'S DEAD!!!*"

"Dad, wake up! *Daaaaaaaaaad!*"

Cheyenne was shaking him hard by both shoulders. The force was knocking aside the sheets and pillows. He snapped out of the dream, the fugue state. Whatever he was going through, he didn't know the difference between dreams and reality or sleep and insanity. He was about to point at the wall, to say the doorway was dangerous, so get out of the room, but the perimeter of the doorway wasn't burning anymore.

Morty's throat was ragged.

How long had he been yelling?

She's dead.

She's dead.

She's dead.

How many times had he shouted those words at the top of his lungs? Poor Cheyenne. Morty considered how it must've been for her to wake up with her father shouting those horrible things. He kept apologizing to her. He was so, so sorry.

Cheyenne told him to breathe and not say a word.

She pressed her hand against his forehead. "Oh my God. You're burning up, Dad."

Cheyenne took his temperature. "You've got a fever. You need rest. This has been too much for you. You poor thing."

"It's been too much for everyone." Every syllable made his throat seize up in pain. "Glenda needs me. There's so much we don't know. I should be scouring the streets. I should be doing more than just—"

"We're doing everything in our power to find Mom. You can't keep on like this. You have to rest. I know it's the last thing you want to do. But look at you. You sound awful, and you're so pale. You have to keep yourself healthy."

Cheyenne gave him whatever over-the-counter fever and cold medicine Morty had in the medicine cabinet. Cheyenne brewed some hot tea. He sipped on it. Every little bit he forced down made him wince in pain.

"Sleep, Dad. Try not to think about anything else for now. We'll see how you feel in the morning. Deal?"

"Yes. Okay."

Morty checked the digital clock beside the bed. It was three in the morning. He did need rest. An overwhelming fatigue suddenly hit him. Whether it was the cold medicine kicking in or his body forcing him to close his eyes, Morty was fast asleep in minutes.

Cheyenne returned to bed.

She was very worried about her father.

Chapter Eight

Morty wanted to scour the earth for Glenda. He would search every house, question every citizen and replay the events of that night until he came up with something he missed. The problem: Morty simply couldn't move. Dr. Hillman, a doctor who lived four houses down from Morty's, was summoned by Cheyenne to check in on her ailing father. The doctor's assessment: he was overstressed, and he had succumbed to a mean virus. Dr. Hillman wrote a prescription for some antibiotics and medicine that would knock him out. Rest was what he needed, the doctor kept emphasizing. Cheyenne drove to the local Walgreen's to fill the prescriptions, while Dr. Hillman kept talking to Morty.

"I know you've had a hard few days, but you have to take care of yourself. Stress can do very bad things to the body. It's obvious you're not in a good place in your head, Morty, and it's perfectly understandable why. Everybody wants to see Glenda back home safe and sound. But you can't go against what your body is telling you. Cheyenne is doing a wonderful job with things here. She's going around town putting up flyers with that woman, what's her name? *Hannah*, yes, that's right. Everybody in town is doing their part. Everything is being done that can be done. You've already worried yourself sick, Morty. There's no need to make it worse. Rest. That's an order."

Morty promised he'd stay in bed. Not that he had a choice. The swelling in his head, the skull-compressing migraine, the burning hot fever, how he ached from head to toe, it kept him anchored down in bed.

Soon after Dr. Hillman wished him well and left the house, Cheyenne returned. She gave Morty the proper doses of pills from three different bottles. She assured him he would soon be asleep. Before he did slip back into a pharmaceutical slumber, the knock at the door concerned him.

It was Detective Larson.

Morty heard the detective talk at the front door to Cheyenne.

"Can I visit with Morty? Apparently he talked to a reporter the other day. The article is in the morning newspaper. It goes on about a doorway in this house. There's a whole supernatural slant to the case now. I'm getting all kinds of weird calls down at the station. People who think they have leads when all they have is a fabricated story to tell. I *really* need to talk to Morty and find out exactly what he told that reporter."

Cheyenne remained calm against the detective's urgency. "He's sick in bed. He's not well. I can give him a message later."

"Are you sure he can't talk now? It's really important that I—"

"My dad's stressed himself out to the point he's got a fever. He's asleep. If there's anything you need to tell him, you can tell me. The poor guy's been through enough already. We've all been through hell lately. Go easy on us, if you can. Please, Detective."

A long silence followed Cheyenne's response.

"Yes, you're right. I apologize. It's just that talking to press can complicate things. Even talking to the small-time local papers can cause a media firestorm. I've made a statement to the press about the case, and that's all the media needs to know. Please tell Morty not to give any more statements to anybody. Everything I'm doing is on the behalf of your mother. I'm doing everything I can to bring her home. I can't let a dumb reporter get in the way of finding Glenda safely."

Cheyenne thanked him, and said she understood his position. They went on to say a few things about arranging a voluntary search party to cover more ground tomorrow. By then, Morty had fallen into a deep medicated sleep.

Chapter Nine

Morty tossed and turned in bed. He wasn't in any better shape when he woke up, however many hours he had snoozed away. Tears streamed down from his eyes. Had he been sobbing? How did someone cry when they were asleep? His throat was so dry. When he coughed up mucous from the pit of his throat, his vision went double, and his skull tightened around his brains. *Such agony!*

Unable to will his body to get up from the bed for a drink of water, it was a matter of seconds after being awake that it didn't matter how much his body ailed him. The room was cast in that awful red color again. The room was a hot box of fire and cooking blood. Awful smells betrayed his nostrils of things that shouldn't be burned.

The outline around the bedroom doorway was so blaring bright he squinted against its powerful intensity. Morty shouted many things: questions, accusations, horror. The outline kept burning brighter with every word Morty spat in its direction. Then with all the power Morty could muster in his weakened state, he threw aside the blankets and sheets, lifted himself up off the bed, lunged for the wall and—

"—*I'm sorry, please don't hurt me! I only wanted to ask you some more questions. Jesus Christ, I'm so sorry. I shouldn't have let myself into the house. Please don't call the police. I didn't mean any harm. I only want to help your wife. Everybody in the community has good things to say about your wife. Hey, let me go you son of a bitch. What are you doing? You're HURTING me!*"

The blonde woman in Morty's clutches slipped from his grip and hit the floor hard. Her face was scrunched up in horror. A scream was about to leave her lips. Arms shielded her body from harm. Harm from him. Morty had been clutching her in one hand, and the other hand had torn a streak down her sweater, parting her bra, and revealing one of her breasts. Appalled, angry and terrified of the sickly man who suddenly sprang alive to assault her, Janet Ranscombe got back to her feet and fled the house. A collection of curses escaped the reporter's lips during every step of her fast retreat.

Morty collapsed back into bed and fell asleep again.

He would forget this moment ever happened.

The colors burning around the bedroom doorway were gone.

Chapter Ten

Janet Ranscombe buttoned her pea coat over her torn sweater to protect her decency as she fled Morty's house. Nail marks raked down her sternum and across her right breast. One of the bastard's nails had split her nipple. The wound stung, issuing a small amount of blood. The shock of it was still setting in. Janet stayed in her car parked across the street and collected herself. Her breath was starting to even out again. Her boss told her she needed a follow-up to her first story on the disappearance of Glenda Saggs. One just as sensational. People loved ghosts stories and missing persons cases, and put them together, it was investigative gold.

Looking in the rearview mirror, she saw her long blonde hair was undone. Morty had yanked on her ponytail as if to rip it from her scalp. Morty slapped her face and almost got a hold of her neck after clawing her chest.

What else would he have done to me if I didn't escape?

It was clear there was something wrong with Morty Saggs. He was psychotic and on the verge of a nervous breakdown. When psychotic people had breakdowns, innocent people were in danger. The burning question on her mind was, was his breakdown because of Glenda Saggs's strange disappearance, or was it because the man had something to do with her vanishing?

Was Morty Saggs a killer?

The possibility was strong.

More troubling still, when Janet knocked on the man's door earlier, she heard Morty call out to her from his bedroom. He said it was okay for her to come inside for a talk. He apologized for being sick and told her to keep his distance if she didn't want to catch his virus. Janet felt guilty exploiting him, but Morty was so friendly and welcoming. He said he'd do anything to have Glenda back home safe and sound. He was genuine. How could she not let her guard down? The man let her ask any question on her mind. Most of those questions pertained to the burning doorway he mentioned the other day. She asked him where this burning doorway had appeared. Morty pointed right behind her at the bedroom's doorway. She traced the edges of the doorway with her hand, merely grazing the surface. There was nothing special there. She felt like an idiot during that moment, then she was screaming. Morty rose up from bed and assaulted her. The altercation had happened in seconds.

Morty's wicked facial expression was etched into her memory. She feared the man. She feared for Glenda's whereabouts. Sure, she had done bad things in the past to get a story. Those were matters of bending the rules, but this, THIS, was morally reprehensible.

Janet had to do the right thing and tell the police that Morty Saggs could very much be a killer.

Chapter Eleven

Judging by the color of the drawn window shades in Morty's bedroom window, it was nighttime. Morty had slept through the entire day. He didn't feel much better after so much sleep. Morty would've slept longer if it weren't for the sound of the front door opening and closing and the sound of Hannah and Cheyenne talking to each other. Hannah checked in on Morty, peeking her head through the bedroom doorway. The woman looked absolutely exhausted. Hannah said there was a wide-scale search party happening, and everybody was hoping new facts pertaining to the case might surface. That Glenda would come home safe. He could only thank Hannah over and over again for everything she was doing for Glenda. Hannah told him to rest and to get better as soon as possible. When Hannah left the house, Cheyenne came into the room and checked his temperature.

"The fever's gone down a little bit. It's still too high. How do you feel?"

"About the same," Morty said, looking at his daughter, who was very tired. "This isn't just hard on me. It's hard on you too. Are you taking care of yourself?"

Cheyenne gave him that smile that said she was fine even though everything in her eyes said the very opposite.

"I bought you some egg drop soup. I know how much you like it."

Morty was starving. The very mention of egg drop soup had him perking up in bed. He ate the soup while Cheyenne took a shower.

When Morty ate the food, he noticed there was a speck of red under his pointer finger's nail. The red flaked away when he rubbed his fingers together.

Odd, he thought. *Where did that come from?*

Cheyenne was asleep in the other room. After eating, Morty too had fallen asleep for a few more hours. His dreams were empty and black, unlike his bedroom. The room was bright with that intense red. It stayed that color for minutes, painting Morty with its strange firelight color. Morty came out of his sleep only when the smell intensified. Sulfur infused with burning wood. He stared at the burning outline of the doorway. He had to understand it. The outline was cooking, smoldering and reeking. Morty wanted to make the pain in his eye sockets stop, but he couldn't draw his eyes from what was happening. Daggers of heat soldered his retinas. The room was burning his skin. The room was an oven, and he was being cooked alive.

Make it stop make it stop make it stop oh my God MAKE IT STOP!

He shielded his face with his hands. It didn't help, because the intensity of the light bled right through his hands. He could see his bones, like he was viewing a CAT scan picture.

Cheyenne! Cheyenne, are you out there? Stay away from this house. It's not safe here. Something is very wrong. I don't know what it is, but it's done something to Glenda. I just know it.

Morty, trying to escape the room, collapsed onto the floor. He was so weak. As he lay splayed on the ground, the red light eased up enough he could see more of the room again. He was facing underneath the bed. Morty saw it within arm's reach. The item had been hidden under the bed this whole time.

He reached out and touched it.

Glenda's slipper.

It was covered in dried blood.

Chapter Twelve

Morty woke in bed feeling like he never had a fever. In fact, he felt refreshed. That relief was curtailed when he remembered last night. The burning doorway. The horrible red color. And Glenda's bloody slipper under the bed. Morty shot up out of bed, lowered onto his stomach, and reached under the bed. He couldn't look. He was so afraid what he thought he recalled could be true. It would mean so many new things. Terrible, horrible things.

Uncovering the mystery, Morty gasped when his finger touched the slipper. When he retrieved it and put it up to the light, it was in fact Glenda's slipper. The toe was covered in three wild spots of blood.

Oh no, Glenda.

His heart sank. This proved foul play. Glenda was in danger. It wasn't speculation. It was fact. Something terrible had happened to Glenda. She wasn't just missing. She could be dead. Before Cheyenne woke up, Morty called Detective Larson with the startling news.

Detective Larson asked Morty to step outside when the crew arrived on the scene. Cops were canvassing the house and treating it like an actual crime scene. Detective Larson kept telling Morty it was only a formality. *Simple procedure. It means nothing against you. It's to find your wife, Morty. And we all want to find her in a safe and good way.*

Cheyenne stayed at Morty's side while this was happening. She was horrified to learn one of Glenda's slippers was found covered in blood. The lab was going to test the blood and confirm or disconfirm that it was actually Glenda's blood. People were coming and going in the house, like cops, investigators and anybody else who was involved in this type of investigation. Morty and his daughter stood there as quiet, concerned spectators.

Forty-five minutes into the home search, Cheyenne didn't like it when Detective

Larson asked if Morty would go down to the police station to answer some more questions.

"It's only some questions. There's no need to worry. I'm only trying to piece together my investigation with this new evidence."

Cheyenne wasn't so trustful. She wasn't afraid to speak her mind in front of the detective either.

"If he grills you too hard, don't say anything you don't mean. Ask for a lawyer if the detective starts treating you like a criminal. I know how these things go."

"I wouldn't force your father to say anything untrue. I'm not a detective from one of those TV crime shows. I genuinely care about you and your family. I'm only doing my job to the best of my abilities. So if you would, please, Mr. Saggs, come down to the station with me. We'll get this over with quickly."

Cheyenne was protective over her father, thinking that perhaps he could be the only living parent she had left. "You treat him right, Detective. He has rights."

Morty held his daughter in his arms.

"Like he said, it's only some questions. I'll do anything to find Glenda. I'm scared like you are, Cheyenne. It's natural to be scared. And we're going to stick together and bring our family back together. I promise nothing bad will happen. I trust the detective. He's worked very hard up to this point. Stay here. I want you to be here if anything turns up. Can you do that for me, honey?"

Cheyenne had tears in her eyes. There was nothing good to draw from this predicament, and they both knew it. Finding blood in a missing person's case was never a positive thing.

Morty left the house with the detective. They drove in the detective's vehicle. As they drove to the station, Morty looked back at his home as it grew smaller in the rearview mirror. The police were hard at work checking out the property. He couldn't lie to himself. Sure, he could stretch the truth with Cheyenne if it meant not breaking her heart, but in his own mind, there was no lying. This was looking more and more like a murder case.

Chapter Thirteen

They weren't in Detective Larson's office this time. They were in an interrogation room. The walls were a cold institutional white. The ceiling lights were two times brighter than they should be. Maybe it made the room slightly hotter, Morty thought, so he'd spill whatever information the police believed he was holding back that much quicker. The table between them had a greasy top, making Morty keep his hands off of it. He noticed the two-way mirror and a warm pang of dread covered him from head to toe. Morty felt sick to his stomach when it dipped hard and fast. He closed his eyes, sucked in two great gulps of air, and kept thinking: *This is for Glenda. Everything you're doing here is for your wife's safe return. You have to get through this for her.*

Detective Larson had left Morty in the room alone for five minutes. Larson said he was getting a cup of coffee, and did Morty want anything? Morty didn't feel like ingesting anything with the cramps in his stomach and the ache in his head. A bad feeling coursed through him from top to bottom. Whatever he drank, it would come right back up.

Was Cheyenne correct to assume this investigator was targeting him as a suspect? If that was the case, it would be a helluva tall tale. Put it in a novel and send it to a publisher, he thought, wanting to leave this room with every conviction in his body. And while he was here, was somebody else doing harm to Glenda? Was it already too late? Would somebody turn over a pile in an alleyway, junkyard or empty lot and discover the pale and very dead body of Glenda Saggs?

Jesus, I don't want to imagine it!

Stop thinking that way.

Time is being wasted here.

Morty kept his eye on the door. Should he leave? Tell the detective that he couldn't do this right now? It was a legitimate reaction to thinking his wife really could be dead. This was an emotional time for him, and why wasn't he being handled with more care? Why did they put him in this room all alone for so long? Was Larson, the smug prick, behind the double-sided mirror watching Morty sweat? Was each bead going down the side of his head somehow proving his guilt or innocence?

He was seconds from pounding the door with both fists when Detective Larson finally returned. He was holding a steaming cup of coffee in one hand and a pack of cigarettes in the other, both for himself, and sat down with Morty.

He also had a mini tape recorder.

"May I record this?"

"Yes, but what for? I feel like I'm in trouble. Am I in trouble?"

The detective did his best to offer a reassuring smile. His eyes were too cunning to offer anything of the sort. He was a vulture about to peck into a steaming pile of dead remains.

"It's for our records, Morty. Now that our investigation has made a sudden turn, I want to re-ask some questions and maybe throw in a few new ones. Nobody's suspecting you of anything. This is how every investigation is conducted. I'm working on your behalf. If there's any problem, you may end this interview and request a lawyer. Do you request a lawyer?"

"Not at this moment." *But try me. I know my rights.*

"Very good. And thank you so much for your full cooperation. I understand your daughter's concern. She loves you very much. It's a tough time for you guys. Know that I see that. You're very courageous, handling this the way you've been handling it, Morty. I want to backpedal to the other day. A reporter interviewed you. You told her something about a doorway. Is there anything you can elaborate for me? Have you seen this door before?"

"Not before Glenda went missing. No. Never. And it's not just a doorway. Somebody traced my bedroom door with black."

"So why did you tell the reporter about the doorway? Do you feel it has any real significance to the case?"

"I was in a bad state of mind. The woman, that reporter, she pressured me. I had to run into my car to avoid her. I probably said things in haste that I normally wouldn't say."

I smelled burning things. It keeps me up at night. I think it made me sick the other day. But I don't know if it's real. God help me, I might be going crazy. I don't know what to think or do about it—

"Janet Ranscombe is reprehensible. She'll swoop down and pick on people until she gets her story, then she'll fly away without another care for your well-being. She's one of those young kiddoes who thinks being unkind gets them farther in their careers than finesse. I'm very sorry she pressured you in any way. I'm also very sorry for the disrespectful article she wrote in that rag paper."

Detective Larson had printed off the article from an Internet website. Morty read it with severe displeasure. There were quotes Morty didn't remember making, mostly about a mysterious "ghostly" doorway that appeared shortly after Glenda disappeared. The article went on about ritual killings, local cults and Morty's questionable state of mind during Glenda's disappearance. He couldn't finish reading it, the article was so leading about Morty's role in Glenda's vanishing.

Detective Larson sensed the change in Morty.

"It makes me cringe, Mr. Saggs. It's total and complete bullshit. A lot of theories are posed without evidence. Janet's a rebel rouser. I'll arrange for her to print a retraction, and an apology. You might get away with suing her too."

Morty wasn't sure what to say, so he didn't say anything.

"I talked to the officers who came onto the scene when you first called the police about Glenda. There wasn't a single sign of a break-in or foul play. It's just strange that after being sick as a dog, Morty, that you'd make a complete healthy comeback and find this slipper. I mean, you don't look sick at all to me today."

That was the punch in the gut that about knocked Morty from his chair. So the detective really was interrogating him, not casually running through a few things.

Detective Larson anticipated the rise from Morty, so the man raised his hands to calm him.

"Look, I'm only posing what other third parties might say about the case. I'm giving you a chance to clear the air. Man-to-man. Straight-talk. No bullshit, Morty. The truth. That's all I want."

Morty wasn't sure why he was saying what he was saying. Scared for his wife, worried that he might be going crazy seeing burning doorways, the words came right out of him in a hurry.

"I'm stressed, I'm overtired and I'm, I'm emotional. I think I'm seeing things, Detective. The burning doorway. It appeared the night Glenda vanished. The doorway glowed like it was on fire. Yes, I was drunk that night. I walked home from Side Pockets, but that's got nothing to do with what I saw, because the burning doorway keeps coming back. It scares me that it's real, and I'm also scared that it might not be real. I don't know for sure. Am I going crazy? Please tell me, Detective. Am I losing my mind? Does seeing burning doorways on my bedroom wall mean I'm slipping into insanity? It's grief, right? I didn't hurt Glenda. I love her. She's my everything. I'm not a bad person. I wouldn't hurt anybody, especially my wife. But what am I saying? How do I know I wouldn't do these things? If I'm seeing burning doorways, maybe there's other things going on in my head I can't explain. Things I might not be aware of. I might be going fucking crazy, so do what you need to do. Detective, please. Yes, maybe you're onto something. I could've done these things without even knowing it. It horrifies me that it could be true. So book me, arrest me, psychoanalyze me, but please, please, whatever happens, *please please please tell me if I'm going insane!"*

Chapter Fourteen

How he ended up in a holding cell, Morty couldn't recall no matter how hard he tried. He was lying on a wooden bench, muttering to himself to calm down right now, or they'll think he's crazy. After an hour or so of lying there, the rage of his thoughts calmed. Then he was embarrassed and concerned. Would the investigation turn completely to him? Surely it would. Would Detective Larson push him in the direction of a doctor who would open up that brain of his and then the state could answer that sixty-thousand-dollar question: is Morty Saggs sane, or insane? Or better yet, did Morty Saggs in fact kill his wife?

Morty's gone postal, he imagined Hannah, the gossip queen, saying when the shocking news hit the airwaves. Hannah could go on and on under his back porch awning drinking wine with Glenda and talking bullshit about their coworkers at the hospital. Glenda would nod and agree, and Hannah would keep dishing it out like a shovel slinging shit. Morty imagined Hannah's response to Morty being insane had to do with his job with the post office. Hannah would suggest Morty walking the same route shoving letters into the same mailboxes for far too long had caused him to snap. Maybe Hannah would go deeper and bring up the old resentment of having a kid too early with Glenda. That giving up his hopes and dreams of doing anything beyond menial or labor-intensive caused Morty to snap. Hannah would tell anybody anything about Morty the murderer, Morty the psychotic, Morty the human piece of garbage who ended the life of a wonderful woman.

But that wasn't right. He loved Glenda. He wasn't postal, and he wasn't a bad guy. Just ask his daughter. Cheyenne believed in him. Cheyenne knew him the best out of everybody. Better than Bruce Spaniel. Imagining Cheyenne speaking on his behalf tuned down the intensity of his thoughts. Cheyenne would clear up any misunderstanding. He did nothing wrong. He was a loving husband. He wasn't a murderer. Yes, he was seeing burning doorways, yes, he could be crazy, but—

The door opened, and Cheyenne entered. She helped him up off the bench.

"I told them to let you out right now. I knew that asshole detective was trying something funny. They're trying to take advantage of you, Dad. They think you're stupid, but you're not stupid. Damn it, I don't trust these guys. We're going home. If they want to press charges, they can."

Cheyenne guided him out of the station and to her car. She kept saying over and over, "Total and complete bullshit. It's all bullshit. The police are so wrong about this. So wrong it worries me."

They drove home while Cheyenne kept cursing the police. When they returned home, the police investigating the house were gone. They collected all the information they needed, Morty supposed, and had packed up their operation. Cheyenne explained how the cops took pictures of rooms, *but why?* Cheyenne asked him. The bloody slipper was random. Nothing else in the room was touched. The slipper could've been placed by the one perpetrating Glenda's disappearance. The slipper could mean a wide variety of things.

They were going back and forth when Cheyenne's cell phone rang. She took a call from her husband. She went outside on the back porch to take it.

Morty couldn't help but go to his bedroom. If he looked hard enough, would he see something else the police had missed?

He lowered onto all fours, peered underneath the bed and there was nothing but a few dust bunnies. Morty pictured the single slipper. He wondered where the second one was. He searched for it. It wasn't in Glenda's closet, the living room, dining room, bathroom, or anywhere. So where was the other slipper?

Morty returned to the bedroom thinking about the whereabouts of the slipper. He stared at the bed, then he looked at the bedroom doorway. He pictured the scene in his mind with Glenda kicking off her slipper and it landing under the bed the way it did. The angle of the slipper, the way everything else in the room was untouched, Morty wasn't an expert in forensic science, but this seemed elementary.

This was obvious.

He wanted to shout for Cheyenne about his idea, but what would that do? Cheyenne wouldn't believe his speculation. Cheyenne was his strongest ally right now. The way the investigation was going, Morty's character would be put into question. He needed those who loved him here by his side vouching on the behalf of Morty Saggs's good name and character. Cheyenne was that person, and to lose that, it would be devastating.

But it didn't change Morty's concern.

Think about it.

I mean REALLY think about it.

Glenda's slipper had been on its side, as if flung off of Glenda's foot. It landed crookedly under the bed. Morty imagined it happening, so he decided to actually play it out as if he were Glenda. Morty stood in front of the doorway. He loosened his shoe, and he flung it out as if he were struggling against somebody's hold. His shoe landed right about where he located Glenda's slipper.

By doing this simple experiment and seeing the result, Morty was attacked by too many feelings at once to properly interpret them. Much like the moment Glenda went missing. Was it really possible that somebody had dragged Glenda through the burning doorway? What did it mean for something like that to happen?

Right or wrong on his theory, there was one thing Morty had to do.

Chapter Fifteen

Detective Larson did his best not to slam his office door. He'd love to slam Morty Saggs instead. The bastard had fooled him from the start. Morty played up the part of being an innocent and grieving husband. If it weren't for Morty freaking out in the interrogation room, he would have a full confession. The problem was, Larson still didn't have any solid evidence. Circumstantial wouldn't be enough. Conjectures didn't cut it. He needed hard evidence. Something hard like a confession.

Morty was guilty of killing his wife. Larson didn't need the evidence to put it together, the feeling in his gut was so strong, but the detective believed in the justice system. Due process. Against his judgment, there were still things missing in the case. The timetable for Morty to kill Glenda and to stash her body somewhere didn't add up. Hannah and two other of Glenda's friends visited their house that Friday night until about ten-thirty. Morty left Side Pockets at roughly midnight. Morty had walked three blocks to get home. Make it about twenty after midnight, maybe thirty after, and Morty shows up at home and does the deed to his wife. This was quick and clean. *Very clean.* Then to move Glenda's body and hide it well was tough enough to explain. On top of that, Morty had made various calls, including calls to his daughter and Hannah, and then the police at about fifteen after one o'clock.

So Larson set it up in his head. Forty-five minutes to kill a woman, hide her body, clean the mess, make various calls and come away clean didn't sit well with Larson. Morty was in his early sixties. He wasn't the smartest guy ever known to mankind, nor was he the dumbest. Morty was more of a crazy kidder, fun-loving, beer-drinking, get 'er done blue-collar type, but when it came to book smarts, he was limited. It didn't mean he wasn't capable of cunning murder. It was just highly improbable.

Morty was also lacking in motive. Hannah, Cheyenne and everybody else Larson had interviewed in the neighborhood were unanimous in how strong Morty and Glenda's marriage was. There were no signs of tension between the two. No reason for Morty to suddenly snap and kill his wife. It didn't mean it didn't happen. The warning signs weren't always there. And people weren't always looking either.

So why did Larson keep thinking there was something off about the whole deal?

Morty's talk of a burning doorway bothered him. Morty said something to amateur reporter Janet Ranscombe about it, but why? That article made Morty sound like a loony. Fortunately for Morty, not many people read the small-time paper Janet wrote for. She was no Diane Sawyer. She was a twenty-something wannabe journalist who was balancing using her journalism degree for a career or letting her lawyer husband put some buns in her oven and becoming a housewife. If anybody asked Larson, she should let the rich lawyer knock her up and be done with the deal. Put the pen down and start breast-feeding, lady.

So was Morty preparing himself for an insanity plea by mentioning a burning doorway in the house? Was he that smart? Was he that forward thinking? And what was up with him being sick, bedridden actually, and then bouncing back in twenty-four hours' time? Too much wasn't right, and Larson hated toiling with the information in his head to no clear conclusion.

Larson sat at his desk and eyed his bookshelf with titles like *Unsolved Crimes of the Century* and *The Criminal Mind Versus the Investigative Mind*. He enjoyed cases that were impossible to solve, and yet somehow a relentless investigator tackled it and got a conviction. Larson also read a ton of true crime novels and pulpy crime fiction. He also owned twelve different books on historical killers, anything from Ed Gein to Jack the Ripper.

Morty was no Jack the Ripper.

But something wasn't right about the man.

Larson couldn't prove it.

But he would.

Soon.

Chapter Sixteen

Fearing he was going insane, Morty charged into the garage, retrieved his sledgehammer and rushed upstairs into his bedroom. He bashed the business end of the sledgehammer against the wall surrounding the doorway. Morty pounded his message home. *No more.* Morty started laughing hysterically. This would solve everything. He kicked this problem in its ass. Sledgehammer to wood. No more doorway.

The wood surrounding the doorway crumbled to the blows, the sledgehammer breaking through the thin layer easily. Morty kept smashing and breaking. He didn't want to stop. It felt *so* good. So many pent-up feelings were being channeled into this moment. The longer he did this, though, the more Morty began to realize this would make him look bad. Really, really bad. Covered in dust and standing in a small rubble pile of the wall, Morty *felt* guilty of a crime.

How could he say he wasn't losing his marbles now? That he couldn't be the reason for his wife's bloody slipper, or her disappearance altogether?

He refused to admit things that were lies. Morty Saggs hadn't gone postal. He was happy-go-lucky Morty. Funny Morty who would rather pay more money buying candy bars from a vending machine than buy them from the store in bulk. Morty who fell asleep while fishing because he'd had too much to drink and woke up in the middle of the lake confused as hell. Morty who had accidentally hit Bruce in the ear with a dart during a game of darts at Side Pockets, and the sight of blood made him so queasy he threw up. But it wasn't the blood. It was the concern for Bruce that had him so worked up. That he was the one responsible for Bruce's pain. So he couldn't have harmed Glenda, right? *Right?* He wasn't a sadistic person. He was fun-loving Morty without a mean bone in his body.

"Dad, are you upstairs?"

Cheyenne.

Oh my God, no.

Cheyenne kept calling out to him.

What do I say? I have to keep her from coming upstairs and seeing me like this. She'll ask me about the wall, and I'll have to tell her—but what will I tell her? What could I possibly tell her?

Cheyenne was coming up the stairs. She was closing in on the bedroom. Morty did the only thing he could and hid the sledgehammer in the closet.

Morty was spinning responses in his head.

Cheyenne, dear, I was…/Cheyenne, I wasn't sure about something, so I…/It seems like I'm losing control of myself, so I…/I'm so scared right now, I had to do…/I didn't want to tell you, but there's this burning doorway, and it keeps appearing on my wall, and it scares the hell out of me, so I had to…/I think, no, I know, the doorway had something to do with your mother's disappearance, so that's why I…

"Dad, why are you looking at me like that?"

Cheyenne's face was ugly because of her strange expressions.

Her concern for him was that intense.

"I…I don't know what I'm doing. I don't—"

Morty broke down into heavy sobs. He retreated into Cheyenne's arms whispering nonsense. What meant to be apologies.

"*What's come over me I don't know why I'm acting this way I need help I need serious help.*"

Cheyenne helped him out of the room, led him downstairs, and set him down on the couch until he was done crying. When he calmed, Morty came to his senses. Morty was so deep in thought, so entrenched in his head, that he hadn't noticed Cheyenne slip back upstairs. She was in the bedroom. What was she seeing?

Morty was about to launch upstairs and try and attempt an explanation, but it wasn't necessary. Cheyenne wasn't worked up when she returned. Instead, she gave him a sad expression.

"You poor man. That detective really did a number on you. Whatever you're going through, I'm going to help you, Dad. Now go upstairs and get some rest. I'll work on making you some dinner, okay?"

Morty was dumbfounded.

Why wasn't she asking him about the torn-up wall? *Why, damn it!*

Maybe she didn't go in his bedroom? Maybe she didn't see the mess? The possibility was strong. It was the only thing that made sense.

So Morty went upstairs. He could clean up the mess, figure things out, and go from there. Cheyenne didn't need to know about what he'd done with a sledgehammer until Morty had the facts sorted out. Until he was absolutely certain about the strange burning doorway.

He entered the bedroom and wasn't prepared for what he was going to find.

Just what the hell was he going to do to fix this surreal situation?

He'd ask himself these kinds of questions all night, alongside the best question of all: why was the wall around the doorway undamaged when he had just taken a fucking sledgehammer to it?

Chapter Seventeen

Janet Ranscombe came so close to calling the police on Morty Saggs's sick ass. She had her finger on the send button of her cell phone after dialing 9-1-1 right after the man had assaulted her. Morty Saggs was a madman, the way he launched out of his bed with that insane expression. The only thing she did was touch the wall where he pointed, saying there was a burning doorway there. Janet only humored the old man, but the second she touched the wall, he went psycho bat shit crazy.

At home, after locking herself in her bathroom so her husband wouldn't see the collection of bruises on her bicep and shoulders, and worse, the tear through her right nipple, Janet Ranscombe mended her wounds. What would she tell her husband the next time they were intimate? She avoided his sexual advances last night by using the 'I have a headache' excuse. She knew it was lame, but what else could she do? Tell him what happened? No, she wasn't ready to do that just yet. There was a special motive for her silence.

Her husband was set in a career. Blake made partner at a local law firm. So why did she need to work? Blake asked her. Her parents were of the same mind as her husband. Investigative journalism was a waste of time. She should be having babies and letting her husband win the bread. When she graduated college, she landed a local job on Channel 4 News. It didn't pay shit, well under twenty grand a year, and the news was boring. Local stories. Fluffy fillers to make small communities smile. Bake sales and new traffic signs, that kind of shit. She talked to a lot of stay-at-home-Moms and churchgoers and community leaders. Janet wanted something more ambitious and world changing.

If her husband knew she had been attacked by Morty Saggs, forget her chances of taking her career to another level. He would insist she quit the business immediately. Demand it, actually. She would start being a stay-at-home mother. Blake wasn't shy about his intentions with their marriage. He wanted to keep working as a lawyer, and she could have all the babies she desired. The plan was simple.

Janet wanted children too, but not yet, not now, not when Morty Saggs's story was on the verge of breaking. This could potentially kick-start her career. Sensational stories of murder always hit the national circuit, especially the kind of story involving Morty Saggs. She wouldn't be writing articles about fall festivals and local flavor. Janet would tackle real stories. Edgy stories. After Morty, she could become a name. She'd be on *Dateline* or *20/20*. Diane Sawyer-level reporting.

Growing up in Massachusetts, Janet lived next door to a true crime writer. The woman was retired at the time, but re-runs of the television show called *Deadly Mothers* still played late at night. Janet watched the shows religiously. Whenever Marty Fielding was pruning her hedges, working in her garden or was outside on her front porch reading a book with a cigarette dangling from her mouth, Janet would sneak out of the house and ask her questions about the cases she wrote books on. Marty Fielding fascinated her. Janet wanted to be Marty Fielding. It's the only reasons she considered journalism as a career. While other kids her age wanted to be *Barbie*, Janet said she wanted to apprehend serial killers and deliver them to justice. Because Janet was only ten years old at the time, Marty Fielding was limited on her details about the murderers she wrote about, but Marty said one thing that stuck with Janet to this day.

"*If you want to make a name for yourself, you have to break an incredible story before anybody else does. A real sensational story that will keep a neighborhood up at night. The kind of story that will make husbands hug their wives at night tighter and for wives to count the children in their beds. If you're the first to tell the story, to be the face of the story, they'll remember you. And if you're put in any kind of danger in the process, they'll consider you a hero. You'll be remarkable.*"

Janet wanted to be a mother, but first, she was going to do as Marty Fielding suggested and break Morty Saggs's story. It had the right ingredients. Danger and intrigue. Motive and murder. This was the moment of truth for Janet. How many more chances would she have to report this developing story, especially when in all likelihood it would turn out to be a sensational murder story? Oh, how the public ate this kind of shit up! Marty Fielding was absolutely right.

From the moment after she was assaulted, Janet kept watch over Morty's house. He wasn't right in the head. The man was unbalanced, on the brink of more murders, and whatever mask he wore to cover up his psychotic tendencies was slipping big time.

Janet began today's stakeout early this morning. She witnessed Morty go to the police station, and the police comb through the man's house. She stayed parked on the street waiting for something else to happen. Two people arrived at Morty's house. A man and a woman. Cheyenne let them inside. The sun was starting to go down. Soon, it would be nighttime. Blake probably thought she was crazy doing this. If it weren't for his most recent client keeping him busy, Janet wouldn't be getting away with this kind of stakeout.

Janet didn't care. The way this was going, she might even be able to write a non-fiction account of Morty Saggs, the sociopath who murdered his wife. Janet imagined a book jacket with *#1 Bestseller* emblazoned on the cover. Everything in her life was coming full circle, Janet thought. Her heart was fluttering. She was high on her own prospects.

Then Janet's processes were racing for a new reason.

The violent red light blaring from what she assumed was Morty's bedroom window had her running towards the house. She dialed the police on her cell phone, then she dug into her purse for her 9mm pistol.

Camera, check.

9mm, check.

She hesitated at the front doorway. Was she running into certain danger? Would Morty try to kill her? Those questions and worries fled her mind when she heard the harsh screams coming from the house.

Chapter Eighteen

Morty woke up in bed from another long sleep. It was dark outside. The whole day, gone. The window shades were drawn. He could see the slight tinge of orange coming off of the streetlight in front of his house. How he ended up in bed eluded him. Morty had taken a sledgehammer to the wall, and then Cheyenne came home, and the rest of it, he couldn't remember.

Where was Cheyenne?

He heard several people talking downstairs.

The first voice he picked out was Hannah's. *Poor Morty, he's going through such a terrible ordeal. He's not doing so well, is he?*

Then it was Bruce's voice. *They've got another thing coming if they think they can push Morty around like that. Cops think they can do anything they want. Morty didn't do anything wrong. You guys need a lawyer. Did you get a lawyer?*

Cheyenne spoke up next. *Yes, I made the arrangements for a lawyer. I'm scared, guys. I needed to talk to somebody. Thanks for coming over. It's just that Morty's coming undone. I don't know if I can keep him together. I'm not sure what to do for him. They said at the police station, Morty was asking that detective if he was insane or not. And I mean he was shrieking it at the top of his lungs.*

Hannah said, *I've got a few downers I could give him.*

Bruce said, *He's stressed. You can't leave a grieving man to a detective's interrogation. There wasn't a lawyer present. There's no telling what the asshole did to poor Morty. They grill people hard, and Morty can't handle it. He's a softy. And with Glenda missing, I'm sure it was even harder on the guy.*

Morty couldn't listen to anymore. How much longer before the people who knew and loved him began to doubt his state of mind? He could stay in this bed and never move again. Maybe that was the way to avoid people finding out he was going insane? Stay in bed.

"So are you ready to confess?"

The voice wasn't Cheyenne's, Hannah's or Bruce's. The words were harsh and accusatory. Morty feared saying the wrong thing to this mystery voice. He stayed on the bed, glued in place, fearing if he did anything at all, this person could come out of hiding and really hurt him.

Hurt him like they'd hurt Glenda.

Morty couldn't believe he was addressing the voice. He still couldn't pinpoint where the speaker was in the room.

"I haven't done anything to my wife. I wouldn't harm her, ever. I swear to God. What do you know about my wife? Are you the one who did something to her? Answer me, damn you. Face me!"

"*If you ever want your wife back, you're going to have to tell me what happened to* my *wife first. I know you took her somewhere. I know you did terrible things to my wife. So where is she? You can't lie to me. Not me. If you think you can play games with me, you're fucking mistaken, buddy.*"

"Who are you? Who is *your* wife? I don't know what you're talking about. You're confusing me. You're talking crazy, whoever you are! Show yourself so we can really talk. Do you have a special reason you're hiding from me?"

Morty was so enraged that somebody was accusing him of harming not only Glenda, but also somebody else's wife, he growled, "I wouldn't hurt anybody, not ever!"

"*Liar! Liar! You lie! You fucking lie! It was you, Morty Saggs. It was you!*"

Morty got up out of the bed and threw open the closet door. Nobody was inside. Under the bed, in the hallway, nobody was there.

So who was talking to him?

Who the hell was it?

"I haven't done anything to anybody. I don't know what you're talking about. Why are you hiding from me? Come on out!"

"*You come talk to me if you want Glenda back. I'll make you crack. I make them all crack when I put them in my special room. I'll make you spill the truth to me. I have my methods. Then, and only then, can you have your wife back, Morty. I want a confession. I want the truth spoken from your lips. I want to know what you did to my poor wife. Join me on the other side of this doorway, and let's finish our business together, Morty.*"

The voice on the air, so ghost-like, stopped speaking.

That terrible smell of burning started filling up the room. Morty was choking on it so hard it knocked him onto all fours. Unable to breathe, he couldn't move. Morty could only keep his eyes open and watch as the room was consumed by burning red.

Chapter Nineteen

Cheyenne sat with Hannah and Bruce downstairs in the living room. They were drinking coffee and quietly talking about Morty. Cheyenne called the two of them over because she could trust their opinions and advice. Clearly her father wasn't acting right, even up against Glenda's disappearance. What had he been doing when Cheyenne was out? Why did her father panic when she went upstairs to the bedroom today? Why did the man collapse in bed and sleep all day? Bruce and Hannah argued that Morty's actions weren't anything beyond stress and being concerned about Glenda. People reacted differently to extreme situations. They also agreed Morty wasn't handling it well. Any husband wouldn't be handling it well. And Bruce mentioned how Detective Larson probably came down hard on Morty. It wasn't until after that questioning that Morty started acting different. It was the damn detective's fault.

Cheyenne was beginning to feel a little better about her father. Yes, he had gone through a terrible ordeal from the start. Then stack on a hard-ass detective's interrogation, and that horrible article that reporter wrote, making her father look crazy, possibly guilty, how would she fare in her old man's shoes? Not very good.

They agreed they had to be there for Morty. Stay positive about Glenda and the investigation. Give the man support when he needed it the most.

They were quiet for a moment, then Bruce started talking.

"I was at the front of the search party today. We combed the Hillsdale Lake area. So many miles we searched. It's so frustrating. Anything can be evidence. Cigarette butts. Clothing. A broken bottle. It's hard to know if you're missing something or not."

Hannah was with him during the search party, and added, "We can't forget why we're doing this. I know it's hard. It seems pointless searching through acres of woods and fields when you don't come up with anything, but we have to do as the police say. They're professionals."

Cheyenne's eyes welled with tears.

"What if this is one of those unsolved cases? Like ten years from now we're still searching for my mom? I don't think I can handle it. How can I go back to work, raise my kids, and *live* without knowing what happened to her? I can't eat, I can't sleep. What's happening to my father is happening to me. I'm being hopeful, I'm being realistic, but I may never know what happened to my mom, no matter how many rocks we turn over or missing posters we hang up. It's so damn frustrating. It's not fair. My mother never did anything to anybody."

Before Bruce or Hannah could try and inject more hope into the situation, they overheard heavy footsteps upstairs. Thuds.

"Morty's awake," Hanna said. "We should see how he's doing."

"It might make you feel better to talk to your father, Cheyenne," Bruce said, getting up to lead the way. "I know you're hurting right now, sweetie. You have to be tough. I know you can pull through this. We're not going anywhere. We're going to see you through this difficult time."

Morty was shrieking, "*I'm not crazy! I wouldn't hurt anybody, not ever!*"

Bruce stormed up the stairs ahead of Cheyenne and Hannah. "Jesus, what's wrong with him? What's he going on about?"

Cheyenne was right behind him.

"I don't know. It's like he's being attacked. He sounded like that the night he was doing that in his sleep."

Hannah was the last up the stairs.

Bruce reached the doorway, then Cheyenne, then Hannah. When they stepped into the bedroom, Morty was missing.

Bruce: "What's burning?"

Cheyenne: "And that smell?"

Hannah wrinkled her face. "It smells like fire."

Before any of them could question any further, they were covering their faces, shouting in horror, calling out for help, when the violent red light burst from the bedroom doorway.

They were consumed instantly.

Janet was hot on the heels of the noises. Strange red lights kept flashing from upstairs. She could see the flashes from the bottom of the stairway now. 9mm drawn,

Janet charged up the stairs. The screams, the peals of horror. What had happened to the man and the woman who entered the house earlier? Janet was hesitant to thrust herself in the middle of it, yet the curiosity was so strong, she abandoned all sense of safety in exchange for the answers.

Was Morty a killer?

Was there something else going on in this house?

The red lights were like lashings against her skin. Janet was screaming with each step she climbed higher. She couldn't open her eyes. Through her eyelids, red blazed into her retinas. Janet moved blindly. She couldn't turn back even if she wanted to. A force was compelling her up each stair. Her joints bent and flexed against her brain's command to turn around, to run the hell out of there, to fuck the story, to go home where it was safe. The 9mm fired twice at empty air. Helpless, Janet was forced into Morty's room.

She too crossed through the burning doorway.

Chapter Twenty

Detective Larson stood among the many officers waiting in the street outside of Morty Saggs's residence. When the detective was called out onto the scene, Larson already knew they had a hostage situation on their hands. Morty had finally come to terms with the fact he had lost his mind and killed his wife. And now, they were at a stand-off. This could go all night. People might die, Cheyenne Saggs included. Two others were also inside, including Bruce Spaniel and Hannah Albertson.

Larson watched the other officers at work, including a sharpshooter who positioned himself behind the line of police vehicles facing Morty's house. Another crew was circling the perimeter of the house, taking point. They would do anything to disarm the hostage taker. It was confirmed two gunshots were heard fired in the house. Another fact: Janet Ranscombe's vehicle was located on the block. Better yet, the reporter was missing. Most likely, she was inside the house as well. That would mean another head to account for. Another hostage in Morty's crosshairs.

Things were heading in a sour direction and fast. Morty had the control and power, and give a psychotic both those things, it created a solid equation for a high body count. Larson would have to call in a negotiator, learn Morty's demands, and then everybody would have to team up to lure Morty out of the house without bullets being fired.

This was going to be one long night.

None of the steps Larson had considered would be necessary. Morty called down to them from the upstairs window. The blinds were drawn, so nobody could see him. Morty said he was surrendering, but only on one condition. Detective Larson had to come upstairs alone. He only wanted a minute of the detective's time, and then they could arrest him. The hostages would be released. Morty was in fact the one responsible for Glenda's disappearance. He would give the detective a full detailed confession, but first, Morty needed to talk to Larson upstairs, and most importantly, alone.

His fellow officers warned Larson of the potential danger of this proposition, but

Larson had been through this scenario before. The detective knew this could be a psycho's ruse to kill him, another play in the man's sick-ass game. Morty played him good in the interrogation room the other day. When Morty mentally collapsed, freaked out and raised hell in that room, the man slipped right out of his hands. Larson gave Morty that point. But this time Morty wasn't getting away with anything else.

Larson strapped on a bulletproof vest just in case Morty opened fire on him. Once Larson was ready to approach the house, he used the bullhorn to announce that he was coming into the house and not to shoot. Morty called back down that he heard the detective loud and clear and to come on up.

The detective approached the house, entering slowly through the front door. He exercised universal precautions by sweeping the living room with his .28 police issue revolver. The strangest odor hit him immediately of something burning. It didn't smell like firewood or food burning on a grill. It was noxious, offensive and most of all, unnatural.

What the hell was going on in this house?

The detective expected to turn a corner, venture into another room and step into a mass sacrifice. Larson imagined body parts on the ground and pieces hanging from the ceiling fan. Maybe be more creative, add Satanic symbols drawn in blood on the walls, or some other fucked up dark demonic rites. But there wasn't a single drop of blood anywhere.

Only that damnable burning smell.

Morty's voice called down to him, saying to go up the stairs and meet him in the bedroom. It would only take a minute. Nobody was hurt. Nobody was going to die. Nothing bad was going to happen to anybody if Larson just came upstairs for a second to clear up a few things before being arrested.

Larson didn't trust anybody, especially a hostage taker, a psycho like Morty Saggs. The detective kept the gun trained in front of him, promises be damned.

Up the stairs he crept. Every creak announced his position. Outside the room Morty was hiding in, Larson said, "I'm coming in the room. Please don't shoot me."

Morty indicated everything was safe. He could come inside. No harm was coming his way.

When he entered, Larson stepped into an empty room.

Where the hell did Morty go?

Where did Cheyenne, Hannah, Bruce and Janet go?

Morty couldn't stash that many people by himself. Did the son of a bitch have an accomplice?

The burning smell doubled. He gagged on it, his eyes leaking tears, because the stench was as strong as cut onions and high proof rotgut alcohol. All at once, a red light was shooting out of the room's doorway, blinding him.

He heard Morty shouting for him to run and get away before it was too late.

Janet Ranscombe was pleading for her life.

Hannah lost herself in a fit of uncontrollable emotions.

The sheer impossibility of the doorway being on fire hit the detective. Deny it all he wanted, there it fucking was. The bastard was telling the truth.

"JESUS NO!!!"

Larson was consumed by the raging red colors and forced through to the other side of the doorway.

Chapter Twenty-One

Things had taken a terrible turn. That's why Officer Chris Wright was called out onto the scene along with a dozen other officers. After hearing Detective Larson pleading for his life from Morty Saggs's residence, Wright knew action had to be taken. Entering the house with the terrible smells of burning hitting each of the officers, like charcoal briquettes doused in something chemical, Wright heard Detective Larson unleash a terrible call of agony from upstairs. Larson shouted for backup, that there were innocent people in danger in the upstairs bedroom. *Send every cop in the house through the doorway, and do it NOW.*

Officer Wright headed the charge upstairs. Officers were behind him, ready to back him up. He expected to see Larson shot up and on the ground covered in blood, and anticipated dodging bullets, but neither of those things occurred. Wright stepped foot into a bedroom. The moment he crossed the threshold, the doorway appeared to be on fire, burning with the intensity of the sun. The colors instantly ruined his vision. Wright was consumed by the raging colors of red and the burning. He wasn't sure where he was anymore. It was as if the room, and himself, were being consumed by the colors. Other officers were shrieking in reaction, unable to contain their horror at the impossible situation.

It wasn't much longer before the doorway vanished.

Morty Saggs's bedroom was empty.

Officer Wright and his backup were gone.

Captain Murtaugh toured the house of Morty Saggs for the fourth time and things still didn't add up. Where did his officers and Detective Larson go? The one remaining officer on the scene who hadn't seemingly vanished into thin air all said to Murtaugh: *I have no fucking clue what the hell happened.* How did all of those cops and a detective disappear? How did Morty Saggs, his daughter, two family friends and an amateur reporter disappear as well?

No.

Fucking.

Clue.

Captain Murtaugh tried Detective Larson's cell phone. He didn't get an answer, and he couldn't leave a message. It just kept ringing.

The captain didn't like this at all.

Maybe there was a hidden compartment in the house they didn't know about, where the twelve cops were stashed, along with the detective.

That made bullshit sense. With twelve cops, there would've been a firefight. Bullet holes in the walls, and more probable, a dead hostage taker. Worst case, dead police. Throughout the rest of the house, there wasn't a speck of blood or a shred of evidence indicating where anybody could've gone.

That was almost twenty people the house had taken in mysteriously. There were calls to make. Interviews with the neighbors to conduct. Rational explanations to find.

Murtaugh wished he was like his best friend who had retired a year ago, Chief Darrel Perry. The bastard could smoke his cigars, enjoy his bourbon nightcaps and not have to worry about messed-up investigations that were like puzzles without the pieces.

The captain was in for a long fucking night.

Chapter Twenty-Two

What happened was only something you could describe after the fact. If you survived it, then you registered the details. Then you reacted. That was Morty's present situation. He ended up on his hands and knees trying to catch his breath. Pearls of sticky sweat covered his face and neck. Every part of him was high on adrenaline. His heart was beating like a heavy metal double bass drum. He feared he was going to have a deadly heart attack. Still trying to catch his breath, he swept the area with his eyes. The intense red light was gone. Cheyenne was on the ground nearby, also out of breath, her eyes wide as if she was staring insanity in the face. Bruce was curled up on his side as if he'd broken his ribs. Morty couldn't move yet. Everything was an effort just to breathe and slow down his chugging heart.

Entering the violent red light, it was like jumping into fire. Morty felt flames eat into his skin. He smelled his own flesh burn. Felt the agony of his muscle tissue bubbling and boiling from the heat. But he wasn't burned. His skin was intact. Other than shock, Morty was untouched.

Blinking the red spots out of his eyes, Morty's vision adjusted. His eyes went from squinting to gaping wide. Shattered and broken dark brown brick was scattered around him. The floor was solid concrete. They were in the basement of Morty's house. Strange, though, because nothing that belonged to Morty was here anymore. Something was very wrong here. The lights coming from the ceiling didn't exude yellow. The lights shed a burning coal red. Everything appeared to be bathed in blood; a trick of the lights. Morty was already rubbing at his eyes. They ached against the harsh color.

The rest of the details in the room would come to him later.

Right now, all that mattered was his precious daughter.

Morty rushed over to Cheyenne who was sprawled on the floor clutching her arm as if she'd landed hard on it.

"You okay, honey?" He panicked when she didn't respond. "*Tell me you're okay.*"

Cheyenne could only nod. She couldn't speak. Her breath was uneven. She was panting. Morty held her close and did his best to soothe his poor daughter. Morty checked her over. She wasn't bleeding or damaged besides her arm.

"Is anybody hurt?" Morty asked everybody in the room. "Speak up."

Hearing Morty's voice rocked Bruce out of whatever mental hell he was trapped in.

"I landed funny, man. I might've broke my ribs. It's like somebody picked us up and dropped us down several flights of stairs."

Morty didn't hear half of what his best friend said. His focus was stolen by the table that took up a quarter of the open area in the basement. The table was of thick stock. Mighty oak varnished with a cherry veneer. A giant light bulb housed in a wire cage hung right above the table casting down that unnerving color of red.

Stranger still, surrounding the table were more of those broken bricks. Morty thought about it for a time and realized the table used to be surrounded by four walls of bricks. The walls were broken, but by what, and why? So much didn't make sense in the room.

It wasn't just the table that gripped Morty in horror. Hannah was sitting in a chair with her head, chest and arms slumped over the tabletop. Her right hand was flat on the table. Five nails had been driven into her hand. The nails were at least five to six inches long. Around the entry points, ragged flesh showed between exposed bone. Hannah had tried to work her hand free from its forced down position with no success except to further her own agony. The circle of blood on the tabletop continued to widen. There was also a larger pool at Hannah's feet that had curdled. The blood looked plastic in the light.

The facts weren't adding up in Morty's mind. Hannah staked down to a table. Hannah pale as death. Her eyes remained open in terror. Those eyes seemed to be looking right at Morty for answers. *Why did this happen to me?*

Hannah wasn't recently dead. She had been dead for several hours even though they had just passed through the burning doorway minutes ago.

"Oh my God, Hannah!" Cheyenne was at her father's side. "Who would do such a thing to her?"

Morty heard Bruce grumble "*Sick*" under his breath.

The three of them stood in the room trying to figure out how they winded up in Morty's basement and why Hannah was dead on the table.

Morty thought out loud because he couldn't stand the silence.

The silence scared the shit out of him.

"This table's not mine. I mean, it wasn't in my basement. I've never owned it. And these broken bricks are strange. It's like someone walled up the table then shattered the bricks. Why would, I mean—?"

"So how's any of that supposed to explain Hannah's death?" Bruce motioned around the room with his hands. "This is *your* basement. This is happening in *your* house. *Your* wife is missing. This all has to do with *you*, Morty. *You. You. You.* So do *you* have something *you* need to tell us?"

The sight of blood and a corpse had turned Bruce into a crazed bully. The man was poised to take a swing at Morty at the best opportunity. Cheyenne squeezed her father's arm harder, either showing support for him or fear of Bruce.

Morty chose his words carefully. He knew this situation could escalate no matter what he said in the coming moments.

"I can't explain any of this. Look, if I could, I would. I promise you guys I would. How could anyone explain this? I didn't see Hannah murdered. I don't know who did this. I know only as much as you guys do. If we're going to figure things out, we're going to have to work together. We can't turn on each other. I promise I have nothing to do with this. Let me make that clear. What human being can make a doorway burn? What human being can make a doorway suck people in? Think logically. We're all angry, confused and in shock. But if we come undone, how are we going to survive this? I am not the one you should be worried about right now. It's whoever killed poor Hannah we should be watching for."

Bruce's eyes were a snake's. They called bullshit against Morty. He didn't say it, but the man was thinking it.

Morty didn't know if everybody in this room considered him a suspect for a crime yet to be identified. There was one thing he did know.

"What happened to us happened to Glenda. My wife is here somewhere, and I am going to find her."

Chapter Twenty-Three

The horrible red lights, the burning heat against her flesh, the feeling of being pulled forward by an invisible force, the assault didn't end until Janet was on all fours against a cold tile floor. "*Ahhhhhhhh-gawwwwwwwwwd!*" Janet repeated the wailing scream until her throat gave out. Unable to see where she was, Janet crab-walked backwards and soon hit a wall. She screamed out on impact, got to her feet, ran forward and hit another wall. She banged her forehead. Janet stumbled in confusion, then stayed still. She stared at her reflection in a mirror. The surface was caked in rust, dirt and smears resembling blood spatter. The entire room was the definition of grime. She smelled the mixture of stale unkempt bodies, and even worse, death. The room resembled the inside of a brown bottle that had grown moldy on the inside. It was stifling hot. Janet had trouble breathing.

The room wasn't lit very well. Weak amber light filtered into the room from the crack at the bottom of the doorway. Janet turned the knob. It crunched, being locked.

Janet saw the curtains of a bathtub and quickly drew the curtain back. It was an instinctive reaction to seeing so many horror movies in her lifetime.

She doubled back and screamed again.

A woman was in the tub, as pale as the white porcelain. Her throat had been slit at the femoral artery. The tub was filling up with blood. Trails of red ran down the curves of her breasts, belly and the dips of her pelvis.

Janet stayed up against the wall, wanting to curl up into a protective ball and shield herself from this horrible sight.

The corpse's eyes were wide in a morbid death stare. The eyes made a squeaking sound as they turned in their sockets to regard Janet.

The corpse said this under its breath: "*I couldn't help him. I knew nothing. That's why I had to die. Just like you will, Janet. You better know something, or you will be next. You will be like me. Dead and forever trapped in this house.*"

Janet unleashed a scream as the corpse's eyes were pushed out of her head by giant clods of black dirt. More dirt pushed itself out from her ears and mouth, and ripped through her sinus cavity until her head split down the middle to unleash what fought so hard to escape. Janet watched the corpse's flesh and muscle tear as dirt exploded at high pressures from the corpse's body until the bathtub overflowed with earth.

The corpse had buried itself.

Janet threw aside the curtain in revulsion. She closed her eyes, shook her head, counted to ten and timed her breathing. Each breath steered her away from hyperventilation. From insanity.

Access the situation. Access the situation. Access the situation.

The burning doorway. The heat, what could've been flames, brushing up against her body. What exactly had brought her here in this apparent trap without an exit?

Maybe trap wasn't the correct word.

I'm in a room. I don't have a clue how I got here. I could leave this room if it wasn't locked. Who locked me in? Who put me here?

The concern for her safety deepened. The sinking feeling of helplessness dissolved her ability to stay calm. She could use every breathing technique known to man, but it wasn't going to help.

You wanted a story. Well, lady, you got your fucking story. Morty Saggs and his wife are God knows where, and you're here alone and nobody's looking for you. Nobody's going to help you.

Pray that corpse doesn't leave the tub.

Don't think about the corpse.

What are you going to do now? You could be home, making house and spending your time with your wonderful husband. Why did you throw yourself into somebody else's problem? You don't have a career. Nobody cares about you as a journalist. You're an amateur. You might as well be a blogger. You're not going national. You're a nobody. You're a nothing. You're going to suffocate in this room. You're going to die all alone. You're going to die a horrible, unimaginable death.

Janet banged her fists against the mirror in anger. She had been staring into it with each mean hurtful thought she hurled at herself. The mirror could shatter if she punched it hard enough, but she feared breaking the glass and cutting herself. She could get an infection. This room could harbor every disease known to man. Flesh-eating bacteria and plagues. Malignant cancers. It was easy to believe, considering how foul this glass box stank of that woman's dead body in the tub.

Her striking the mirror revealed more surface to reflect. Janet saw herself, how her eyes were giant globes, and how her mouth was drawn in a tight frown. The very essence of fear. She was a living example of vulnerability.

Janet kept crying out to anybody and anyone.

"Help me! Please, please, *pleeeeeeeeeeease! Heeeeeeeeeelp!*"

The shower curtain was torn from the pole. Shower rings clanged against the floor. A deflated corpse charged with dangling arms to choke her. Janet's eyed doubled at how the woman's face hung in ribbons. The mouth and tongue, what was left of it, kept spitting out dirt.

"*They will never find your body, Janet! You shall die here with me!*"

The doorway leading out of the room blazed red.

Janet didn't care about the scary light. She chose the door. Anything to get away from that corpse!

Chapter Twenty-Four

Red hot heat, red hot light, red hot everything, Detective Larson was overwhelmed by the transition from Morty Saggs's bedroom to *this*. He was blinded, and a sense of weightlessness attached itself to his body. The air went from red hot molten heat to an icy barren cold. Larson's neck was turned awkwardly. He was forced into a sitting position. His arms were forced at his sides. The detective's legs were bent as if he were sitting down and turned at an odd angle. Not upside down, but not right side up either. Everything was in pitch black darkness. He didn't smell that terrible burning smell anymore. That didn't mean the awful odors had ceased. A new odor replaced the previous one. Did he hear the slither of maggots swimming in a fetid body? And what was up with the sound of a motor chugging on its last life?

Coughing against a disgusting smell the detective couldn't put a name to, he tried to shift in the tight cramped space and bumped full-on into something wet and cold. He pivoted right, and he hit something else damp. Larson had little leverage to maneuver. He would surely freeze if he didn't find escape soon. Another problem, his air was running thin. He was dizzy from taking in his own exhalations. Larson fought against himself and the objects in the tight space that seemed to make the area tighter by the second.

Then came two gunshots. Loud enough to be coming from nearby. The detective trained his ears to the slightest noise. He needed an indication of where the fuck he was so he could get out of here. Something had happened to him, Larson easily gathered. Maybe Morty saw him enter the house and clubbed him over the head. It wasn't impossible Morty stashed him in a closet or a hideaway for safekeeping as he dealt with the cops outside his house.

Larson tried to call out to whoever was on the scene, that he was here, that he needed saving, and for them not to shoot him. From another corner, there was the sound of a hard and awkward landing. Shrills defining high levels of excruciating pain. Even more gunshots rang out. Shotguns being pumped. Disoriented voices clashed against sharp deliveries of panic. Footsteps drummed upstairs and downstairs in droves. Movement came from everywhere. Shots. Running. Falling. Retreating. Advancing. Agony and discord. Repeat.

Larson had to escape this cramped space and help his officers. Morty Saggs had really lost his mind. He imagined the investigative team would find Glenda's dead body. Larson prayed Cheyenne wasn't killed as well. The psycho was going to kill as many people as he could before the good guys could take him down. It always happened that way with the serious psychos.

Larson tried to batter his way out of the tight nook. So cold, he was shivering. How much longer could he survive in this black box? Even if he could survive another hour, Larson refused to stay in here another minute.

Struggling to make sense of the darkness to locate a switch, a doorknob, anything to open the trap he found himself in, Larson continued hearing gunplay. The blasts echoed from up high, from low, and even yards out from his position.

Was Morty packing a machine gun up there?

It didn't matter what Morty was doing. Larson couldn't do a damn thing to help matters until he escaped this box. He fought harder and gained nothing. The weight of something pressed harder against him and further limited his mobility. Larson bent his left arm in, forced his left leg back so his other leg could rear back like a kicking horse. He gave the escape one last shot before giving in to exhaustion. He channeled every bit of momentum and strength into that one kick. Larson's foot connected with a flat surface. A burst of light made him shut his eyes. He rolled forward, collapsing onto the floor. Glass shattered all around him. Something landed on top of him, and he couldn't get up. Pinned down by something hideous, Larson could only shout out in terror.

Chapter Twenty-Five

It was only moments after Morty made his declaration about finding his wife when he started paying closer attention to the things that were off about the basement. One corner of the room was occupied by a row of female mannequins. The mannequins were completely white except for the blue eye shadow over their eyes and the neon pink lipstick painted on. There were also supplies for a seamstress stowed away in a tall wooden hutch. Everything else in the basement was somebody else's. Nothing down here belonged to Morty.

"What the fuck is going on with this house?" Bruce paraded about the room turning over boxes and spilling spools of thread and dress patterns, as if searching for the answer. "I saw it change. One second, your shit is here, and then the next, somebody else's shit. Tell me I'm not crazy."

"You're not crazy," Morty said. "Or maybe we're both crazy."

Cheyenne dispelled the notion.

"This room, that doorway, that's crazy, but we're not crazy. It's this house. There's something about that doorway. What do we know about this house anyway?"

Bruce's astonishment hadn't changed. He was eyeballing the ceiling, the walls and the new items occupying the space.

"It's a house. What else can you say about it? Morty, things like this have never happened before in the years you've lived here, right?"

"No. Absolutely not. I've lived here for almost ten years. We got the house for a really good price. Almost fifteen grand cheaper than its true market value."

"Just because it's on sale doesn't mean a fucking thing," Bruce said. "Tell me something that matters, you idiot. Who owned this house before you?"

"Everything was done by a realtor. I didn't meet the previous owners."

Bruce kept scanning the mannequins and the sewing equipment. "I don't know. I'm trying, guys. I don't know what's going on here. This is impossible to figure out."

Morty held his daughter by the arm and said, "We need to get out of this room now."

Morty noticed a long sheet of burgundy fabric folded on top of a worktable. Measurements covered the sides of the table. Inch and centimeter markings. It was the seamstress's work station. He decided to cover Hannah's body with the fabric.

"Just for now."

Everybody agreed covering Hannah up was the right thing to do.

Bruce noticed the sink in the corner. He hurried to it, splashing cold water in his face and lapping up water he collected in his turned-up hands. Bruce drank the water with increasing fervor.

"That's better. I'd rather have a beer. That'd really give me back my composure. Pale ale. The darkest Guinness you got. How about a finger of scotch? Fuck it. Water will do. I don't know what I'm going to tell my girlfriend when I get out of this situation. Hell, what are we going to tell the police? I guess we can pretend we suffered some group psychosis. Yeah, officer, a burning door sucked us all in, and we ended up in the basement of Morty's house. But it wasn't Morty's house, you see. There were mannequins and sewing equipment instead of Morty's shit. The new stuff just *appeared.* Good enough explanation, copper? You believe me, don't you? I wouldn't lie to the law, would I?"

Morty stared at his babbling friend talking and talking. Bruce couldn't see it. Bruce couldn't taste it. His bald head down to his chest was covered in the brightest of blood. The sink was coughing up blood like a spewing artery. The red came out in clots. The sink was filled with floating things. Tidbits from the human anatomy. Cheyenne couldn't look. She was crying hysterically and yanking on Morty's arm to tell the man—*for God's sake tell the man he's covered in blood!*

Morty forced out the warning, "Bruce, look in the mirror!"

Bruce looked up in the mirror. His body locked up for a second. Then he released a yawp of shock. Bruce started coughing. Revulsion destroyed his face. He was on his hands and knees sticking his finger down his throat to cough up the tainted water. After burping and gagging himself for what felt like minutes, he puked up a wide puddle of red.

Morty kept his daughter from seeing the flapping tongue in the red puddle and the twitching pointer finger. How had Bruce swallowed a tongue and a finger without noticing? Morty dared to look in the sink. It was filled halfway, brimming with nasty worms, and plated insects, and eyeballs of unknown life forms.

Morty said it for himself as much as his suffering friend and daughter. "This house can't be trusted. Bruce, are you okay? *Jesus*, what happened?"

Bruce sensed him coming near and urged Morty away.

"Stay back. We know nothing about what came out of that sink. I don't want anybody else getting hurt. I, I—Morty, I felt things moving inside my stomach! I felt fingers twitching. It's so disgusting."

With the sickening expression of horror on Bruce's face, added to the blood coloring his skin, it was hard for Morty to stay by his friend's side, but he did. Morty tore a square of fabric from one of the many tall fabric rolls that were up against the wall. He helped Bruce clean off his face and hands to the best of his ability. Without water, that was almost impossible.

Bruce kept making himself throw up. He was at the point he was only coughing up bile and nothing else. Bruce got back up to his feet and clutched his stomach.

"I don't feel right."

"Just stay calm," was the best Morty could come up with.

Cheyenne was already across the room and treading up the wooden staircase to the first floor. She wanted nothing to do with the bloody sink or what Bruce puked up. The tongue and finger were motionless on the ground in the circle of sticky blood. Morty didn't know what to make of it except to believe this house was haunted.

Cheyenne cursed at the top of the stairs. "*Goddamn door!*"

Morty launched up the wooden stairs. Cheyenne kept turning the knob, furious. It wouldn't open.

"Let me through," Bruce said. "I'll knock the bitch down."

"Bruce, wait—just hold on!"

Morty helped his daughter scramble down the stairs and clear the way because Bruce was already positioning himself to turn into a human battering ram. "Hurry, Cheyenne. Once he gets an idea in his head, he won't back off until he does it."

"I just swallowed a bunch of fucking blood and gross shit. Nothing except getting the hell out of here will make me feel better. So get the fuck out of my way!"

Morty and Cheyenne scrambled away from the staircase. It wasn't but a second later the large man was charging up the stairs. When Bruce was halfway up, that burning smell filled the air. The red was so bright at the doorway, Bruce shielded his eyes and faltered. He crashed through the staircase steps when he collapsed backwards.

When the burning red eased up, Morty raced over to Bruce. The man was sprawled out in the nook under the stairs. He had landed on the bare concrete. Bruce moaned in pain. He was clutching his right arm. A circle of blood on the side of his bicep was mushrooming. Morty thought the man had broken his arm, but the wound didn't match that hypothesis.

Bruce, wincing, warned Morty, "Get down! I heard a gunshot! Somebody's shooting up the place."

Bruce was right.

Bang-bang-bang-bang-bang-bang-bang.

Fast successions of shots were issued by many guns upstairs. Morty dove for cover, putting his body over Cheyenne's.

Various people were shouting and talking over each other. Morty wanted to run up the stairs, bang on the door and beg for help, but the bullets were flying fast. There was no way to know for sure who was firing those shots. Stray bullets pounded through the ceiling and hit things in the basement. One hit Hannah's body under the blanket between the shoulders. Another hit one of the mannequins. Three bullets hit the washer and dryer. Morty prayed they didn't get hit with a bullet like Bruce did. The man wasn't faring so well. This situation was getting out of hand, and there wasn't any way to make it any better except to duck for cover and pray for the best.

Cheyenne's body jerked with each shot that ripped through the ceiling. How many more shots were coming? Morty heard people crashing onto the floor and shouting. Sounds of hysteria. Ten agonizingly long minutes passed before the gunshots ended.

Morty said to everybody, "Wait. Don't get up just yet. They might not be done up there."

"What is going on in this goddamn house?" Bruce kept repeating the question. "Those assholes up there shot me in the arm!"

"It has to be the police," Morty guessed. "Who else could it be? It sounded like a dozen people stomping around up there."

"Nobody's doing anything now. Maybe they're all dead."

Cheyenne didn't like hearing that their help could be dead.

Morty was quick to correct that thinking. "It could be anything. There's so little we can figure out from down here."

"Why don't you take a peek up there, Morty? Since you know so much about what's happening and everything? After all, this is your house. If there's something fucked up going on, wouldn't you be the most likely to know about it? Don't you think, Cheyenne? This is happening in *Morty's* house. Doesn't that bother you? And your mom disappearing like she did. It makes a person think. I'm only connecting the dots here."

Cheyenne was very upset in the moment, but not too upset to defend her father.

"What's happening is happening to all of us at the same time. My dad's not crazy. He didn't make the house the way it is. He didn't do anything to my mother. How dare you, Bruce? This isn't like you. My dad didn't bring on those people shooting at each other upstairs. I might be worked up, but I'm not pointing fingers at anybody. What, did my father make the sink run with blood? You're talking crazy. This is all crazy."

Bruce was silent a moment, then he lowered his voice. "I'm sorry. I'm in a lot of pain. I'm scared, and I'm taking it out on you people. Forgive me."

"Apologize by buying me and my daughter a pitcher of beer and the first game of pool at Side Pockets."

"You got it, man. Let's make it five pitchers of beer."

"Five it is. Then we'll—"

Morty looked up to case the room when he saw something that horrified him. The sight made no sense. It was so illogical. He blinked his eyes several times trying to un-see it. How many times would he need to fact check what was right in front of him before they escaped this house?

Bruce saw it too, then Cheyenne did.

Bruce stood near the stairwell and stayed there. Cheyenne remained cautiously behind her father. Morty kept his distance from the mannequin. His eyes were glued to the mannequin's head. It had taken a bullet. Half the head had shattered. Real bone, blood and brain oozed down the plastic body.

Morty didn't know what to make of it.

Chapter Twenty-Six

Officer Chris Wright was upstairs one moment with the rest of the squad, then the next moment he was shielding his eyes from the blasts of searing bright red light. Consumed by the strange heat, unable to do anything but let whatever happened happen, it wasn't until that insane red vanished that he could open his eyes again. He was standing in a living room.

Officer Wright wasn't alone.

He hit the deck, dodging bullets. From the kitchen, from the upstairs staircase, from behind and in front of him, his fellow officers were blasting their firearms.

"Who killed my wife?"

Officer Wright stayed low, trying to figure out who was being shot and asking that strange question. It sounded like the words were coming from a jilted psycho fresh from a sanitarium breakout.

Shotguns tore up chunks of the wall in mighty blasts. Single shots quickly turned into sporadic death warnings as the officers' desperation increased.

Desperation from what, Wright couldn't tell from his position hiding behind a couch. Bullets were breaking things everywhere, going astray, pounding through the floor and raining chunks down from the ceiling. It's like everybody had lost their minds going trigger happy.

"Who killed her? Why don't you know? Why didn't you find out?"

Wright rolled to his right when a series of bullets shot up the couch, sending up tufts of cotton and padding into the air.

They're shooting everything except the goddamn perp!

Retrieving his .28-issue revolver from his holster, Wright was about to do some shooting of his own when he saw Officer Sarah Greene suspended in the air. A machete's blade stuck out of her lower back. She was being held up so high that gravity and her body weight caused the machete to slide up. Greene screamed as the machete slid upwards until the blade *schlicked* out of the crown of her skull. She tumbled down onto the floor, everything inside her spilling and slopping onto the wood floor as her body performed wild death spasms.

Officer Wright had dated Sarah Greene twice, and things weren't going so bad. It wasn't third base territory, but he was beyond first base. Plus, he knew enough about her to admire the woman, and here she was damn near split in half by this psycho!

Wright unloaded six shots into the towering man who did this center masse. Wright would stop the fucker's cold heart. The bullets entered and exited the man's body, awarding Wright the sight of high spattering blood. What it didn't award him was pain or death.

The man stood there as if he'd been hit by snowballs.

The bullets meant nothing.

This guy's high on PCP. Cranked up. I guess I'll have to keep shooting him.

Wright was disturbed by the sight of the man who was now studying him closely. The perp wore eye gear over his head, like one would in woodshop to avoid flying splinters in the eyes. The man also wore a paper-thin surgical mask covered in shades of dried and fresh blood. He was dressed in a dark blue painter's suit with black boots. In each hand he clutched a hammer.

The deranged man with the wicked bulging eyes and raging voice shouted again, "*Who killed my wife?*"

The killer turned to the left.

"*Was it you?*"

Both hammers swung on either side of Officer Ray Tompkin's head, the collision making the man's dome erupt. The crack of hammers against skull was like concrete wrecking into concrete. Wright watched Ray's features disintegrate into red motion.

"*Did you murder her?*"

The hammers vanished from the psycho's hands to be replaced by a huge roaring chainsaw. How he did it, how it was fucking possible…Officer Wright couldn't react or think hard enough to come even close to producing a reasonable explanation.

The killer charged into the living room, and in his wake, claimed hands from almost half a dozen wrists so nobody else could fire their guns. Every officer in the room was in a panic as their stumps-for-hands bled in generous spurts onto the floor.

Officer Wright backed into a corner behind a lone standing chair, staying silent. He feared it could be him too with the spurting stumps for hands. The victimized cops stood there screaming in shock, losing stream after stream of blood onto the wood floor. The killer double backed, swinging the chainsaw higher, shifting about the room at impossible speeds, swinging, arcing the menacing murder machine in his hands to deadly precision. Officers' heads came off their necks as if flesh and bone were butter and popsicle sticks. Lobbing off their heads so fast, heads crashing against one another in mid-air.

The murderer shrieked:

"You're supposed to protect and serve!"

"So why is my wife dead? Why is her killer still out there?"

"I guess I have to do everything myself!"

"I don't need you people! I'll find the killer myself."

"Is it you?"

"I will find you and murder you like you murdered my wife!"

"The pain will be worse! Much worse! I will paint this room with your blood!"

Wright replayed the moment the hammers turned into a chainsaw. How was it possible? And the doorway that seemed to be burning earlier, what was up with that? He still smelled the stench of flesh, hair and bones being cooked over roaring flames. Wright could barely breathe. All he could do was channel his will into watching the killing scene and process it without making a sound or drawing attention to himself. He could be one of the armless, headless victims if he wasn't careful.

One by one, the decapitated cops tumbled to the ground. Wright could hear arteries spit their contents onto the floor, forming ever-widening crimson pools. He stayed where he was, waiting for the psycho to come after him. The killer only smiled at his work and the corpses spread about the room. Then Wright was taken aback when the killer started to sob.

"I still don't know who killed you, my love."

The chainsaw vanished.

The door that led to the front yard lit up in that blazing red color. The killer stepped into the red and was gone, but not before saying, *"…I never will stop looking for the one who killed you."*

Officer Wright ran to the hallway closet, opened the door, shut it and hid in terror.

Chapter Twenty-Seven

Janet remembered a moment in her college years at Ohio State. She was living in an apartment shared by two other girls. They were party girls, and so was Janet. Jungle juice and keg beer galore on weekends, especially Friday nights. This was a particularly wild Friday night because finals week had ended right up against winter vacation. Their apartment was packed with students de-stressing. Janet was drinking, but she wasn't wasted at the point this moment happened. She had to pee, and when she stumbled into the bathroom, somebody had taken a shit on the toilet. It was one of those moments where the repulsion took its sweet time sinking in. Her mind refused to accept the problem, this being the shit on the toilet, because Janet knew she would be the one to clean it up. That hesitation was similar to right now. She would have to do something she very much didn't want to do.

Janet stood in place thinking about what to do next after she'd left the tiny room with the dirt-leaking corpse attacking her. She hadn't taken any steps forward because she was afraid to do so. What took her out of the moment was the scratching on the door behind her.

It was that damned corpse.

Get out of here before that corpse bashes through the door.

Janet was now standing in a bedroom. A woman's bedroom. She had to find a way out of this house. Janet threw open a closet door, thinking it led to another room. With no other doors to choose from except the one being scratched on by the dirt corpse, she had no choice but to search the bedroom. Janet rushed to the windows first. She was on the second floor of a house. She looked out onto a street. The streetlight on the sidewalk shed a red color, coloring everything in harsh tones. Nobody walked outside. The windows in every house in eyeshot had their lights off, including their porch lights. She saw the awning below the window. Janet could crawl across the awning and make a short jump onto the front lawn and run for her life. The plan seemed feasible.

This would make one hell of a story if she survived this. This property would be dubbed The Morty Saggs House. The Burning Doorway House. No, even better, The Bleeding Doorway House. Janet imagined herself standing in an expensive dress outside Morty Saggs's house to film her TV special. She'd get a full two hours of network time going through each room, describing how Morty Saggs murdered his wife, and how the house manipulated the man into becoming a murderer. Janet would have a nation on the edge of their seats. She's open up the human psyche and have it bleed all over the viewers. They would know every taste, smell and horror she had endured tonight. A level of embellishment was necessary, of course. But maybe not. She was seeing ghostly visions. Corpses in bathtubs. Something was indeed very wrong with Morty Saggs's house. The problem was, would anybody believe her?

What had Morty done to make the house this way?

The answers to the questions didn't matter.

Getting out of here safely mattered.

Janet attempted to raise the window up. She checked to make sure the latches weren't in the locked position. They weren't. Janet tried again. The windows wouldn't budge. They were sealed into place. Had they been painted shut?

Morty Saggs was thinking ahead of the situation. If his wife tried to escape when he was murdering her, Glenda might attempt to jump out of the second story window. It made sense to paint the windows shut from a killer's perspective.

Fuck it, she thought. She had her own key.

Janet grabbed a heavy wooden chair placed in front of a vanity mirror and heaved it at the window. She expected to be rewarded with the pleasant shattering of glass. Instead, the chair broke into many pieces. The barrier was too strong. But *how*? It was just made of glass. Janet hit the damn thing so hard she hurt her back and shoulders slamming the chair down.

Frustrated, Janet grabbed the table beside the bed and hurled the fixture at the window. Again, the table erupted into pieces.

Janet pounded the window with her fists. She was doing more harm to herself than the window, not that she cared in the moment. Adrenaline erased the pain. Fear made pain insignificant. Janet could still hear that broken corpse scratch at the door.

What would it do to her if that corpse cornered her?

Disturbed from that concern, Janet heard the voices of men and woman shouting in terror downstairs. It sounded like dozens of people were stampeding forward. Screams and fighting followed. The blasting guns covered up any sense she could make of what was transpiring downstairs. So many bullets were fired. Most of them went wild as they ripped through the floor and created holes in the wood. One bullet ricocheted off the window. Nothing happened.

A fucking bullet couldn't shatter the windows!

How was she going to escape?

No time to think. The bullets kept coming. Janet curled up in the corner and prayed one didn't come her way.

Staying rigidly still, she waited for the onslaught of gunfire and the sounds of people being terrorized to end. When it did, Janet once again opened her eyes.

Somebody was standing in the room with her.

Oh, how she screamed!

Chapter Twenty-Eight

Detective Larson was face to face with the dead corpse of a man well over three hundred pounds. The corpse's eyes were carved out of their sockets and leaking black blood. The rest of him was rotting from the inside out and weighing Larson down against the kitchen floor.

"Fucking goddamn!"

Larson kept wrestling with the corpse who was dressed in a yellow stained undershirt and boxer shorts. His struggle was a losing battle. The detective literally had to scoot out from under the corpse to escape, and that took several minutes. When he was free, he stood up to survey the scene. First, he considered how he'd fallen out of a running refrigerator. The shelves and items inside of it had been cleared out, and the corpse and him were stuffed inside the box together. But when was he placed into the box? Larson checked his head for a wound, a place where somebody could've knocked him unconscious. There was no blood or mark on his skull. He wasn't coming down from a drug dose either. Then the detective remembered the bright red doorway, and then being blinded by a great blast of light, and then waking up in a tight and dark place. That's how he remembered things, but the scene still wasn't adding up.

The detective eyed the corpse and the fridge for several minutes interchangeably. A level of recognition kept his eyes glued on the body. That recognition grew into something more disturbing. The corpse on the ground had no eyes. Gouged out clean. Scooped hollow. On both the corpse's hands were circular wounds that showed through to the other side of the hand. The hand was covered in ugly yellows, purples, and pustules. The wounds had become infected when the man was still alive. The man's fingernails were missing on random fingers. Parts of his scalp were set on fire. Larson could smell the burnt hair and flesh, and he curled up his nose in repugnance.

Larson remembered this man.

His name was Jimmy Loomis.

His body can't be here. No fucking way. It's impossible.

Observations were turning into new connections. This kitchen, this house, there was something seriously wrong going on here.

The detective raced across the kitchen to the door that led into the backyard. He turned the knob, but the door wouldn't open. He checked the locks. It was unlocked. The door should've opened. But it wouldn't. The detective punched and kicked at the barrier and got nowhere except more angry and pissed off.

Turning around to face the living room behind him, Larson could see gunpowder clouds hanging about the air. He hadn't seen the clouds earlier. It was a rich haze of blue smoke. The hot heavy cordite smell was just as potent. The bodies of more than ten officers were scattered about the room. Bullet casings covered the floor. Over a hundred rounds were spent in this room. Holes ravaged the wall, tearing open the wallpaper to reveal the panels underneath. The ceiling and floor were also chock-full of holes. These were wild shots. Guns blazing in a moment of serious panic.

The bullets weren't the only concern.

Hands were cut off from wrists. Heads were chopped off from necks. There was so much blood everywhere.

Larson didn't have to check the bodies to see if anybody was alive. Everybody in the room was clearly dead.

The room of grizzly death compelled the detective to try the front door, which was also stuck in place. The door wouldn't budge.

Larson un-holstered his pistol and aimed it at the doorknob. Before he squeezed off a shot, the corpse of Jimmy Loomis brought itself to a standing position in the kitchen. Larson heard the pulls of rigor mortis.

The blued corpse, marbled by blacks, yellows, purples and dark reds, spoke with fluids boiling in his throat. Every word popped.

"You're wasting your bullets, Detective. You may need them later. Those bullets could buy you time later on, or they can buy you a merciful death if it comes down to that. We're patient for now because we summoned you here. But our patience will wear thin, and when it does, you'll need every last bullet to protect yourself. Do your best work tonight, Detective. You can only count on yourself if you want out of this house alive."

As if on cue, the doorway in the kitchen lit up that awful bright red. The detective smelled burning. That awful tang of charred things. Jimmy limped towards the red doorway, walked through it and disappeared.

The door was solid again.

Where did the corpse of Jimmy Loomis go?

Another question, where did the people who viciously slaughtered those officers go?

Larson kept telling himself this wasn't right. The couch, the television, the pictures on the wall of a husband and wife, he recognized them all, and those pictures didn't belong to Morty Saggs and his family. This was Morty Saggs's house, yes, but it had also been somebody else's house at one point in time. The detective didn't want the logic of what he was seeing to set in too deeply. If he allowed those facts to be real, what else would he have to accept?

He refused to look too deeply into things. Doorways didn't turn red. Corpses didn't walk. Something real had killed these officers and brought him here. In the very back of his mind, Larson kept thinking, *Things like this don't happen for real.*

Larson aimed the barrel of his Glock at the front doorknob. Before he pulled the trigger, somebody from the hallway called out to him.

Chapter Twenty-Nine

The mannequin's head kept bleeding real blood. Inside its plastic head, Morty noticed the inner workings of a skull, brains and everything that would normally be inside a real human being's head. Cheyenne also noticed it and quickly stood back in repulsion.

"Get away from that, Dad. You don't know what it means."

Morty kept shaking his head at what didn't make sense. Inanimate objects didn't have blood to bleed and brains to spill. How could he twist this sight into something logical?

Bruce got up and asked for help with his wounds, disturbing Morty from scrutinizing the mannequin. Bruce's arm was dripping with blood from the stray bullet that came from upstairs. Together, Morty and Cheyenne tore more fabric from the rolls of material in the corner and wrapped it around Bruce's arm wound.

"I have to get to a hospital," Bruce said, eying the blood. He was pale in the skin and purple in the lips. "That bullet can't say in there. We have to get it out."

"We will, I promise," Morty reassured his friend as he wrapped the fabric around the man's biceps three times. "Keep pressure on it. We'll find a way out of here."

"If we can't get through that upstairs door, we're not going anywhere. I'm going to die." Bruce headed up the stairs, determined to escape now that he had lost so much blood. "I have to get to a hospital. And soon."

Morty could hear Bruce stop at the giant hole in the steps where he had crashed through earlier. He stepped around it, then he started turning the doorknob and banging it with his good arm.

"Let us out! Let us out, right now! I'm dying down here! You can't do this to us! Tell us what you want. Why are you locking us down here?"

Bruce was losing himself to the panic of the situation. Morty stared at the amount of blood that had exited his friend's body and knew the man didn't have a lot of time. It was only an arm wound, but if he didn't get the bullet out, it would mean bad things.

There were so many problems, Morty couldn't focus on a single challenge. Morty kicked over the mannequin, grabbed the steel scissors and shouted, "Why is this mannequin bleeding? Why aren't you asking yourself that, Bruce? The door won't open no matter how hard you bang on it. Something is keeping us here against our will. It's not a person. It's, it's something else. They took Glenda, and now they took us. We have to figure out what it wants."

Morty turned his head up at the ceiling. "What do you want? Say it, and I'll do it! None of this is necessary! Anything you want. *Anything*. We'll do it."

Bruce kept banging against the door. "Don't waste your breath. This isn't a situation for talking. I'll get us out of here. Watch me. I've had enough of this house."

Cheyenne was at the bottom of the stairs. She was right between the two men who were competing to correct an insane situation. She was so unsure of what was going on, she could only frown and beg her father and Bruce to stop what they were doing. They were scaring her.

Morty was so frustrated, scared and unable to do anything to help himself, he didn't hear his daughter until Cheyenne grabbed him and shook him hard.

"Look! Hannah's moving!"

Chapter Thirty

Detective Larson turned around to find a young officer pop out of the living room closet. He recognized the cop.

Officer Wright kept pointing at the floor, saying real fast, "They're gone. Where did the bodies go? Twelve cops were here. *Right here*. The man, that man, he slaughtered them all. I saw it happen. But where's the blood? Where's the blood? I'm not making this shit up. And I'm not crazy either. None of this makes any sense. I'm going out of my mind."

"Boy, you need to take a deep breath and calm the fuck down." Larson grabbed the cop by both arms and sunk his fingers in real deep until it hurt. The pain got the young cop's attention. "I just got out of a refrigerator trapped with a corpse. When I got out, the body started talking to me. If I can get a grip after that, so can you."

"Why were you in the fridge?"

"I didn't voluntarily go into the fridge, dumbass. I was forced through this burning doorway, or something like that, you see. It was red—"

"—Me too, me too! Yes, all of us entered Morty Saggs's house like that. The squad went upstairs to the bedroom. Morty was calling out to us, and BAM, we're in this room being attacked by this tall, burly guy wearing plastic eye gear, a doctor's mask and a painter's outfit. The guy slaughtered everybody. Well, everybody except for me. I hid from him. I'm not ashamed to admit it. I would be dead right now if I stood there like an idiot and let him slaughter me. None of us stood a chance against him. You believe me, don't you? I had no choice but to hide. I didn't want to die."

"Shut up, boy. I'm thinking. Sit down on the couch and calm down. Listening to you talk is starting to seriously aggravate me."

Larson was thinking all right.

The connections were missing, that vital glue to keep it all together. Corpses didn't come back to life. Houses didn't trap people. Red burning light didn't transport persons from one place to another. Dead killers like Ted Lindsey didn't return to life to take out an entire squad of policemen.

"You said a dozen cops died in this room?"

Wright shot up from the couch. He had so much nervous energy. He'd been repeating the explanation to himself under his breath the entire time the detective was thinking over the matter.

"Yes. I mean, blood was everywhere. He had hammers and a chainsaw, and he kept shouting something about his wife. *'Who killed my wife?'* That's what he kept shouting. *'Who killed my wife?'* Dude was scary. Even if I tried, there was nothing, and I mean nothing, I could do. He killed all of those cops in under a minute flat. No exaggeration. I'm not a coward. I was scared, yes, but I'm not a fucking coward. I did what I had to do to save my life."

"Shut up, you hear me? Calm down, or I'll calm you down for you. I understand you were under duress, so drop it. No more explanations."

The detective recognized Officer Wright from the precinct. He was Dean Wright's boy. Judging by the kid's lack of toughness and wherewithal, even in this situation, the detective knew the boy had a heaping dose of nepotism to get him through the academy and into that uniform. The officer needed validation and something to do, so that's what Larson did. Anything to shut the young pup up would serve well to help improve this tricky situation.

"I'm going to have you check every door in the house. See if one is unlocked. I couldn't get them open earlier. Yell at me if you can open one of these doors."

Wright was covered in a nervous sweat. He stumbled from one room to the next, trying to force open doors and failing.

"It's like the doors don't function like they should, you know what I mean? If the classic way doesn't work, I guess I can try *this*."

Wright turned over the kitchen table, broke off one of its thick wooden legs and bashed it across one of the living room windows. The makeshift bludgeon split down the middle. Wright smashed it over the glass again and again until what he had in his hand was decimated.

Wright gave the detective a helpless look. *What now* showed in his eyes.

The detective moved to the front bay window and peered outside. The streetlight shed that ambient red. It was pure night without a moon or any stars in the sky. The block was silent. Nobody had their lights on. No cars were in the driveways. No barking dogs in people's backyards. Nothing.

What was he supposed to draw from this scene?

"Okay," Larson said, thinking out loud. "We're not where we're supposed to be anymore. Whenever we crossed that doorway, we went somewhere else."

"But we're in someone's house. This is real."

"Corpses don't come back to life. And that man you say killed all those cops—even though there's no trace of blood or their bodies—has been dead for well over ten years. This used to be Ted Lindsey's house. And however this is happening, maybe the knock-off killer mimicking Ted Lindsey wants something from us."

"What does this fucker want?"

"You said it yourself, Officer. This guy wants us to solve the case of Deborah Lindsey's murder. And we're not leaving this house until we do."

From downstairs, they heard a woman's scream.

Chapter Thirty-One

The bullets that had been tearing through the house earlier mattered little up against the corpse standing in the room with Janet. The corpse was a younger man, high school age, maybe in his twenties. It was hard to distinguish these details under the glow of the red light bulb shedding its mean color. The sunken contours of the boy's face, the skin thinning and turning into a black bruise color, sullied any ability to truly determine the boy's age. Not that it mattered. Janet focused more on how the young man's hands were constantly issuing blood from dozens of crude holes the size of BB pellets. In one of the young man's eyes, over a dozen ink pens were jammed through the cortex.

The young boy acted oblivious to his inflictions.

He was too busy pointing at the floor.

Janet screamed yet again. "*Oh my God!*"

Yet another body was on the ground. It was a woman in a pink evening gown. Her black hair was soaked in blood. Janet could see a dent in the back of her skull.

The corpse spoke, though when he opened his mouth, a collection of beetles and centipedes crawled free, slithering down the boy's body and onto the floor, soon hiding in the shadows of the room. Crunching through exoskeletons and insect bodies, the corpse spoke without affectation. Those vocal cords were good and dead.

"Don't run from me. My name is Chad Neilson. I'm not here to hurt you. At least not now. I'm doing my best to hold back the evil inside of me. Evil has inhabited this house, and evil has summoned you here. Once you crossed that door, you entered a new plane of existence. This is where the dead reside who seek justice for the wrongs perpetrated against them. We're waiting for someone, anyone, to mend our broken souls. We were all brought to this house and murdered at one point.

"There's only one thing we want, Janet, and only you and the others here can give it to us. The way back for you will only be available for so long. If you don't give us what we want before the doorway closes in on itself, you'll be trapped here with us for all eternity.

I promise you'll suffer in torment. Not you, nor anybody else, is leaving until we get what we want. I'm trying to help you before I go bad again. You don't want to be around when I go bad. So you better hear me out. I need your undivided attention. I beg of you."

Every alarm and red flag in Janet's mind went off. Janet searched the room for a weapon. Anything to defend an attack, be it against a corpse or anybody. A heavy book from a nearby shelf. The bedside lamp. There wasn't much here in the room to use.

She could sprint for the door, but she knew it wouldn't open. She was trapped. This house was controlled by something evil.

Janet did her best to stay calm. That was a tall order indeed. She had to hear this ghost/corpse/aberration out. The more information she gathered, the more likely she might survive this nightmare. The reporter in her had enough backbone to stand in place and listen to this dead man speak.

"I died in this house. Nails were driven through my hands downstairs in that damn basement. I was forced to eat insects. The son of a bitch burned my genitals. He even," the corpse pulled up his shirt, revealing his stomach with a "T" of stitching, "cut me open. You see my flesh move along my belly? Those are rats inside of me. He cut a hole into me, shoved rats inside, and then sewed me up. Those rats were nice and hungry. They're still eating my insides, tunneling through my intestines and scouring every inch of me for a new morsel to eat.

"At that point in his interrogation, whatever he wanted me to say, I shouted it with every conviction a man in agony could muster. It still wasn't enough for the sick bastard. Nothing could appease that lunatic sadist. It will be you next, Janet, if you don't solve this poor woman's death. Nobody knows who killed her. To this day, even. You must find out. While there's still humanity in those who died in this house, you must solve Deborah Lindsey's murder."

Janet, unable to restrict her inquisitive nature as a reporter, even under these extreme circumstances, asked, "Who is Deborah Lindsey? How did she die?"

The corpse cringed as if suffering a fresh round of cruelty against his body.

"The murder weapon was left on the scene. It was a failed robbery. Deborah died for nothing. Whoever broke in didn't steal anything. Someone took a nine iron and bashed in her skull. One thwack was all it required to cave in the back of her head. Dead," he snapped his finger, breaking both of the digits off in the process, "like *that*."

Chad eyed the broken bits of bones extending out of his shattered hands. It was as if the reality of his death was closing in on him even harder.

"I can't hold it back much longer, Janet. I have so much hate and evil locked up inside of me. When you die like I did, in total agony, it follows you to the grave. It follows you into eternity. I can't rest until the one responsible for what happened to me is held accountable. My soul will always be broken, and it's up to you people to mend it. If you fail, you shall suffer the consequences."

"Wait, who else is here?"

"You'll find out very soon, Janet." Chad pointed at the bedroom door. "You may leave now. They'll be waiting for you downstairs."

"*Wait, wait, wait.* Don't go." She couldn't believe she was asking Chad to stay. The corpse wasn't getting any easier to look at, but he had such vital information. "Why was I forced through that doorway? Why me?"

Chad's face contorted into a sinister smile. The movement caused two of the pens jammed into his eye socket to fall onto the ground.

"Not counting the cops who got sucked in the doorway on accident, everybody was brought here for a reason. Together, you can solve the crime. You can find out who killed Deborah Lindsey. The living owe us that much. The way we suffered, please, give us what we need to rest in peace. Before it's too late. I'm not the only one who will be sorry if you fail."

The light bulb in the ceiling started to glow an even brighter red. Janet had to squint against its intensity. She covered her face with her hands to fend off the sharp light. Once the red reached its height, the color vanished altogether. The room was bathed in normal light. Chad was gone. Deborah's body had vanished.

The bedroom door creaked open by itself.

Janet heard the screams coming from downstairs and hurried down the staircase to find out who else was trapped in the house with her.

Chapter Thirty-Two

Morty was the first to hurry to the table and lift the sheet over Hannah's body. Hannah was indeed alive. She tried her best to sit up, but the collection of nails driven through her hand kept her sitting in the chair. Hannah's eyes were full of tears. He words were bogged down with the tortures inflicted against her body.

"Wait," Morty said, "I'll find something to get those nails out. Hannah, we're going to get you out of here and to a hospital, I promise."

Morty's words were cut off by a bitter Hannah.

"I'm dead, Morty. *You stupid shit.* What that horror of a man did to me I pray none of you have to endure. But you will. Worse than me. Oh, so much worse. What he expects from you is impossible to fulfill. With every new nail he drove into my hand, with every fingernail he ripped out, that bastard made me say things that weren't true. *Lies, lies, LIES!"*

Cheyenne teetered between comforting Hannah and keeping her distance. Morty and Bruce were searching the room for tools to free Hannah from the table. So far, their search was fruitless.

Morty kept talking. "Who is this guy? Do we know who this man is?"

"Yes. His name is Ted. He used to live in this house. Your house, Morty. He took Glenda. He reached through the doorway and pulled her in. Ted wants to know who killed his wife. He will make you find out, or what happened to me will happen to you. He used Glenda to bring all of you here. Ted thinks someone among us knows what happened to his wife."

Morty was trying to take in what she was saying without studying her wounds too much. Her flesh was changing. What was once cycling blood and pumping with life was degrading. Even Hannah's eyes were drying out and shrinking in their sockets, yet still she talked, and what she said was terrible.

"Ted will interrogate you to the end of your sanity. Find out who killed Deborah

Lindsey. You must. She died in this house. Ted's victims all died in this house AND SO WILL YOU!"

Hannah's face was a melting candle. Morty gasped watching her mandible, tongue and teeth shape the words through liquid see-through skin. The madwoman jerked her hand upwards, ripping it from the table. Half of her hand remained stuck by the nails. Her hand was a mitt of spurting blood and broken fingers. She used that hand and swung it against Morty's chest. He was thrown across the room by the force of the blow. Morty crashed into the mannequins who suddenly came to life, holding him down, choking him. Two of the mannequins leaned on his stomach and lungs to snuff him where he lay.

Morty briefly caught Hannah leaning over a cowering Cheyenne, who had fallen onto the ground in horror. Hannah's face was dripping flesh onto her body. The flesh was actively moving, combining and coagulating into a noose that slithered like a snake up to Cheyenne's throat. Once that boiling flesh noose had wrapped around Cheyenne's neck, the noose shot up to the ceiling with a wet *thack* and held Cheyenne high up in the air. He could hear his daughter choking. Cheyenne's eyes were as wide as they could get, bulging from the sockets.

Hannah's face, only a skull with strands of muscle tissue and hair, cackled at Cheyenne's pain. Morty was ripped from his daughter's situation watching the mannequin's features writhe and shape intense animosity. There were no eyes, just the pink lips and blue eye shadow. If only he could gain leverage, the mannequins were hollow on the inside. Four of them on top of him, he was outnumbered and overpowered.

"*Ahahahahahahahahahahahahahah!*"

Hannah's delight was grating to Morty's ears. Cheyenne's frantic choking noises told him time was burning fast in favor of his daughter's death by strangulation. Her face was a violent shade of blue. How much longer before death claimed her?

Enraged, Morty slipped one of his hands free of the mannequin's hold. He swung, and he swung hard, winning a punch to the mannequin's head on top of him. His fist was wedged between shards of broken plastic. Jerking his arm to reclaim his fist, he ended up throwing the mannequin backwards. The body was off of him, but a new body had already taken its place. Its painted-on pink mouth opened to reveal teeth like a snarling dog's.

Cheyenne's struggles were slowing down. Enough oxygen had been deprived from the brain that she was starting to slip into unconsciousness. If she slipped, she would die.

The flesh noose continued to boil and let off steam.

So unreal. Morty couldn't deal with the horror surrounding him. He kicked upwards and the attacking mannequin sailed up over his head. Rising from the ground, Morty thrashed aside the other mannequins until he was clear of them.

Bruce warned him, "Morty, watch out!"

Hannah was behind him, the skull-faced madwoman. She was about to drive a pair of steel sewing scissors into his back when Bruce swung a wooden chair. The chair caved in the top of Hannah's skull. Her body dropped to the floor.

The moment Hannah hit the ground, Cheyenne's body was released. The liquid noose vanished. Hannah's body hit the ground. It kept melting, the sound of it a sickening boil. The mannequins each toppled over and hit the ground with the sound of hollow plastic.

Bruce set down the chair. Morty rushed to his daughter who was gasping for breath. She was alive, Morty thought, and thank God. Father helped daughter to her feet.

Bruce's gait was uncertain. He was still losing blood from the bullet he took to the arm, but the man was determined to help them stay alive.

"What happened to Hannah?" Cheyenne asked them. "She turned into a monster. What did they do to her?"

"First thing is finding out who *they* are," Morty said. "Somebody tortured Hannah in this basement. I don't know when they did it, or how, considering we each went through that doorway at the same time."

"This place isn't right," Bruce said. "It's your house, and it's not your house, Morty. Whatever that doorway did, it has warped things. That doorway is evil. It's making things come to life. For God's sake, Cheyenne was hanging by a noose fashioned from flesh. Explain how that's possible. We're not in a safe place anymore. We're somewhere we shouldn't be."

"Hannah said something about a murder," Morty said, already understanding this house, this place, wasn't right. That much was very fucking clear. "If this is my house, and we never left it, who died in my house? I still don't know what happened to Glenda. She has to be here somewhere."

"If she's here, she has to be dead—I'm sorry to say it, Morty. I know it's hard to think in those terms, but on her own, how could she make it in a place like this? We're barely holding up, and there's three of us."

Morty was chilled by the thought Glenda was dead, but his best friend was right. It was very much a possibility.

"Then where's her corpse? Who were those people firing guns up there? We haven't searched this house enough. We've only been in the basement. That doorway appeared for a reason. We were sucked through it for a reason. I still don't know what Hannah was talking about earlier. Did somebody die in my house? If they did, I know nothing about it."

Bruce forced out a single note of wry amusement.

"I guess the realtor forgot to tell you a few details. I just assumed you knew, Morty. When you moved into this place ten years ago, I kept my mouth shut. You and Glenda were so happy to get into a house you could afford. You bragged and bragged about the price as if you didn't care this was the infamous Interrogation House. I didn't put any stock into earlier, because I refused to believe this place was haunted, or that anything supernatural was going on."

Morty had to backtrack. "Excuse me. Wait a second. The *what* house?"

Before Bruce could say anything more, the door at the top of the stairs opened.

Chapter Thirty-Three

Detective Larson was surprised when the door to the basement came right open. He was also taken aback by the three people standing at the foot of the stairs staring up at him with terror on their faces. Larson noticed at the middle of the staircase, several of the wooden steps were broken. The taller, bald man of the group had a bleeding arm. That was Bruce Spaniel. He recognized the other two as Morty Saggs and his daughter. The three of them were covered in blood. The detective couldn't help but wonder what these people knew about the doorway, the house and the living corpses.

The detective aimed his Glock at the three of them. "I want you upstairs right now. No tricks. If you've done nothing wrong, you have nothing to worry about. Now, if you would, please, come on up."

Larson whispered to Officer Wright, "Back me up."

The cop aimed his .28 pistol, the gun already in his hands before the detective had opened the basement door. The officer continued to be spooked. If the novice couldn't handle basic police work, there was no way the officer was going to take on what was happening in this house, Larson thought.

The three downstairs were slow to edge up the stairs.

Larson spoke sternly. "Up the stairs. Come on. I don't have all night. One behind the other."

"We're moving as face as we can, Detective. We've had a long night ourselves," Morty said. "One of you up there shot Bruce in the arm. Stray bullets were flying everywhere. What's going on, huh? You care to tell us, or are we on a need-to-know basis, and we don't need to know? Is it one of those bullshit police situations?"

"This isn't the time for sarcasm, Mr. Saggs. You did something to this house, and you're going to tell me what."

"I did something to this house?" Morty hurried up the stairs. He was in the detective's face despite the gun being aimed at him. "You had me pegged from the start, didn't you?

You think I murdered my wife, that I'm the one making red doorways appear out of thin air. Now you probably want to blame me for Hannah's death as well. Why not blame me for her resurrection too? I have Christ-like abilities. All this time, and I never knew. *A-fucking-mazing.*"

"Wait, Hannah's dead?"

Morty hesitated. "I *think* she's dead. I don't even want to try and explain what happened down there."

Larson didn't like the way Morty was coming at him.

What had happened to Hannah?

The three were in the living room now. Officer Wright kept his gun trained on them. Nobody trusted anyone in this house.

"I want you to watch these three, Officer. If they try anything, you shoot them. This is that kind of situation. You three sit on that couch. Relax. I'm checking out the basement. Don't move."

"Don't go," Cheyenne said. "It's not safe down there."

"I'm carrying a gun. I'm sure I'll be fine. I appreciate the concern."

Morty scoffed when he sat on the couch. He had a "fuck it" expression on his face. So did Bruce. Cheyenne sat down only after warning the detective two more times that the basement was dangerous. The detective ignored her. He didn't like unanswered questions banging around in his head, and the sight of blood on the three of them inspired many question marks.

"Go ahead, Detective," Morty antagonized. "Be a fool. If you start screaming in terror, I'm sure your buddy here will come to your rescue. They hire just about anybody to be a cop these days."

"No kidding," Bruce chimed in. "The kid looks like he shit his pants. I've got two kids of my own, and I know what it looks like when someone's filled their shorts."

"Hey, fuck you," Officer Wright barked. "Say what you want. Just do as you're told. Sit down and shut up."

Morty raised a brow. "Wait, there were shots being fired from all directions earlier. There were more people in the house. I mean people were blasting each other left and right. Where are the other shooters?"

Detective Larson was also going to tell Morty to shut up and be quiet when Wright answered the question.

"Twelve other cops were with me, and, well, they were killed, and their bodies just up and disappeared."

Morty was incredulous. "They, *what?*"

"E-nough." Detective Larson stomped his foot. "No more questions. Nobody talks. If I hear a word coming from anybody, I'm going to cuff you to something, and considering what's been going on, you don't want that, do you? Okay. Now nobody says another word. I'm going downstairs to check things out. I'll make it quick. Sit tight."

Larson eased down the rickety staircase. He thought if someone placed a lit match to it, the whole wobbly thing could burn in seconds. Three stairs were missing, reduced to broken tatters and blank spaces. Larson eased past the gaps. He was happy to hear nobody was talking upstairs. It took a professional to shut up people who were nice and worked up. Panic control was the key. Finding answers was another matter altogether.

Nothing going on in this house made a lick of sense. He wasn't a believer in the supernatural, but then again, he believed in what his eyes were telling him.

His eyes were telling him a murder took place here.

Hannah's corpse lay on her side on the floor. Her head was missing. He couldn't see her features through the glaze of black cherry splashed on her skin. Blood was spattered on the walls and the ceiling. Judging by how that wooden chair was tipped on its side and strewn across the room far away from the table, the detective considered that to be the murder weapon.

What was on the table horrified him.

Five nails were driven into the wood. On those nails were three fingers and a large hunk of meat and bones from a hand. He imagined the gristle of a devoured steak.

A pang hit him. Warm with concern, Larson broke out in a sweat. A realization was hitting him hard. He recognized the basement. The placement of things. The washing machine and dryer. The archaic furnace that was a coal-black box waiting for wood to be thrown inside and burned. The corner with items a seamstress would use, including a work table and mannequins to fit dresses on. The mannequins were tipped over on their side. One had a broken head, showing through to the hollow plastic on the inside.

Jimmy Loomis's corpse in the fridge.

This house.

This basement.

The table with the nails in it.

Officer Wright describing a man wearing eye gear, a doctor's mask and a painter's suit.

This wasn't the place to be.

Hannah's corpse shifted on the floor. Her head squished when it craned itself up to look at the detective. Both her eyes were squashed in the sockets, but the ocular tissue still moved as if perceiving images.

"Someone in this house knows who killed Deborah, and until they confess, Ted will interrogate each and every one of you. Do it your way, Detective, or Ted will do it his way."

The light bulb changed from yellow to electric red in two seconds. The red pushed him backwards. Larson stumbled against the stairs, landing hard against his back. Shielding his eyes, crying out in horror, it was several seconds before the red bulb turned back to yellow. When the change occurred, it didn't make matters any better.

It had made them much worse.

Ted Lindsey stood under the light bulb, wearing that plastic eye gear, paper face mask and the painter's outfit. A hammer was clutched in one hand. A bundle of six-inch nails were clutched in the other. The hulking six-foot tall man was breathing hard, his chest heaving, his breath under the mask audible, like a snarling dog's.

Behind Ted, the twelve missing officers, each white as corpses, their expressions vacant of humanity and replaced by vile evil, riddled with bullet holes and more insane damage, stood with torture tools in their hands. Wire ropes. Wooden buckets. Tongue pullers. Eyelid rippers. Leather whips. Archaic devices Larson had little knowledge of, but knew their purposes were purely for torture.

"Find out who killed my wife," Ted said, kicking Hannah's battered and motionless corpse. "One interrogation down. I'll give you some time to talk it over with the others. Get your facts together, Detective. I'm coming for the next one of you very soon. I have so many questions to ask everybody. Soon, it'll be interrogation time again."

Detective Larson couldn't move. He gawked at the officers he once knew, who were now covered in decaying flesh. Worms crawled in their sockets. They were torn up by bullets. Gangrene infection tainted the air. Some officers were pulling worms and insects from underneath their skin, digging in real deep to stop the infernal itch. Some didn't even have heads or hands.

The light bulb spat out that blinding crimson light once again with renewed intensity. Ted, the corpses and Hannah all vanished.

The bulb's light returned to normal.

Larson was alone in the basement.

He heard Ted's jarring words on the air.

"Soon, *INTERROGATION TIME!*"

Larson ran up the stairs as fast as his feet would carry him.

Chapter Thirty-Four

Janet braved coming downstairs when she heard Detective Larson argue with someone that sounded like Morty Saggs. Could she really be hearing those men speaking? Janet took a chance and obeyed her first instinct to run to familiar people. She prayed for safety. Maybe these people knew the way out.

The moment she came downstairs and found the three sitting on the couch and the young officer pointing a gun at them, Detective Larson shot up the basement stairs, slammed the door behind him and trained his gun at everybody.

"Everybody does what I say. Nobody moves. I have to think for a minute."

Janet stood at the end of the stairs. Nobody had seemed to notice her arrival. She only got out three words, "Hello, I'm sorry—" when Detective Larson shot around, startled. He came at her and forced Janet onto the love seat.

"Nobody sneaks up on me again, or you're going to get shot!"

Detective Larson was on edge. The man's eyes were casing the people in the room. Everybody was a suspect according to those shifty eyes.

"Where did you come from, Janet?"

The answer was obvious. "Um, from upstairs."

"Goddamn it, I'm serious!"

Morty realized who she was. "Wait, what are *you* doing here? It's your fault everybody thinks I killed Glenda. I didn't kill my wife. I don't know what happened to her. Why did you do this to me, lady? That's some underhanded shit you pulled writing that article."

Officer Wright stepped between Janet and Morty. "Calm down, Mr. Saggs, or do I need to mace you?"

"I'm trying to get some answers about my wife, and you're threatening me with mace?"

Larson had zero patience. "You want to continue to be a problem, go ahead, Morty. I'll laugh when he sprays that shit in your face. It'll hurt like hell. Maybe then you'll shut up."

Janet was scared of everybody in the room. She was beginning to think it was a mistake coming down from upstairs. Detective Larson's dismayed face offered nothing in the way of relief. The young cop's face didn't offer any confidence either.

Larson asked her, "How did you get here, Janet? Why would you be at the house when the rest of us were?"

"I was tracking the case, or rather, I was tracking Morty, and I heard screams coming from the house." She pulled out her 9mm to demonstrate purpose. "I came in the house fearing Cheyenne was going to die. Those screams were so intense. I thought Morty killed his wife, then he was—"

"I did no such thing to my wife! You bitch, you made everybody believe I was a killer, why, I should—"

Wright removed the can of mace and waved it in Morty's face. "Sit down, Mr. Saggs, or else."

"Fuck you all," Morty said, angrily sitting back down. "I didn't murder my wife. I didn't. I thought this messed-up situation would prove it."

"Yeah, he's innocent," Bruce agreed. "We've been through a lot, but Morty's been through the most shit. He still hasn't found Glenda. You guys are pissing me off as much as you're pissing off my buddy here with that kinda talk, especially you, lady. You call yourself a journalist, I call you a bullshit artist."

Detective Larson motioned for everybody to be quiet.

"Stop it. I ask the questions. I do the talking. When I address you, you're allowed to talk. Only then. Otherwise, be quiet. If anybody talks out of line, I'm allowing my partner here to shoot you with mace. I'm sorry for the harsh tactics, but I'm afraid we've got little time here. I need to find out what's happening, and fast. If you don't like it, tough shit, because it's going to go the way I say it goes.

"Now, Janet, how did you get here?"

"I heard screams coming from Morty's house. I followed the noises upstairs. I brought my gun to stop Morty from killing his daughter," Morty growled under his breath but didn't say anything, "and I ended up in his upstairs bedroom. A red light blinds me, and after that, I found myself upstairs in a room. I, this will sound crazy..."

"Just tell me, Janet. Please. Everybody in this room has been served a heaping dose of crazy tonight."

"I'm suddenly in the upstairs room, but it's not right. A woman's dead body is on the ground. Then a corpse appears in the room with me. He said his name was Chris Neilson. Chris said the body on the floor was Deborah Lindsey's corpse. Chris said I had to find out who murdered this woman, or else Ted Lindsey would kill us all."

"That man I told you about," Officer Wright said. "The one that killed all those cops earlier. That was Ted Lindsey too. He was here, then he vanished into the red light. You think he's coming back?"

The words shot out of Morty's mouth, "Of course he's coming back!"

Officer Wright was so startled by the sudden outburst that he shot a jet of mace into Morty's eyes.

"Fuck! *Ahhhhhh* fuck! Why'd you do that? Asshole. Asshole. *You stupid asshole!*"

Morty hit the ground. His was rubbing furiously at his eyes. No matter what he did, the pain increased. It felt like paprika powder was thrown into his eyeballs.

"Sorry, sorry, I didn't mean to do that. He scared me. Everybody's so jumpy."

Cheyenne tended to her father. "I'm going to get some water. We have to wash that stuff out of his eyes. You two make a great team, you know that, officers?"

She rushed into the kitchen, stopped at the sink, and fumbled in the cupboards for a glass of water to pour into her father's eyes. When she found a glass, she turned on the tap.

Bruce, holding a rag wet with blood to his bicep wound, realized too late what would happen. "Cheyenne, no! Remember what happened to me earlier?"

Cheyenne turned on the faucet. Long earthworms slithered from the faucet, mixed with clods of soil. "Oh my God!"

The smell was atrocious. Cheyenne saw a half rotted nose. A deflated eyeball attached to connective tissue that resembled old rope. Individual teeth. She turned before seeing anything more. It was just too much!

Bruce grabbed the couch coverlet, ran to her kitchen, and covered the writhing worms and mess up. "Out of sight, out of mind."

Bruce turned Cheyenne away from the sink. "Come on, let's help Morty. There's nothing we can do here. Maybe there's water in the fridge."

Detective Larson said not to open the fridge.

"Stay away from the fridge. Trust me on that one. Things seem to be popping out of everything."

Bruce looked on the floor finding shattered ketchup bottles and broken glass.

"I'll take your word for it," Bruce said, helping Cheyenne back into the room. "You going to be okay, Morty?'

Morty was in the corner with his back against the wall. He used his shirt to rub at his eyes. The pain was incredible.

"What if that was a gun instead of a can of mace? You people could've accidentally shot any one of us because of your nerves. And why does that stupid reporter get a gun? If you haven't noticed, she's pointing it right at me."

Janet noticed the barrel of the 9mm was in fact pointed at Morty, though her hand was resting against the top of her leg. She had done it unconsciously. *Maybe.*

Detective Larson made a proposal.

"How about we promise to be calm. Nobody yells at anybody. I put my gun away, my buddy puts his away, and you too, Janet, you put that bad boy 9mm on the arm of the couch. We have a lot to talk about. The faster we do it, the faster we get to the bottom of things. The faster we might be able to leave."

"I don't trust Morty," Janet insisted, keeping the gun tight in her hand. And it stayed trained on Morty. "You see, I visited him the other day. He invited me into his house. He was lying in bed because he was sick. He said he'd do anything to help the investigation of his wife's disappearance. I was asking questions, then the old man launches out of the bed, grabs my breast and assaults me."

"*I did no such thing!* You're full of incredible stories, aren't you, reporter bitch? I never let you into my home. I wouldn't dream of it after that article you wrote full of lies. You made me look like I was insane. I should sue your ass, lady. You're a liar!"

Janet gripped the 9mm.

Her intentions were clear.

"Stay the fuck away from me, Mr. Saggs. Don't. Come. Near. Me. I'll shoot you dead. If you killed your wife, you could easily kill me."

"How dare you?"

Morty's eyes were irritated raw, making him look like a fuming maniac.

Cheyenne pointed a stern finger at Janet. "Morty's the victim here. You've been no help to anybody."

"Oh bullshit. Nobody wants to believe their father is capable of murdering anybody, but I know otherwise. My hunches are correct."

"Your hunches are correct?" Morty was cornered by Bruce who kept telling him to cool it. "You haven't been sniffing leads. You've been sniffing your own ass, lady. I've done absolutely nothing to anybody. I know how you reporters are! Whatever preconceived notions you have about me, you better start shaking them, because you're so very wrong about me."

"It's your fault the detective hounded my father so hard," Cheyenne accused. "You've got nothing better to do than make somebody's tragedy even worse for your own personal gain. You make me sick."

"Morty assaulted me," Janet said. "He hurt me. It happened."

"Bullshit," Bruce said. "When did he have the chance?"

"I haven't laid a finger on you," Morty insisted.

Janet unbuttoned her top. She parted her bra to show her bruised breast. The nipple was covered in bandages. The bandages were spotting red.

"He grabbed me. The man was screaming nonsense at me. He leaped out of bed as if to rape me."

"Now you're saying Morty wanted to rape you!" Bruce was aghast. "You've got something coming to you all right."

The pain in Morty's eyes was still intense, but something rang true to him. He remembered the days he couldn't leave the bed. The days the doorway was messing with his mind.

Morty had to ask Janet a question.

"Janet, was I in bed when you say I did this? Did I get up to answer the door? Was anybody else home at the time?"

"Nobody else was home. You called me from upstairs, and you sounded all nice and friendly. Too bad it was all a set-up. I took your bait hook, line and sinker."

"You swear I did this to you?"

"Quit talking like you didn't do anything wrong. Yes, I swear on my dead mother's grave. It was you who assaulted me. You're a monster. You killed your wife, and I will prove it."

"I DIDN'T KILL MY WIFE!!!"

Detective Larson fired a round into the ceiling. It quieted everybody. The detective was done with the public relations campaign. Forget diplomacy. This was his show and he was going to run it to his liking.

"Give me the gun, Janet. *Now.*"

"But Morty will—"

"Right now. I can handle Morty, if need be."

Instead of waiting for Janet to give up the gun, Larson forced it from her hand.

"Thank you. Let's put things in perspective. None of the doors in this house will open. The windows are impenetrable. We're not getting out of here until we figure out some things. We must work together. Now Janet, you said you saw a corpse upstairs?"

"Two corpses," Janet corrected.

"Okay, two corpses. I want to have a look around with you up there soon. Do you know much about the Deborah Lindsey case?"

"You mean about what happened at The Interrogation House?"

"There's that name again," Morty said. "Why do you keep calling my home The Interrogation House? Everybody seems to know all about it except for me and my daughter."

The detective decided to play it straight with the hard truth. "Ten years ago, before you lived in this house, I answered a call here. Deborah Lindsey was found dead in her upstairs bedroom."

"So somebody died in my house?" Morty posed. "It happens. People are killed on properties all the time. What's special this time around?"

"What's so special is that this house, right now, matches the murder scene that night. This house is as it was ten years ago on the day Deborah Lindsey was murdered. It doesn't do much to explain the red doorways—"

"It sure as shit doesn't," Bruce said. "None of this scary crap makes sense. I'm going to bleed to death before we figure it out. And even if we do figure this out, does that mean we get to leave? It's like we're playing a game without the rules."

"I might have a strong idea about what's going on here," Larson said. "And it has to do with Deborah's husband, Ted. Do you know why they call this house The Interrogation House?"

"I sure don't," Morty said. "I never knew anything about anybody dying in my house ever until now."

"That's because what happened here ten years ago was pretty sick. People in town still talk about it sometimes, but they don't have the whole story, which is why you don't know the sick history of this house, Morty. Nobody knows everything, except for the unlucky few, like me. But I'm going to tell you all about it, because it was my case. And it was a case that went cold. I failed to solve Deborah's murder. And now it seems we've all been summoned to solve it ourselves, or we all die. I understand why it chose me, but I don't understand why everybody else here is involved."

Larson didn't realize how much clarity his statement gave to everybody in the room. The words were just came out of his lips. The explanation quieted everybody.

"So let me tell you why they call this house what they do. Then we can get on with putting our heads together and getting the hell out of here."

Chapter Thirty-Five

"Ted Lindsey was scraping together money to make a living. He was a do-it-yourself guy. He hired himself out as a jack of all trades in the neighborhood. He re-shingled houses, performed basic plumbing work, painted houses and put down sod. His wife, Deborah, was a schoolteacher. They were in their early thirties and thinking about having children. They were both well-to-do people, honest and hard working. So Ted and Deborah had lived in this area for about a couple of years. They established themselves in the community. They went to church and had many friends.

"Nothing went wrong until that night about ten years ago. Ted frequented the bar downtown on Friday nights. People bought each other beers back then, because the community was a lot smaller ten years ago. Everybody knew everybody. One Friday night, Ted comes home late. He's in walking distance from the bar, so he goes home on foot. All the while, he's enjoying the night air and taking in his buzz.

"Between approximately one-thirty and two a.m., Ted arrives home. All the house lights are still on. Deborah was known to leave the porch light and kitchen lights on so Ted wouldn't trip over himself in the dark. She knew what he did at the bar, and that was drink himself silly. But it strikes Ted as odd that *all* the lights are on. Even the television is on in the living room. Ted goes inside, turns off the TV, but when he enters the living room, he notices the back door through the kitchen is wide open. Ted calls out for his wife, and she doesn't answer. Ted cases the house, and it isn't until he arrives upstairs in his bedroom that he finds Deborah Lindsey on the ground, dead. She's bleeding from the back of the head. The murder weapon was left in the room. A nine iron golf club was used to smash in her skull.

"Ted's devastated. He calls the police, and things are set in motion. I was called onto the crime scene, and there was no evidence. I mean no fingerprints, traces of blood or anything stolen. My guess, it was a botched burglary. Odd though, how the person didn't steal anything. Deborah's fine jewelry was on the vanity near her dead body and not a single thing was taken. I couldn't make sense of it.

"I ask Ted questions down at the station. The man's not in a good place. He can barely speak, and he's jittery. I would say it was suspicious, but it was the man's nerves, in this case. So I let Ted go. The case goes on, and I find no new evidence, witnesses, or any leads. Even the reward put up for information in regards to Deborah's death didn't award a single phone call. That has never happened before. Even the crackpots who always call in attempting to cash in on reward money didn't do so this time. Not a soul called.

"I'm doing everything I can do to put together a case, and I'm getting nowhere. No fingerprints, no footprints, no blood, no real witnesses, no nothing. The case goes cold. After so many months with nothing, you can't proceed. New cases come in. You can only hope a witness turns up or a piece of the puzzle falls from the sky and onto your desk. Unfortunately, it didn't happen. Meanwhile, Ted goes off the deep end. Nobody knew this until it was too late. The man kept working, fixing people's leaky faucets, loose gutters, and performing basic home maintenance for the neighborhood. Ted has as much work as he wanted. Everybody in the community was pulling for Ted.

"Ted put on a good show. He wore his nice man in the community face during the day, but during the night, he tore that mask off. While he was doing odd jobs at people's houses, he was compiling facts, observations and clues. After everything was said and done, I found fifty spiral notebooks full of notations that didn't make sense. How people looked at him. The arrangements of people's bedrooms. He was obsessed with rooms and how objects were put together. Ted was clearly going off the deep end.

"I wish the man would've stuck to his simple observations, but the guy took it to the next level. When he got home after a long day, Ted didn't take off his work clothes. He stalked the streets, following anybody he suspected could've harmed his wife. Ted became a detective and vigilante. He kidnapped people and took them into the basement of his house. He built a small room made of bricks. From the outside, it was virtually soundproof. Ted placed a table in that room where he asked innocent people questions about Deborah's death. He kept them chained to the floor by the ankles. Even if they escaped, the door out of the room was triple padlocked from the inside, and Ted was the only one with the key.

"If Ted wasn't hearing what he wanted, and he never did, because he'd gone completely insane with grief, he would drive nails through the person's hands. He tortured people for hours on end. Ted would bash toes out with hammers. Dip people's feet in boiling pots of water. He resorted to ripping out fingernails. Busting kneecaps. He murdered fourteen people by the time someone witnessed Ted kidnap a local in the neighborhood. When the police busted in on his house, the man had torture tools lined up on the walls of his basement. Things I couldn't even tell you what they did. Some crazy shit.

"Ted insisted the person he had in the concrete room was his wife's killer. He had a knife held to their throat. We were at a standoff in his basement. I was on the staircase, and he was standing in the threshold of the concrete room. Ted kept saying, "*One more time. I only need one more chance. I'll prove this bastard killed my wife! Just give me an hour. Maybe two.*" Things got out of control real fast. Ted made a move to stab this poor random guy he selected from the street when I shot him. Ted takes the shot in the shoulder. He slashes his victim's throat, then he dodges my next shot. He darts across the room, finds a sledgehammer and starts breaking down the brick walls in a fury. Ted was going mad. After bashing the brick wall into rubble, he came at me with the weapon, so I had to shoot him again. That second shot ended Ted's life. He died right here in the basement.

"Things were bad enough already, but there's more to the story. Ted accumulated bodies during his so-called investigations. We found a corpse in the refrigerator. Another corpse was placed in the upstairs bathtub, buried in dirt. Ted had built a sandbox in the yard before Deborah had passed. They were going to have children, like I said. Two bodies were buried under the sand. Most of the victims, he drove to Hillsdale Lake and dumped them, though from a criminal's standpoint, he was smart enough to weigh down the legs with cinder blocks to keep them from floating to the surface. We checked the lake on a tip. Somebody had seen Ted driving in his work van around the area late at night numerous times."

Detective Larson paused a moment.

It took a lot out of him to tell the story.

"When I crossed through that red doorway, I was, I don't know, displaced, into that fridge in the kitchen. I was trapped inside with one of Ted's murdered bodies. Janet said Deborah's body was lying upstairs. And Officer Wright saw Ted murder the rest of his fellow officers. Look, I know this sounds crazy, and it is, by God it's bat shit crazy, but we've been summoned here to solve Deborah's murder once and for all. *And I think one of us is responsible for her death.*"

Chapter Thirty-Six

Detective Larson expected an outburst from everybody in the group. He indirectly accused everybody of murder. His words had the opposite expected effect. Everybody was silenced. Larson knew this was his chance to reclaim control of the situation. Considering Officer Wright was such a young pup, and everybody else was too scared to be a leader, the detective chose his next words carefully. These people needed a job, a role to play in the situation, and if they didn't have one, they would argue with each other pointlessly until somebody, or everybody, ended up dead.

"I want to take a look upstairs with Janet. I'll inspect Deborah's body for myself. If this house is as it was that night she was murdered, I have to look for new evidence. We have to give these living corpses what they want, or we'll end up like Hannah. Officer Wright, I want you to stay down here with the others. Keep everybody safe. Try the doors and windows again. After that, stay put and stay calm."

Morty and Bruce were muttering things to each other. Both of their eyes shifted between Janet and Officer Wright. They were hatching a plan, and the detective knew it.

Larson had to keep them in check.

"Bruce, you stay here. You're wounded, and I don't want you expending anymore energy than you need to right now. Morty, I want you upstairs as extra backup in case anything funny should happen. Everybody else, do as I say. Does everybody understand what's been asked of them?"

Cheyenne didn't like the plan.

"I don't want you to leave me, Dad. I'm so scared."

Bruce held Cheyenne close. "I'll stay with you. It's okay, Morty. Go. You guys won't be long. This is something we have to do, right? We weren't given a choice. I'm not feeling very good right now anyway. I've lost a lot of blood. I should stay down here, you're right. You go, Morty. I'll watch her."

Janet wasn't happy with the idea of Morty going upstairs with her.

The detective didn't leave them any choice.

"One more thing before we go upstairs, people. I don't want anybody going after anybody. It's up to me to piece together the facts. You uncover something interesting, you tell me first before sharing with it with others, even you, Officer Wright."

Everybody agreed.

Larson went upstairs hoping he was going about the situation the right way.

Like Bruce had said earlier, they had no choice.

Morty was fuming on the way upstairs. How come nobody cared about the whereabouts of Glenda? If this crime involving Ted Lindsey took place ten years ago, why was *he* considered a suspect in any capacity? He didn't live in the area at the time. He was well out of range of this town and its people. So why was he implicated?

What kept him from shouting these facts from the top of his lungs was the one thing he could not account for. Janet's battered breast. The bruises on her shoulder. He couldn't say he did or didn't do that to her.

The doorway.

This house.

It had done something to him.

Heading up the staircase, Morty called back to Janet. "You were just up here. Is something going to jump out at me? It's dark up there. I can't see anything."

"Then turn on a light," Janet said. "Figure it out for yourself, Morty."

The detective didn't like her tone. "Take this seriously. We're all in danger. We're all in the shit. Don't make it worse by antagonizing each other."

"Good idea and all, Detective, but the problem is I don't trust Morty. Supposed he didn't kill his wife. He still assaulted me. It was hard enough showing you people my body. But I proved my case."

Morty stopped in the middle of the staircase. "When you came to my house, Janet, I was sick, wasn't I?"

"Yeah. You were in bed. You didn't even get up to answer the door."

"That doorway had appeared several times before we all got forced through it tonight. It was messing with my mind."

Janet sprung on his statement. "So you can't account for all of your actions?"

"That's what scares me. No, I can't account for my actions. What I do know is that the doorway didn't first appear until the night Glenda disappeared. I did not harm my wife. That is one thing I know for certain. Everything else after that doorway appeared, I can't say one way or the other. I may have hurt you, Janet, and if I did, it wasn't me. I promise you it wasn't me. It was something in this house."

Janet sneered. The expression cut deep trenches in her skin.

"Do you hear this guy? He's full of all kinds of bullshit. You said it like you expect me to believe you, or something."

Morty's anger turned against him. He started to sob.

"Whether you believe one thing or the other, I just want Glenda back. If I did harm her, prove it. Please God, prove it so I know for certain. I must know for a fact what happened to her. If I did anything to her, you can shoot me on sight."

"Nice speech," Janet said. "Oh, and he's crying. That must mean he's innocent. Exhibit A for the defense. Morty's tears. They're so sparkly and exonerating."

Morty had to keep his composure not only for Glenda but also for Cheyenne.

"Say what you want. Believe what you want. Let's just solve this case. I want my wife back."

Larson didn't expect Morty to keep his anger in check.

The detective was impressed.

"Janet, I'm going to ask you to lay off Morty until we get some answers. I need to see the body of Deborah Lindsey before any more speculations are thrown out there. We have to treat this like a fresh crime scene. Both of you have to be my eyes and ears. No more bickering and accusing anybody of anything. If either of you had anything to do with Deborah's death, or Glenda's disappearance, I will find out. That's a promise."

Morty started walking up the stairs again. He entered the top floor hallway. The area was dark, but when both of his feet touched the carpet, the bulb in the ceiling turned a harsh red.

Morty covered his eyes. "What's with that shit?"

"I don't know," Larson said, "but it keeps happening."

Janet pointed at the second door on the right. "That's Deborah's room."

"Morty, you first."

Morty didn't hesitate a moment to stalk down the hallway and put his hand on the doorknob.

"Wait, Morty."

Detective Larson handed Janet back her 9mm. "I need cover. But if I give you this, you promise me you won't shoot Morty."

"Only if he doesn't give me a reason."

Morty scoffed. "I won't."

Both guns were pointed at the door. Morty counted backwards from three. On three, he threw open the door. The room's light was also red. Morty was startled by the corpse lying on the floor. Worse, the back of her head was bashed in.

Janet snuck past Morty. "Where's the other guy? There was another corpse in the room. He talked to me. Why isn't he here?"

"I don't know what corpse you're talking about. Just keep your eyes peeled for more of them, or Ted. Ted murdered over a dozen officers. He won't hesitate to slaughter us too."

"Where are the bodies?" Morty asked. "I mean, twelve cops don't just vanish."

"I don't know what happened to the cops."

Morty studied the room. "It sounds like we don't know shit."

Janet stayed in the door's threshold. Half her body was in the room, the other half ready to bolt. "That's the first true statement I've heard you say, Morty."

Larson was sick of Janet going on.

"Enough, Janet. Why don't you go down the hallway and check the other rooms with Morty. I need to look at Deborah's body for a while. You guys aren't investigators. The red lights are hurting my eyes. It's going to take all of my concentration just to do an average job here."

The detective surveyed the room. He leaned in real close to Deborah's body. Her long dark hair was sodden in blood. She was face down. Larson turned her over and studied every inch of skin and stitch of clothing for any clues. The room was as it was the night she was found dead. Nothing was missing or changed. A nine iron lay on the floor about a yard from her body. Dropped after it was used. The nine iron was taken from the golf bag in the corner. Ted played golf before he took up the hobby of murder and interrogation.

He realized Morty and Janet hadn't left the room.

"Get out of here, you two. You got your gun, Janet. Yell at me if anything happens. Morty will help you, and I won't hear another word about it."

Morty decided if the reporter didn't trust him, he'd stake it out on his own. He exited the room, choosing the first door nearest him and opened it. Braving anything for Glenda's sake, he stepped into a bathroom.

"Don't open that door!"

Janet raced to his side.

"What is it? *Jesus*, you make me nervous."

"There's a corpse in there."

"If you saw it earlier, it's not in there anymore."

Janet blinked her eyes twice. "I shut it up in this room. So where did it go?"

The room was cased in the same red light.

"The detective said to look for anything suspicious. Other than the red light, I say this room's clear."

Morty started to regard this house as haunted. Thinking that way, he checked under the sink, rooted through every drawer, the supply closet, and then he opened the toilet. There was only water. Nothing evil. No floating body parts or blood. Relief wasn't a strong enough word. Morty turned to leave the room and saw Janet standing there.

Her eyes were fixed on the drawn shower curtain.

"Why don't you look behind the curtain?"

Morty immediately perceived the threat.

What if Glenda's behind that curtain?

"If anything scary jumps out at me, you're going to shoot it, right?"

"Right."

"Try and not shoot me on accident."

Janet was serious. "If I ever shoot you, it will be on purpose."

Morty had a feeling he really did attack Janet. Even if it was in his fever state, it happened all the same. So he let her hold onto her animosity. There was no other way around it. Not in this situation.

"I'm going to draw back the curtain. I'll do a three count."

Janet nodded her head once.

"Okay, on three."

He counted to three.

Jerking back the curtain, Morty couldn't peel his eyes from what was inside the tub.

Chapter Thirty-Seven

"Do you believe my father's innocent?"

Bruce's heart went out to Cheyenne, especially after she asked him that question. This had been a long few days, and tonight wasn't getting any better.

"You shouldn't let that reporter get to you. Morty didn't do shit. Janet probably did it to herself. She sees Morty's vulnerability as a way to exploit him. Think about it? The reporter came to the house when you were gone. Morty didn't answer the door. The reporter claims to have *let* herself in. Funny how she went into Morty's bedroom, and Morty assaulted her. Morty was sick. He was out cold. No way did he hurt that stupid bitch. She's working a story. The bitch is sneaky. They all are when they work in that field."

Bruce tightened the bolt of cloth around his arm. The bleeding had slowed. The pain hadn't weakened. He kept feeling the bullet going into his arm again and again. The bullet had scraped bone, and that was where the real pain resided.

Cheyenne sensed his pain and experienced a wave of fear.

"We're going to make it out of this, aren't we?"

"I don't know. I wish I could say for sure."

Officer Wright tried the front door.

"We are getting out of here. You'll see."

Bruce looked at the officer at work. "It's not opening?"

"The door's jammed, or something."

The officer rammed his shoulder into the door and kicked it for two minutes before giving up, out of breath. "No use, guys. The door's not budging."

"What did you see down here when all those bullets were flying?"

The officer's brow lifted. "Do you really want to know?"

"Of course we do," Cheyenne insisted. "Why else would we ask? I can handle myself. Tell us what you saw. We have a right to know."

Officer Wright got more than he bargained for by guarding his information. "Fine, fair enough. No need to get angry at me. I think Detective Larson is right. Ted Lindsey was down here when the bullets were flying. He killed just about everybody. Ted's still here somewhere."

Bruce removed any accusation from his question. "And how come you survived?"

"Because, I don't know. Everything happened so fast. You heard the bullets. It was under a minute everything went down. The guy doing the killing was here, then he walked through a doorway with red flames coming out of it and was gone. It was fucked up. I can't control what's fucked up."

The moment of silence stretched for too long. The officer couldn't stand it. "Fuck it. I got scared, so I hid. Wouldn't you?"

Bruce recalled Hannah coming back to life and attacking Cheyenne. She was being strangled with a noose made of flesh. Nobody was courageous when shit went down like that. Not even cops.

Officer Wright moved into the kitchen. "I'll try the door in here while I'm at it."

Bruce shook his head in disapproval. "You're wasting your time. The doors won't open. Whoever's doing all of this wants us in here. They, whoever the fuck they are, hold the cards. So in the meantime, we're boxed in."

"If that's the case," Officer Wright swung the kitchen door wide open, "then try explaining *this*."

Chapter Thirty-Eight

Detective Larson cased the bedroom again and again. The red bulb was giving him a terrible migraine. *I can't focus. Damn that light.* He rubbed his eyes hard. When he opened them again, the door to the room slammed closed on its own. Filling up the room were thirteen officers. Those who still had hands trained their Mag flashlights on different sections of the room as if to indicate: *Look here, look there, no look over there, check back behind that, or try up there.*

Larson's jaw dropped.

Crowded by the living dead, Larson was now kneeling over Deborah's corpse. He couldn't move. There wasn't an inch of breathing room between him and the officers.

"You're much too slow."

"You're not looking hard enough, Detective."

"The case went cold because of you."

"Your incompetence will cost these people their lives."

"Nobody's escaping until somebody solves the case."

"Who killed her, Larson? Who murdered this innocent woman?"

"Ted will slaughter everybody. Even you."

"I don't see anything! There's no evidence in this room, in this house, any-fucking-where! It's not my fault. I'm doing my best, GODDAMN you! Can't you see how hard I'm trying?"

"Not good enough."

"Work harder."

"No one leaves until her murder is solved."

"You will die here."

"Everyone will die."

"It's not my fault! Kill me, but don't kill anybody else. They're not investigators. They're not detectives. I am! So kill me! KILL ME! I'm the one to blame."

"*Teddy's getting restless. He has so many burning questions to ask everybody.*"

"*Who will he interrogate first?*"

"*Who has the best information?*"

"*If no one pays for the crime of murder,* everyone *shall pay!*"

"*One of you knows something.*"

"*Solve her murder.*"

"*Teddy is growing restless.*"

"*He's on his way.*"

"*Which one of you will he pick?*"

"*Don't let it be you, Detective.*"

Larson was ready to shove his way through the group of corpses and rush for the door when the cops suddenly vanished.

The red light changed back to yellow.

When Detective Larson got his head together, he realized Deborah's corpse was standing over him.

Chapter Thirty-Nine

Morty expected a thousand possibilities lurking behind that shower curtain. A pair of hands reaching out to throttle him. Hannah's angry corpse grappling him down into the tub. That Ted Lindsey murderer posing with a weapon. Anything vile and evil and horrible could be waiting. Morty wasn't exactly let down when he drew back the shower curtain and there wasn't a creeping dead person waiting to attack him. What turned out to be there was strange nonetheless. The bathtub was filled to the brim with dirt smoothed down over the top. He imagined a set of hands smoothing it out. A perfectionist did this work.

"Stay back," Janet warned him. "I was attacked by something in this bathroom earlier."

"What attacked you? Dirt?"

"No, not dirt, you asshole. There was a female corpse who lunged from beneath the surface. Morty, get back! Hurry! I'm serious."

Morty wasted precious seconds being perplexed by the bathtub of dirt. The tang crept into his nostrils that moment he made the connection. It stank of dead flesh. He remembered the detective talking about what that Ted Lindsey guy did with the people he killed, and—

Two gnarled hands sprouted from the dirt. They grabbed both of his arms, and Morty was forced down over the dirt. The dirt was loose, and with his weight against it, the dirt seemed to be sinking. The hand released Morty's arms. He thought he had a chance of escape. He was wrong. A new hand had him by the back of the head, and the other grabbed a tuft of his hair. The hands were pulling him down. He tried to push off the bottom of the bathtub, but all Morty felt was the shifting of dirt. It was a bottomless pit, and he was dragged deeper and deeper.

Janet was screaming her head off. She had him by his left foot, tugging back with all of her might to reclaim him.

"Morty! Jesus!"

Morty was forced forward, pulled by numerous hands at once. He closed his eyes and mouth anticipating going completely under.

Janet lost her grip.

Morty sank helplessly into the unknown.

Janet could only scream.

Chapter Forty

Bruce and Cheyenne ran into the kitchen after watching the door flap right open.

Cheyenne hugged Bruce. "Thank God."

Officer Wright shouted upstairs. "Hey everybody! We're getting out of here. Come on everybody! Let's blow the fuck out of here."

The night air was cool against Cheyenne's skin. What a relief! They could go to the police. Bruce would get medical attention. Cheyenne would talk to that lawyer and exonerate her father. She'd sue the panties off that bitch reporter. Defamation of character. Slander. Emotional distress. Tons of emotional distress. Bruce could sue too. They would be millionaires after all was said and done.

Bruce was right behind Cheyenne. "They're coming, I'm sure. I'm not staying in that damn house another moment."

Officer Wright propped a small charcoal grill to keep the door open. "Come on, people! I found a way out! Why aren't they coming?"

"Maybe the detective found something," Cheyenne said. "It makes sense, right? He found out who killed Deborah, and the house is letting us go."

Cheyenne decided to call out to the next-door neighbors. Certainly people were on edge since the disappearance of her mother. There was a kidnapper/possible murderer on the loose.

"Help! Call the police! We need an ambulance! Somebody help us!"

Cheyenne did this for several moments before she realized not a single house stirred. No lights turned on. Windows and porch lights remained dark. Dogs didn't bark in their yards.

Nobody had heard her.

"Wait, something's not right."

Cheyenne surveyed the yard. She didn't see anything. She thought of a plan of escape. The tall wooden fence she could climb. She could easily hop over it, run to her car and drive downtown to the station.

Before she made it off the porch and onto the grass to reach the fence gate, Bruce held her back. "Hold on. You see them? Look real close at the gaps in the fence."

Cheyenne had trouble making the details out through the dark shadows. When she eyed the thin openings between the fence, the fence being rickety and old and see-through in certain parts, she screamed. Eyes were watching them. Purple corpse fingers were poking through to tease them. Cheyenne caught bolts of torn blue uniforms. Shiny badges. Torn skin. The gleam of guts. Each of the cops rattled the fence, banging their fists against the wood.

Cheyenne saw the very end of the yard. She could outrun them. Jump the fence, gun it the hell down the street and scream her head off. She was fast, and in her running shoes and the right motivation, which she had plenty of, she could outrun anything.

She bolted towards where the cops weren't banging the fence.

"Cheyenne, no!"

Bruce was hobbling after her.

"Cheyenne, you don't know what's out there!"

Officer Wright was after her in a streak.

Cheyenne sensed the cop and Bruce behind her. They wouldn't stop her. She had to take matters into her own hands. Save herself, then save everybody else. Somebody had to take a chance and do something. Going back into the house wasn't an option. She'd go mad spending another second in that scary place.

Her neck swelled with pain from when the flesh turned into a noose and hung her.

She was so close to dying.

Strangled by fucking flesh.

Cheyenne was nearing the end of the wood fence that was about six feet high. Somehow, she'd have to scale it. She didn't get a chance to decide how to maneuver the jump. A man stood behind a tree. He lingered over the large sandbox. The man was jamming a shovel into the sand and making a hole.

Cheyenne gasped at the corpse of a man lying on the grass beside the sandbox. She only knew it was a man by his general shape. The guy had been skinned alive. His exterior was a cherry gleam of muscle tissue. The corpse's eyes were wide and contorted in agony.

The cops were banging on the fence where Cheyenne was going to jump.

Cheyenne froze. Her plan was ruined.

Officer Wright caught up with her. He saw the corpse and the man who was still digging a hole in the sand box.

"Hold it." Officer Wright drew his gun. "Who are you? Stop what you're doing right now!"

When the man stopped shoveling and stuck the shovel into the dirt, Officer Wright gasped. "Oh no, it's him."

Bruce stood in front of Cheyenne. "Him, who? Who are you, asshole?"

"It's the guy who killed all those officers. It's Ted Lindsey. I saw him do it. He's insane. Stay away from him." Officer Wright drew his .28 pistol and aimed it at the killer. The gun was shaking in his grip. "What do you want with us, huh? Sick fucker, answer me."

Cheyenne sized up the killer in that moment. The clear plastic protective eyewear. The overgrown black beard that covered the bottom half of his face. The dark blue painter's jumpsuit. The black gloves. The man was hulking, standing at well over six foot. The man could snap her in half.

When Ted Lindsey spoke in that sharp gravelly rasp, the cops on the other side of the fence banged harder against the fence. Ted's eyes penetrated each of them. His gaze assigned accusations to each of them.

"Who killed my wife? Was it you? You? How about you? Who wants to confess?"

Officer Wright wasn't sure what to say to those demands. "Let's go downtown. We can talk about this. I assure you the police can help with this investigation—"

"*You had your chance for ten years!* I'm tired of waiting. I can't cross over to the afterlife without knowing who murdered my wife. Those I murdered can't cross over without knowing either. I guess I'm blocking the gates of Heaven and Hell for as long as it takes. For some of us, it'll be Heaven, but for me, it's straight to Hell! I'll be burning in that infernal pit with the rest of the sons-of-bitches. I accept my punishment, but first, someone will pay for killing Debbie."

Bruce tried to reason with Ted.

"What do you know about your wife's death? Help us help you. You're hurting innocent people. Like your Debbie."

"*You know nothing about my Debbie!* It's you people who owe me an explanation. Don't you realize how special of a person died that night? I did my part. I worked day and night to find her killer. I came so close. One of you knows who murdered her. If you're not going to help me, if you're going to play mind games, then I'll take matters into my own hands yet again. If you won't tell me who killed her, then I think it's almost that time again. I already had a nice chat with that Hannah bitch. She didn't know a goddamn thing. She had some juicy details to dish out, though. But it doesn't point me to the killer. One of you knows something. I'll make you tell me. I have my methods. So who's next for questioning?"

Officer Wright fired the gun.

Cheyenne screamed.

The bullet hit Ted in the chest. Blood bloomed from his chest. Ted didn't flinch. He looked down and laughed at the point of entry. Ted's grin was malevolent.

"I think you just volunteered, Officer."

The fence burst into wild tatters. Arms battered and powered through the barrier. Cops and other corpses they hadn't seen before, various victims of Ted's, stampeded towards them. Cheyenne was horrified at the various means of the corpses' damage. Some were crawling on the ground without legs. Others were reaching out with one hand while the other held in their insides. Some were suffering deep stages of decay while others were lightly marbled by decomposition.

"Back into the house!"

Bruce was directing the retreat.

Officer Wright was firing his weapon until the gun went dry. It didn't do a thing to slow the collection of corpses down. Wright gave up using his gun. All three of them were doubling back to the house. Cheyenne didn't make it far. The body lying next to the sand box reached out to grab her ankle. Its grip was tight, and Cheyenne tripped. Bruce stomped the foot at the wrist. Brittle bones shattered. Cheyenne jerked her leg to reclaim it, ripping the hand from the corpse's wrist. Running with a hand squeezing her ankle harder and harder with each stride, Cheyenne wouldn't stop retreating for anything.

The corpses were making their way after them fast.

The stink of dead flesh. The singed smell of scorched flesh. Cheyenne smelled fire. The smell of the burning doorway.

Surging ahead faster, Cheyenne somehow kicked off the hand from her ankle. It rolled into the grass, falling into the window well up against the house. Bruce kicked aside the charcoal grill wedging open the door. He ushered in Cheyenne first. Bruce was right behind her. He kept the door open for Officer Wright, who was a good four seconds behind them.

"Move it! They're closing in!"

Officer Wright's expression was all horror.

Bruce had the door ready to slam closed the second the cop crossed the threshold when the doorway itself started to smolder. A blast of searing hot air ejected Cheyenne and Bruce off of their feet. Bruce slammed into the coffee table inside, breaking it in half. Cheyenne landed on the couch, doing a forced back flip.

Cheyenne tried to get up again when the door exploded again with that intense red light. Flames burned around the doorway. Before she had to close her eyes and cover them with her hands, she caught Officer Wright standing in the threshold. Ted Lindsey had him from behind, one hand around his midsection, the other around his neck. Cheyenne was halfway to the door, racing to grab hold of Officer Wright's extended hand.

"*Heeeeeeeeeeeeelpmeeeeeeeeeeeeeeeee!*"

Cheyenne yelled, "Reach for me!"

Too late.

The red burning stopped.

The door had shut itself.

Officer Wright was gone.

Chapter Forty-One

Morty thought he was buried. The compaction of dirt was so crushing. He had no leverage to move or shift. Morty could only let whatever happened happen. Suffocating, stifling his own cries and forced to be stock still, he could suddenly breathe again. The pressure on his limbs lifted. The weight of the dirt was gone. He didn't fall or land. He simply was one place, then he was another. He dared to open his eyes. The way was dark. He couldn't see his hands in front of his face. Morty lifted his upper half up off the ground, and he smacked his forehead against what he thought was a low ceiling.

He heard the creaking of wood.

Someone exhaled nearby.

"Who's there?"

The voice was whisper soft. "*Only me. Your wife.*"

"Glenda? Glenda!"

Morty reached out his hands to feel around in the dark. The ceiling and floor was so low, he had little room to maneuver. It didn't matter. Glenda was alive. She was here in this house. He had to have her in his arms to prove she was really there.

"Tell me where you are. I'll help you. Honey, oh honey, did that son of a bitch hurt you? I'll get you out of here. I promise, Glenda. Everything's going to be okay."

"Stay away from me."

The way she said it made Morty freeze.

It wasn't a command.

It was a warning.

"You don't want to see me."

Up from the floor, between tufts of attic insulation, poured in red light. Glenda stayed in the very far corner of the attic across from Morty. She kept to the deepest shadows. He couldn't see any of her in detail, only her basic outline. Glenda was an object occupying a space, nothing more.

Morty was on hands and knees. He edged towards her. He only wanted to help. No matter what happened, he loved her, he would support her and he would get her out of this house and away from Ted Lindsey.

"What did he do to you? Tell me, Glenda. I'm here now. I won't leave you alone."

She pounded her fist against a wooden beam twice, shrieking, "*Stay away!*"

Morty was startled by the harsh words. He never heard her make such savage sounds before. She was in shock. The bastard must've hurt her real bad. Then he remembered Hannah. How her hand was nailed into the table. Her fingernails were ripped out. Hannah had been tortured.

Panicked by the very thought of his wife enduring such things, Morty had to ask her, "Did he interrogate you?"

"Downstairs, yes. That evil, evil man asked me questions. You don't want to know the things he did to me. Ted's sadistic and insane. The questions were almost as horrible as the torture."

"Glenda, please, let me see you. Let me help you, please."

"Nobody's going anywhere until you solve that woman's death. You heard Ted Lindsey's question. Do you know who killed his wife?"

"I don't know anything about Deborah's death. That lunatic seems to think one of us does, but we don't. We can't satisfy the lunatic. Nobody can. He murdered innocent people, he's so crazy. He's trying to murder us. For all I know, Ted killed his own goddamn wife."

"One of us killed her. Ted won't let us go until the truth is revealed."

Morty was tired of talking to a shadow.

"This psycho's got you saying things you don't mean. You never harmed anybody. You couldn't even kill the bugs in our house. You're not thinking straight. I understand you've been through a traumatic experience. This has been hard on all of us. Just come on out so I can help you. You have to come out."

Glenda sounded playful. "I've been a really bad girl."

"Glenda, stop. You're not in your right mind."

"When somebody starts torturing you, you can't hold back anything. I told him everything. Deep down personal things. Things I'd never tell you, Morty. It'd break your heart."

Morty didn't like the awful feelings welling up inside of him.

"Glenda, my God, what are you saying? Did you kill Deborah?"

"If it were that easy, Morty!"

"*Did you kill her?*"

"Oh Morty, you're in for a very long night. You and your friends really have to start asking each other the right questions. Ted's busy in the basement as we speak. He's picking out his tools and preparing to shed more blood in the name of justice."

"Who did he take? We have to get down there and save them. It's not Cheyenne, is it?"

Glenda's voice was monstrous.

"If our daughter knew the things I've done she'd never speak to me again. Maybe I deserve this punishment. It doesn't matter if one of us killed Deborah. We're here because it was meant to be."

"Glenda, no. Don't say those things."

"You wanna hear what Ted did to me? How he ripped the secrets from my body?"

Morty extended his hand to her. "Stop talking about these horrible things and take my hand. Let's get you out of here. Let's get everybody out of here safely. That's what matters."

Glenda wasn't listening.

Morty was startled at hearing something *tink* against the ground.

Tink-tink-tink-tink-tink-tink.

Whatever it was making the noise was landing in front of Morty. He looked real hard and finally made sense of the objects hitting the ground. A long tail of pink meat was attached to each tooth. She was throwing teeth at him.

"After nailing my hand to the table, he ripped out all of my teeth."

Morty backed up a half-step.

"Why are you doing this? Let's just leave, please. You don't have to tell me this right now. Later, when we're far, far away from here. Don't say another word about what happened."

Glenda ignored him.

"Then Ted, he had this trick. It's called a Chelsea Grin. I never heard of it before. You see, Ted took a box cutter and he drew a slit on each side of my lips. By that time, I was telling him everything I'd done bad in my life. I even made up things, hoping I would happen upon something that would satisfy him. I didn't say the right things. I didn't satisfy his questions. Not even close. So Ted makes a big show of cutting the heads off a bunch of nails so both ends are sharp. Then he starts replacing my old teeth with the nails.

Now, I've got a mouth full of metal.

"Oh, before I forget, the special thing about the Chelsea Grin: every time he jammed a new nail into my gums, I screamed! Those little cuts at my lips tore right through my cheeks all the way to my ears. R-*rrrrrrrrrrrrrrrrip!*"

The red lights filtering through the tufts of insulation burned brighter and banished the shadows to expose Glenda. She was crouched on all fours about to leap at Morty. Her clothing was in rags, stuck to her body with sweat and blood.

Morty reeled seeing her hideous face. Her head resembled a puppet with a large mouth. The cheeks were torn, exposing rows of jagged nail teeth. Gory slobber actively leaked from her maw.

"It's better I kill you before Ted gets a hold of you. I'll make your death quick. I'll tear out your throat. You'll bleed out and be dead in minutes."

This wasn't his wife. Glenda's pale dead skin. That hideous maw. The way her body was arched. She was compelled by a strength, an evil.

Morty knew his wife was dead.

When Glenda's legs flexed to fling herself in his direction, Morty stumbled between a wooden beam and a row of insulation. His leg broke through the thin layer of wood and plaster. The rest of his weight sent him right through the floor and into the room below. The last thing Morty saw was wicked metal teeth flash before his very eyes.

Chapter Forty-Two

A lightning blast of agony exploded in his hand and shot up his arm. Shouting, crying, cringing, mewling, cursing, sobbing, begging for mercy, blind in the dark, skin going ice cold, nerves cranked on high, Officer Wright didn't know what was happening to him. The room was pitch black. He still felt the pair of strong arms grab him from behind and pull him backwards. Then that fiery heat and the electric red color had enveloped him. And now he was here, sitting in a chair in front of a table.

He couldn't move his right hand.

BANG!

Something else was driven into his hand. Now he really couldn't move it. Wright called out to his attacker to stop, *for God's sake stop!*

A light bulb was turned on overhead.

It cased the room in that deplorable red.

There stood Ted clutching a hammer in one hand and a six-inch nail in the other. Before Wright could react to the light, Ted's face bent in rage, those eyes bulging with ideas and notions, all of them adding up to drive another nail through this man's hand.

BANG!

The nail was driven between the bones of Wright's hand with such force the nail slid through as if his flesh was made of wax. So effortless. Blood mushroomed from the three different entry points. Details rushed in at Officer Wright as his nerves worked overtime to deliver the messages of pain. The red light bulb offered vague dimensions to the room. The concrete walls. The staircase in his peripheral vision. The water heater and furnace, each standing as archaic beasts of rust. Ted Lindsey's hands visibly trembled while clutching the hammer. The surface of the table was gouged and riddled with holes from previous victims. Dried blood stained it.

Officer Wright could only imagine the horrors coming his way.

Hanging from the wall from hooks were torture tools. Prods. Prongs. Spikes. Scythes.

Pitchforks. Tongue rippers. A leather whip. The darkness obscured the rest of the items.

Ted dropped the hammer on the table. It bounced twice. Each bounce made Officer Wright jump with a start.

Officer Wright begged to be set free. He said he'd do anything to solve the murder of Ted's wife. He was a fresh set of eyes. A new perspective on the case. He would work day and night and forever until Deborah's murderer was caught.

"I must know everything you know, Officer," was Ted's response.

Ted's back was to Officer Wright.

The psycho was studying the tools and sizing each of them up.

Officer Wright's throat was ragged from begging the man to reconsider what he was doing. He was seconds from ripping his hand off the table and making a run for the stairs when Ted finally turned around. He had a wooden bucket in his hands.

What *the hell* was he going to do with the bucket?

"Let's begin. Now what do you know about my wife, Officer?"

Chapter Forty-Three

Detective Larson stumbled backwards when Deborah Lindsey stood over him. Blood ran down her neck, trailing from the massive wound to the back of her head. The detective could hear pieces of her skull shift and crack. The blue face of the corpse was offset by the sympathetic eyes and her words of genuine despair.

"Detective, I know you did everything in your power to find my killer. You're someone who respects doing the right thing. This isn't about me. It's about Ted and everybody he killed. My husband isn't the man he used to be when I fell in love with him. He's psychotic. I wish I could've told him to live his life without me. It wouldn't matter, unfortunately. Something in him snapped when I died. I don't know how to stop him. I'm afraid of him. But there's one thing I do know.

"Ted made this entire situation happen. Whatever information he has to go on, whatever he carried with him when he died, he knows that between all of you here, someone knows who killed me. He murdered those cops because he knew they didn't know anything about my death. They were useless. Ted grows impatient, you see. Soon, he won't care what you may or may not know. He'll go on killing everybody who steps into this house forever. More innocent people will die. The sooner you figure out who killed me, the sooner he'll stop the killing.

"Use your skills, Detective. Ask the right questions. Get everybody together and interrogate your witnesses before Ted does. I can't stand the thought of more people dying on my account. Let my soul rest in peace. Let Ted's soul rest in peace. Let everybody's soul finally rest.

"It's already too late for one of you. My husband's interrogating them as we speak. Hurry, before he takes another one of you down into the basement. Detective, it's up to you to finally put it all together."

The detective struggled to form words. "What about the doorway that brought us here? And the red lights? What does it mean? How do we escape?"

Deborah took a moment to enjoy her bedroom. The pictures on the walls. Her vanity mirror. The memories of being alive once upon a time.

"This house is charged up with so much pain and agony. Ted killed so many people in the basement. The burning doorway was a tear in the fabric between the living and the dead world. An opening. These spirits, these people who died under this roof, never left this house. The red has preserved the memory of those who died here, and their dying moment. Their agony is as fresh as the moment it was inflicted."

"The red?"

"Red is the color of the place where we come from. It's the walls between Heaven and Hell. The outer boundaries. The red is a purgatory full of spirits who can't cross over into their appointed eternities, whether they be Heaven or Hell. I too have waited in the red. I only want to know who killed me and why. When I finally understand who killed me, the others who died in the house and I can finally go to our appointed eternities. Ted too.

"This house is charged with so much agony and death, the red has seeped in It has changed the house. Some who have been killed here have held onto themselves, their sanity, while others have turned completely evil. Some of the victims will try and help you, while others may try and hurt you. Don't let me turn evil. If I turn evil, I may not go to Heaven. I might just wind up in Hell like my husband."

Deborah was standing in front of him one moment, the next, she was back on the floor lying there dead. Larson wanted to shake her and beg her to give him more clues, anything at all to go on. Talk of the red confused him. The afterlife, the border between Heaven and Hell, he considered it all nonsense. But she had given him an important clue. Someone among them had the right information to track the killer. All he had to do was employ his skills. No forensic science. No investigative team. Even Officer Wright would be little help, or did he know something?

Larson rubbed at his eyes.

"I don't know what I'm doing."

The pressure was all on him.

He had to get everybody together again and ask them the right questions. Hard questions. Personal questions. He was grabbing at uncertainty here, but he wasn't going to watch everybody die in this house because he hesitated too long to act.

Detective Larson rushed out of the room. He saw the door across the hallway was open. Janet was in the bathroom. She was hunched over the bathtub digging out handfuls of dirt and throwing them onto the floor.

"Where did you go?" Janet kept saying. "Where did you go? *Where* did you go? Morty, please!"

"Janet, what's happening here?"

Janet had tears running down her face.

"Morty, the hands, he was forced down into the dirt." She was scraping the bottom of the bathtub. There was nothing but flat surface. "He was forced down. Where did he go? Where the hell did he go?"

"Beneath the dirt. He fell into the red."

The detective whipped around at the figure standing at the door. Larson stood in front of Janet as a barrier. Janet hurried to her feet, grabbing her 9mm with dirt-covered hands. Larson had his pistol out, but then he lowered it.

"My God, it's you."

"Who is this…*corpse?*"

"I'm here to help you," the corpse spoke. "You remember me, don't you, Detective? I'm Jared Simpson."

"Yes, I remember you."

The corpse was a man in his late forties. He had a graying comb over. Between the thinning threads, the man's bleeding scalp showed through. The man's shirt was soaked in blood.

"Ted kidnapped me. I was driving home from work one night. The mad bastard tails me in my car. He hits me from behind at a stoplight. I get out, and he chloroforms me. I'm dragged into Ted's car, and I wake up in a room surrounded by bricks. The guy goes on and on about how I killed his wife.

"I don't know a damn thing about how Ted's wife died. He keeps questioning me anyway. First, he nails my hand into a table so I can't escape. He drives seven nails in, then one more for good measure, or so Ted said. He laughed at my agony. Then he scalped me by using a scalpel and his bare hands. Then he…he…"

The corpse's scalp started sizzling.

Janet gagged on the smell.

The detective cringed and did his best to keep his gorge down.

"He poured salt on the wounds. Ted heated up the questioning. I never knew a woman named Deborah Lindsey. I'm a married man with three kids. I tell him that, and it means nothing to him. *Absolutely nothing.*"

The corpse's face contorted in horror.

"This guy, he starts making me swallow these small ice cubes. Over the course of many hours, I've swallowed about twenty of these things. The questions keep coming. *Why did you kill my wife? What kind of a person are you? Where were you the night of October 15th between midnight and one-thirty?* The questioning goes nowhere, because I didn't kill his wife. I know nothing. I swear to God. He scalped me for fuck's sake! You would think I would've given him a goddamn confession by then. But Ted keeps on asking me questions. He punches me in the stomach so hard, I throw up. And I find out what was in those ice cubes. Fish hooks. They catch on my stomach and esophagus on the way up. He left me in that horrible brick room to internally bleed to death. *The sick fuck.*"

Janet was horrified by the mental pictures the man's story painted.

Larson was disgusted, but then something struck him as strange. "Hold on, Jared, you said October 15th between midnight and one-thirty?"

"Yes, that's when Deborah was murdered."

Larson snapped his finger once. "Of course, it makes sense. October 15th between midnight and one-thirty. Doesn't that ring a bell? That's when Glenda Saggs went missing. Ted wanted to mimic his wife's scenario. Glenda went missing the same day *and* the same time. Ted brought us all here together on purpose. Ted set it up this way. Ted didn't know who killed his wife, but he might've been onto something. He knew the right people to bring to this house to solve the case. *Yes, yes, yes.*"

Jared was visibly disturbed at the mention of Ted's name.

"Stay away from that murderer. He'll do horrible things to you, and if you can't answer his questions the way he wants you to, the things you'll suffer…"

"Why did he pick us?" Janet asked. She did everything to keep her eyes from how the man's scalp kept bubbling red. "I mean, I know I didn't kill Deborah. You didn't kill Deborah, Detective. Cheyenne and Glenda Saggs didn't kill her. That leaves Bruce, Morty and Officer Wright."

"Officer Wright didn't live in the area when Deborah was killed. It's highly unlikely he murdered her. Plus, he's so young. He would've been a young adult. Maybe not even a teenager yet. Wright is innocent. So I'm not sure if any of us killed Deborah. The thing is, one of us may have the clue that connects it all together. It's coming up with that shred of evidence that's going to be problematic."

Jared wasn't so sure. "Or Ted's so insane, he'll find any excuse to drag people into the red."

"Into the red?" Janet asked.

Larson tried to think of a way to describe it. "It's complicated, and I'm not sure if I believe it myself."

Jared explained the red. "This house is locked in our dying moment. The red has used our pain and agony and unrest and preserved our dying moment. This house is bursting with fucked-up energy. Until we know who murdered Deborah, we can't rest in peace. Ted will continue his interrogations now that he's been able to pull you guys into this house, and into the past. That's why he waited so long. He wanted all of you here at once, and taking Glenda was the only way to draw you in. You see why it's so important you guys work together."

Janet screamed at what appeared from the bathtub. Lying there was the corpse that attacked her when she first arrived here. The woman's broken corpse that was bursting with dirt earlier reached up from the tub and grabbed Jared. The gnarled, broken hand seized Jared by the throat and forced him downwards. The corpse tore the skin down his stomach like a sheet. The skin came away soft, the decayed flesh tearing with little force. Bursting from Jared's midsection were hundreds of jig hooks.

A geyser of red blasted from Jared's lips. He unleashed a single plea before his body dropped to the floor in gory pieces.

"*Ruuuuuuuuuuuuuuuuuuun!*"

There stood the dirt corpse woman. She was in tatters, her limbs rubbery and disjointed. Soil kept leaking out of her wounds. The woman had half a head, what resembled a split section of an anatomical figure. The corpse reached out to throttle the detective's neck, but Larson shot her in the face. The woman's single eye bulged wide before it exploded from the bullet's entry point. Bloody mud shot out the back of her head.

Larson shoved the body aside.

The corpse dropped into the tub.

"Go! Run!"

Larson forced Janet into the hallway. The detective slammed the bathroom door closed behind him. The woman beat against the door. Janet and the detective aimed their guns at the barrier. Any moment the corpse could break down the door and attack.

From the ceiling, they heard stomping. Something heavy went THUD. A circle of plaster cracked, then split open wide. The ceiling was caving in.

The corpse woman's fist punched through the door, breaking the barrier in half.

"Run to the second bedroom! Hurry!"

Janet took the lead, dodging the plaster raining from the ceiling. The bathroom door was ripped from its hinges. The corpse woman's body acted as a spear. She chucked herself through the tatters of the door.

"Jesus!"

Larson fired two wild shots in the corpse woman's direction.

The ceiling bent like a long convex mirror. Weight was bearing down on the diminishing barrier. The ceiling was going to collapse any moment.

"Hurry! This way!"

Larson shoved Janet into the second bedroom. He quickly threw the door shut and started to use the furniture in the room as a barricade. After securing the entrance, they stopped and listened for any more destruction coming their way.

"I think we're okay for a minute," Janet said breathlessly. "What do you think?"

"Yeah. I think we're okay."

Seconds later, the voice in the shadows agreed with them.

Chapter Forty-Four

Everything was collapsing underneath Morty. Glenda was on top of him, clacking those hideous teeth made of nails. Their combined weight sent them through the attic floor down into the room below. Morty was howling in terror, cursing at what used to be his wife as she bit down on his shoulder. He could feel the metal scrape against his collarbone. Morty grabbed her by the neck to keep those horrible teeth away from his flesh. By doing so, he spun her around. When they hit the hallway floor on the second level of the house, Glenda was on the bottom. Breaking the fall had stunned the woman. Morty didn't waste a moment getting up and running down the upstairs hallway.

Names exploded from his lips: "Cheyenne! Bruce! Detective! *Heeeeeeeelp!*"

The moment he ran past the bathroom door, he almost tripped over the piles of wood scattered on the ground. Thrown up against the wall, Morty was once again wrestling with something very dead and pissed off. The corpse was barely there. Dirt kept crumbling free from the broken valleys in her face. Morty was able to throw the corpse woman off, almost spiking the body onto the ground in the process.

"It's easier this way!" Glenda shouted from behind him, crouched again to tackle him. "Ted will torture you. He'll put you through a thousand agonies. Let me kill you. I'll do it fast and easy. Almost no pain at all. I promise you. I won't prolong your demise."

Morty's shoulder was oozing blood. The upturned skin against the open air was so painful he gritted his teeth to force the pain down.

"Stay away from me. You're not touching me or Cheyenne! You're not Glenda anymore. You're a monster."

Glenda launched herself at him. Morty attempted to retreat, but he tripped in his haste and hit the floor. He was dizzier than he thought with the blood loss. Glenda was on top of him, battering him with her limbs. Morty couldn't fight back. The dirt woman's corpse was tugging on one of his arms, and Glenda was tugging on the other.

"RIP YOU IN TWO!" Glenda's nasty nail teeth scraped each other, shedding wild sparks through the lining of her see-through cheeks. "Hold him good! Pull with all of your might! I WANT HIM IN PIECES!!!"

Morty begged for them to stop.

Glenda only laughed.

"PULL!"

Morty thrashed to escape their violence.

He couldn't do anything to stop them.

"HARDER!"

Glenda pulled so hard, the rag doll dirt corpse lost her arm. It sounded like a root being pulled up from the earth. It caused Morty to crash into his demented wife. Everything was flashes of motion. Glenda threw him up against the wall. She reared back her head. She bared her nail teeth. She was about to chomp down on his face. Then out of nowhere, a wooden object swung. One blow, and Glenda's eyes were rolling into the back of her head. With another blow, the object broke the crown of her skull. Glenda hit the floor, unmoving.

Morty's defender shoved Glenda aside and helped him down the stairs. The dirt corpse lay on the floor disembodied and unable to pick itself back up. Rushing down the stairs, Bruce helped Morty into the living room. Cheyenne waited there.

Cheyenne screamed, "*Watch out behind you!*"

Glenda's corpse was looking down at them from the second floor railing. Her head was leaking blood and brains. Cheyenne was horrified to see her mother's face in such a ruined state. The corpse stood there, teetering in place, until she tipped forward over the stoop, did a front flip and crashed down into the living room.

Glenda didn't get up.

Bruce clutched a bloodied wooden rolling pin. Something he'd taken from the kitchen. Shock played out on Bruce's face. Cheyenne kept her head turned away from her mother.

Morty's shoulder bite brought him back to the moment and the situation. As did the red doorway at the living room closet that simply materialized. That awful, foul smell exuded from the rough outline of the door. Then out came a hobbling shape.

Officer Wright.

The man was clearly dead. His eyes were bluish white cataracts. The man's flesh was whiter than bar soap. His cop uniform was soaked through not with blood but water. It was leaking out from his eyes, nose, mouth and ears. Every orifice was actively leaking.

The trickling sound was grating to hear.

Gargling and choking against the ever-flowing tide of water, the officer tried his best to speak.

"You don't have much time before Ted interrogates the next person. Pretty soon no one will be left alive. The red lights are filling up the house. Soon everything will be red. When that happens, when all is red, we'll all be dead and trapped forever in this forsaken house with Ted. You must find out who killed his wife!"

Officer Wright pointed a gray finger at the kitchen light bulb that changed from yellow to red. Then through the crack of the basement door, more red light showed. Bleeding through the drawn curtains, that haunting color burned.

"You see, the house is filling up with red. Soon, the corpses trying to help you will turn against you once they realize you can do nothing to save them from their fate. No Heaven, no Hell, only purgatory red. If Deborah's case isn't solved, Ted will keep bringing in more victims through the doorway. He won't stop until he learns who killed her. Can you imagine how many will die that had absolutely nothing to do with the murder?

"This is our best shot. You people have the most clues. You're so close to the truth. Don't let the red become your afterlife. We'll never see Heaven or Hell. We will suffer on Deborah's dying day for all eternity."

Officer Wright noticed Glenda's corpse.

"When Ted was interrogating me, he strapped me down and waterboarded me. I thought I had drowned a hundred times. Ted was saying things about Glenda. They were quite disturbing. Glenda confessed to certain things when Ted was pulling out her teeth in the basement. There's so much you don't know about your wife, Morty. But Bruce knows plenty. Make him tell you what he knows before Ted gets to him!"

Officer Wright suddenly couldn't talk anymore. Fluids blasted from his mouth. His skull quaked with building pressure, causing the top of his head to erupt. Water kept spewing from the top of his head. Like a broken fire hydrant, the officer's innards were sucked up through his head and spat out until the deflated corpse hit the ground. When it did, the corpse went still.

Red light blasted from the second floor level.

Every light coming from that level was crimson.

Morty held his daughter close. Bruce stood opposite them clutching the rolling pin. His eyes weren't glued on the cop. They were drawn to Cheyenne and Morty.

Morty's voice was accusatory. "You got something to tell me, old friend? What was

Officer Wright getting at? He said you know things about Glenda. What does she have to do with what's happening? Glenda couldn't possibly have caused this, so what do you know?"

Bruce's face went heavy with dread. He could cry or he could go into a rage. The man teetered between the two emotions until his face went neutral.

"I thought I was doing you a favor by keeping the secret. The cop was right. There's a lot you don't know about your wife, Morty. I'm sorry to be the one to tell you. I didn't believe it myself when I first heard it. I blew it off as gossip. As bullshit, because it's just that, bullshit. Keep in mind, I didn't get this information firsthand. I heard it from a friend who heard it from a friend. That kind of gossip. I blew it off, man. You loved that woman, and I wasn't going to ruin that for you. I was only being your friend."

Morty studied the red lights coming from various nooks and corners of the house. There were a few normal burning bulbs in this house. There wasn't much time, if he was going to apply the dead cop's logic to the lights. If they didn't solve Deborah's murder, they would be trapped here in the red forever.

"You better tell me what you know about Glenda. Spare my feelings. I want to know everything."

Bruce issued a long sigh. "Have it your way. You won't like it."

Chapter Forty-Five

The voice in the room was another corpse. It was a woman in her fifties. A cigarette dangled from her mouth, half spent. She wore a pink bathrobe and green curlers in her hair. Her flesh hung loose about her face as she talked. Her back was turned to Larson and Janet. She was cradling something in her hands. The detective kept his gun drawn on the corpse. He knew anything could happen at any moment.

Janet's eyes cased the room. Her inspections stopped on a big box. Inside were the parts for a baby crib. The wallpaper was circus themed, with lions, tigers, elephants and clowns. The way the wallpaper puckered and was water stained, it made the animals and clowns look malicious. There were storage boxes in the room too. Many of them were unopened.

Janet couldn't figure out what the woman was doing here in the room.

The detective's voice trembled. "W-who are you? Answer me, or I'll shoot you."

The woman's voice was nasal and no nonsense. Janet imagined the way old women talked while getting their hair done at the salon. Gossipy.

"No need to point your gun at me, Detective. We've met before. You questioned me at the station the night of Deborah's death. You were so nice to me. And so handsome. My husband and I were divorced then. I would've asked you on a date under better circumstances."

Larson gave Janet a "what the fuck" expression.

Janet mouthed, "*Just let her talk.*"

"This room you two are standing in used to be a storage room. Deborah and Tim were planning on turning it into their first child's room. Deborah was only five months into her pregnancy when she was murdered. I live about three blocks from the young lovers. I welcomed them into the neighborhood with a basket full of goodies. Call me a busybody. Barbie the busybody. That's what they call me. I get my nose into everything. I suppose that might've been the reason Ted went after me after Deborah was killed.

"I was the one who called the police that night. I was taking my dog on a walk the night Deborah was murdered. My German Shepherd's getting old and can't make it beyond a few hours without having to go outside. I used it as an excuse to go on a walk and smoke. My husband hated it. He said it was like kissing an ashtray. He never complained about it when we were fucking. Funny how that works.

"So anyway, that night, I heard a car screech away from this house. I didn't get the plate number because there were no plates. It was a big rust bucket piece of junk. One of those cars that should've been put to rest a long time ago. A real clunker. Funny thing is, there was this bumper sticker. It was a person's hand flipping the bird. I told the police everything I saw. I suppose it didn't help. It was suspicious the way the car just sped away from Ted and Deborah's house. I mean, the driver screeched their tires really late. You tell me that ain't suspicious? I hadn't seen the car before, so you know, Barbie the busybody had to say something to the goddamn cops and get herself into trouble. So much for the ol' friendly neighborhood watch. People aren't kind to each other anymore. Everybody wants to be left alone these days. One day, people might get their wish.

"So anyway, I baked Ted a casserole after Deborah's funeral. I felt for Ted. Everybody could tell he wasn't himself. He was a shell. Ted was much too young to be a widower. I visited him a lot to give him kind words and support. I even did his laundry when he invited me into his house. I cleaned the guy's home, because he simply quit doing anything, and what do I get in return? He bashed me over the head with a hammer and dragged me into his basement. Before I come to, he's got me in this bricked off room sitting in a chair and driving nails through my fucking hand. With every question I can't answer, he drives another nail. *Why was I outside walking my dog that night? Why didn't I see the car's plates? Why didn't I go in and stop Deborah from bleeding to death?*

"I told him I didn't know anything had happened to Deborah. I didn't think much of the car, just that the car was strange. I didn't know that poor Deborah was bleeding to death in the house right after the car drove away. He accuses me of killing Deborah. *Me.* He isn't hearing me anymore. Ted's eyes are different then. The store's open, but nobody's inside to ring you up, if you get what I'm saying. From that point on, it didn't matter what I told ol' Teddy. He was going to hurt me.

"In the corner of that brick room, he had a metal spike standing up from the floor. The tip was rounded off and smooth. He made me stand on that spike in my bare feet. He strung me up by my thumbs. I kept shifting my weight from one foot to the other to keep my balance on the spike, but after so long, I slip off the spike. It isn't long before I break both of my thumbs.

"Teddy enjoyed the sound of my bones breaking. He hung me up by all my fingers until every single bone was broken. Then he grew tired of hurting me. He told me I was useless. Ted strangled me with his bare hands. He buried me in the backyard in a trash bag. It didn't keep the worms away from my body. There's only one thing that soothes away the pain. I could never have children, you see. I had a defective womb. My eggs weren't right. There was nothing I can do. I was just born that way. But this bundle of pure joy in my arms, Deborah's unborn child, erases the pain."

Barbie finally turned around to face them. Crooked, broken boney hands clutched an infant clothed only in dried-up muscle tissue and bone. That little bone mouth was sucking on Barbie's greened nipple. Out the nipple maggots flowed into the baby's mouth. It kept sucking, sucking and sucking at the tit for the dead mother's maggot milk.

The bulb in the room brightened into red.

Barbie smiled, steadying the decayed baby in her hands. "Once all goes red in this house, it'll be too late. You will all be dead. You'll keep me company. We'll have wonderful stories to share with each other for all eternity. I love gossip."

The room's bulb went brighter, blinding Janet and the detective. When the red finally dimmed enough to open their eyes again, Barbie and the baby were both gone.

Janet stared at where the woman was last standing. "I don't know what to make of this shit. It's sounded like a promise of death to me. We're not getting out of this house. How are we supposed to gather evidence to solve a ten-year-old crime when we're trapped here? We don't have witnesses, or testimony or access to records."

Detective Larson couldn't say anything to the contrary, except for one thing. "All we have is each other. Maybe that's all we need. We're going back downstairs. We have to talk to Morty and the rest of them and try again. There's something we're missing."

"What was Barbie saying about when the red fills this house, we're dead?"

Larson's head ached. It always happened when he asked the same question repeatedly in his head and didn't happen upon an answer.

"I don't know, Janet. I could try to explain it, but it's fucking confusing."

They heard the loud and violent crashes in the hallway. The sound of bodies wrestling one another. Something growled. Then they heard Morty sound off in terror.

"Help me remove the barricade."

Janet didn't like the idea of facing off with what was out there.

The lights turned red again. Four corpses appeared. They were moving the dresser pushed up against the door. Detective Larson recognized the three men and the one woman. They were each hapless victims of Ted. People who were going to and from somewhere and unfortunately crossed paths with Ted.

"*You must hurry.*"

"*Barbie's right.*"

"*You'll all be dead if you don't put the facts together.*"

When the barricade was removed, the corpses vanished.

"I can't do this," Janet insisted. "This is just too fucking much."

"Do you have any better suggestions?"

"Yeah, we hide in here, and if anything comes at us, we shoot it."

"If I'm not mistaken, I don't have many bullets left, and your 9mm's rattled off a few times already. The only way out is to investigate. You're a reporter. You should be all over this."

Larson didn't have time for Janet's hesitation.

"I'm going whether you're coming with me or not. And in this house, you don't want to be alone."

The detective opened the door, bolted into the hallway and braced himself for whatever the house had to throw at him.

Chapter Forty-Six

Bruce hadn't ever seen Morty make an expression like the one he was making now. *Give me what I want. If you don't, I'm going to hurt you. You know I mean it. I will hurt you.* Cheyenne's face was anticipatory. *What did my mother do? Please don't let it be that awful. Oh my God, I know it will be.* Having faced off with a cop whose head exploded with water, and Glenda, whose body didn't move an inch after collapsing from upstairs, Bruce feared nothing, not even his best friend's scorn. This wasn't his truth. This was Glenda's truth. They were her secrets to own and to bear. There was no special way he could craft a story to remove the damaging elements. Bruce told the story the way he remembered it best.

"When I tell you this, I beg you to keep in mind it was just gossip at the time. Bullshit. I thought you always knew what people said behind your back about Glenda. Maybe you heard softer versions of the truth, maybe not. I don't know. I just assumed you knew and didn't care, Morty.

"I remember when Glenda moved into our school district. We were freshmen at the time. Glenda had moved from Kirkwood. You know Kirkwood, that small town about a six or seven hour drive from here. I had friends who lived in Kirkwood. They hung out with Glenda. She was only fourteen, but man, they had some wild stories to tell about her.

"I guess her super religious father did everything to keep Glenda out of trouble. Most teenagers rebel against their folks in that situation, but Glenda took it a step further. She snuck out of the house at night to meet with her buddies. Her buddies were a real bad crowd. Two of them were sixteen-year-olds. Another was twenty. I think the oldest was named Ryan Brundage. Bad people, man. Kirkwood was a very small town. Not a whole lot to do in that neck of the woods, right? They don't cut the grass anymore in those parts, you get me?

"Well, these three guys, they start meeting up with Glenda after school. They talk her into hanging out with them on a regular basis. Glenda was pretty and looked older than her age. So Glenda, being repressed by her religious father, is fine with sneaking out of the house and getting high and drunk with these scumbag types. They smoke weed, drink bourbon and even dip their noses in cocaine. Glenda's grades start to slip. She's looking rough, because she's doing drugs and not sleeping at night anymore.

"There was much more going on than drugs and drinking. The twenty-year-old, Ryan Brundage, the tried and true asshole, well, it turns out Ryan's dad is a real piece of shit too. A bigger piece of shit even. A fucking piece of shit. His name is Louie Brundage. The fuckhead is an evening security guard at the local junkyard. He liked to sell drugs to kids. Small time guy. Piece of shit, end of story. I only know all of this because my cousin was friends with the people who hung out with this group. Like I said, my information is secondhand.

"So these guys take Glenda to Louie's house one night. The boys don't have any cash. They never have cash. Louie says it's fine. He can take it out in trade. He gets to have sex with Glenda, and everybody gets free drugs. By then, Glenda's addicted to this shit. She loves the drugs. She'll do anything. And Glenda loves the power she had over Louie Brundage. Over the boys too. My cousin said Glenda really liked fucking the bastard for drug money. She'd go to the house and skip school to meet this guy alone and do other things with Louie. The rumors are harsh. I didn't totally believe it. Looking at Glenda, you wouldn't think. Turns out Louie let his son have turns with her too. And—"

"That's total bullshit. *My wife* doing that shit? Listen to you, man. Do you believe it? I sure as hell don't. No fucking way."

Bruce wasn't saying one way or the other if he believed it or not. "My cousin said—"

"Fuck your cousin."

"—My cousin said Glenda was looking so bad and doing so much drugs at one point, she passed out in school. Her nose was bleeding and her heart was chugging a hundred miles an hour. Her father realizes what has happened. He can't prove it. He can't say who is behind it either. So he doesn't go after anybody. Glenda's father didn't want the public, or anybody, knowing his daughter could do those things. So he moves away, puts Glenda into a new school and keeps a tight leash on her.

"Think about it, Morty. Why do you think you had such a hard time asking Glenda out to the prom? And when you got her pregnant, Glenda's father went right to your parents' house and made your folks do as they demanded. You quit school, started working full time and that was that. You had no say in it, Morty, because her father wouldn't let you. I know it's hearsay. If it wasn't important, why was Officer Wright wanting me to mention it?

"And think on this. These corpses have been trapped in this house. I'm sure they've been talking to each other and trying to add things up about Deborah's death like we're trying to right now. They want out of this house. Glenda's story means something."

Morty scoffed. "Like what? That my wife was a drug-addicted slut when she was too young to be doing that kind of shit? That's going to solve Deborah's death? I don't see what this has to do with Deborah at all."

"It has to mean something. Why would Ted pull us through the door? Collectively, we have the answer, or they think we might have the answer. I don't know, man."

Morty refused to believe the things Bruce said about Glenda.

"Exactly. They *think* we might have an answer. They're all dead, and crazy, and psychotic and don't know why they're doing what they're doing anymore. That's what I believe. Not what you just said."

Bruce cried out, "Stay back!"

There was Ted standing behind Cheyenne. He grabbed her from behind with both hands and dragged her towards the basement door.

"*Daaaaaaaaaaaaaaad!*"

"She has questions to answer! She knows who killed my wife. The bitch is holding back information from me! I'll get the facts. Everything!"

Morty lunged for Ted. The man spiked Cheyenne to the floor, removed a hammer from his belt and swung it hard at Morty's head. The second the hammer hit him, Morty spun and hit the floor. Moments before going unconscious, Morty vaguely heard Bruce fighting with Ted, then the basement door slamming closed.

Cheyenne's screams soon bled through the basement's floorboards.

Chapter Forty-Seven

The darkness asked questions.

"Where were you the night my wife died?"

A sob escaped her throat.

No words could she muster to satisfy the demented man's inquiry.

"Did you enjoy smashing her head in?"

Cheyenne couldn't move. She was sitting in a chair. Her body wasn't tied up. The soft nagging sensation in her hand gradually elevated into a building rage.

"Did you like the sight of Deborah's blood spilling out of her head?"

Outrageous, the question!

What could she say to the maniac in the dark?

"Ted, I've never met your wife. I'll help you find her killer. Everybody else upstairs is with me on that, I swear. You have to believe me. Ted, do you believe me? Please believe me!"

A hard exhalation of breath. *Hmmmmmph.* Steps paced back and forth behind her.

The whisper was a blast of icy air into her ear.

"If it wasn't you, then who?"

Before a syllable could leave her mouth, the light bulb above her flickered on, bathing her in its crude yellow beam. The glint of steel, the hammer swung down. One single POUND, and a second nail was driven into her right hand. Staked down onto the table, blood mushrooming around the coppery nail head sticking out of the top of her hand, Cheyenne reeled in shock.

"*Not me. It's not me! That's all I know!*"

"Maybe it was your father? Or your cunt of a mother?"

"Don't you dare say those things about my—"

POUND. POUND. POUND.

"*Ohhhgaaaaaaaaaawd!*"

In the top of her hand gleamed five nail heads. She could feel blood drip onto the top of her legs beneath the table. The nails were so long.

"Nobody from my family ever hurt you, you sadistic bastard!"

A meanness was produced from the agony of each new nail driven into her hand. It was the pain, and the fear that was boiling over into something new and incredibly powerful, that made Cheyenne lash out.

"If you couldn't figure out who murdered your wife, why do you think we can? That detective has no idea. I have no idea. So everything you're doing here isn't in the name of finding your wife's killer. It's whetting your appetite for bloodshed, because you're one of those sociopathic assholes! Throw you in a rubber room and lock away the key and let you ROT! You murdered Hannah. The poor woman, what did Hannah have to do with your wife?"

Ted was about to drill her hand with another nail before she asked that question.

She thanked God it made the lunatic pause.

How could she take another nail through the hand? What would he do next to her? It'd be a thousand times worse than nails.

There was something worse than nails.

Words.

The light bulb changed to red. It drew Cheyenne's eyes to the wide array of torture implements hanging from the walls.

Ted noticed her eyes go over the bricks scattered about the floor.

"I built brick walls around this table so the neighbors couldn't hear the screams coming from my basement. I didn't want anybody interfering with my interrogations. But now that I'm here, trapped in the red, I don't need walls. I only want to solve my wife's murder. I'll do anything.

"And Hannah, she knew things. Hannah and Glenda, they're nothing more than whores. Hannah knew your mother since they were kids. They grew up together. One and the same. And your dad, he's so clueless. When your dad was younger, and you were just a little child, Morty would drive around and think. He knew he was forced into a life of hard labor and all of that hard luck bullshit. While your dad was driving around and thinking to himself about his life and what it could've been if Glenda didn't get pregnant so early, Glenda was out having fun of her own.

"Hannah and Glenda were both into the same things. Drugs and sex. Louie Brundage, dirty Louie, and his son, Ryan, gave them what they wanted. The two bitches would meet up with them at the Brundage house and have a coke party, or whatever drugs they had on them that night. The woman would do nasty things for free blow. Old habits die hard, right? But you see, Louie and Ryan are older, and their tastes for women continued to delve deeper and deeper into the gutter. As those two scummy bastards were aging, so were Glenda and Hannah. Those guys didn't want those older bitches coming around anymore. Hannah told me all about it during our little talk.

"Louie and Ryan liked the young stuff. They called the young ones twats and baldies. They make me sick. And of course, Hannah and Glenda were too old for their tastes, but the two guys wanted to scare the two ladies away for good. Those guys, father and son, were crafty when they wanted to be. Louie and Ryan liked to watch Hannah and Glenda fuck each other with one of those double-sided dildos. When the ladies were done screwing each other, Louie and Ryan showed them a special trick.

"This dildo was built special. They had a remote control with a single red button. Hannah described it in great detail. When those greaseball dumb fucks were done watching the two high whores go at it, Louie pressed that red button. Spikes came out the tip of the dildo on both ends. Louie and Ryan laughed at their horrified reactions, and then Louie, he's extra perverted, he takes a .28 pistol and shoves it into Hannah's mouth. He cocks back the trigger, and shouts out: BANG BITCH. Your mother and Hannah ran the hell out of there and never came back. Lesson learned. No more trips to Kirkwood. No more drug parties with Louie and Ryan."

The story rocked Cheyenne to the core.

"So it's those guys who murdered your wife, right? L-Louie and Ryan, right? It's them. Murder solved, right? This doesn't have to go on anymore. We figured it out. Right? *Right?*"

"Hannah told me how she loved the day she heard Louie and Ryan had died. They were drunk and on a coke binge. Ryan dared his dad to play chicken with an incoming train. They drove across the tracks, trying to time it just right, so they'd just miss the bullet coming for them. Of course, they timed it wrong. They had to put the Brundage boys in little plastic evidence bags, they were in so many pieces. That happened two years before my wife's murder. So no, her murder is not solved. It very well could be anybody. Even you."

The blood in her veins turned to ice.

That outrage, to accuse her, Cheyenne Saggs, of murdering anybody, was channeled into her next words.

"But you can't think I'm responsible? I was maybe a teenager, maybe in my early twenties, when your wife died, right? How could I have done it?"

"It's not about what you did. It's about what you know that you don't even realize you know."

Ted placed the nails and the hammer on the tabletop. They were just out of her reach, not that there was much she could do with them with her hand stuck to the table.

Ted moved deeper into the room, where the red light didn't scare away the black.

"What are you doing? Please, Ted, I'm in a lot of pain. I'm not trying to stop you from finding your wife's killer. I want you to solve the crime. I swear it. But I don't know anything. Really think about what you're doing here. What do I know? This is between Glenda, Hannah, maybe my dad and those scumbags. I'm completely outside of it. Can't you see what I'm saying?"

Ted was at the other side of the room. Cheyenne had to train her ears harder to hear him. She craved any indication of what was coming her way.

"I can do many things here, being in the red. I can craft any kind of tools to make you talk. I want to believe you, Cheyenne. I really do. But you see, everything Hannah told me, she didn't let a word of it escape her lips until I'd ripped out four of her fingernails. Torture has its merits. I need facts. My wife fears me. Deborah's in this house, and she refuses to see me. Deborah has forsaken me. But when I find her killer, she will take me back. Then, we can all move on from the red, to Heaven, to Hell, to whatever eternity has in store for us. If I can grant Deborah Heaven, surely she'll love me again, don't you think? I can see her again before I face the darkness. That's all I want. One more chance to see my Debbie."

Cheyenne wanted to say a hundred different things but couldn't.

He showed her what he was hiding behind his back.

What would make her talk.

Chapter Forty-Eight

The house still had plenty to throw at the detective. One moment, he was leading Janet from the bedroom and away from Barbie and the dead baby, the next, they were facing the corpse of Heather Mangum in the upstairs hallway. Larson recognized Heather from the first time he saw her, in a body bag. Her corpse was abandoned behind a dumpster of a Family Dollar. Heather was one of Ted's last victims before he died. The man was running out of ideas on how to hide the bodies, and towards the end of his murder spree, Ted stopped cleaning up after himself. From a criminal's standpoint, Ted was getting sloppy.

Poor Heather Mangum.

Janet smelled the air.

"Is that gasoline?"

"Gasoline and bleach," Heather corrected. The muscles of her throat visibly throbbed and jerked with each new word. Every part of her throat was corroded. "He poured both down my throat. My insides were boiling. I was shitting blood before I died. Maybe he won't use those things on you. But knowing Ted, and what he's doing to Cheyenne right now, you'll probably receive something even worse, Janet. Ted's an innovative son of a bitch. He's had plenty of time to perfect his craft."

Larson wasn't sure whether to fear Heather or draw information from the corpse.

"Are you here to help us?"

The lights in the hallway blared red.

Janet was close up against Larson. She whispered, "This bitch might not be like the others. I don't trust anything in this fucking house."

Heather's lips dissolved when they drew into a jester's grin.

"I'm not like the others, no. I say if you're going to force me to stay in the red, I'm going to have some fucking fun!"

Heather dug into her pocket and produced a matchbook. She opened the flap.

"I got a guy's number from Side Pockets the night Ted hit me over the head with a baseball bat and dragged me to this house. I could've fallen in love with the guy who hit on me. I went to high school with the big lug. I love a guy who can make me laugh. You can drink, you can shoot up, you can fuck to get things off of your mind, but there's nothing, and I mean nothing, like a genuine laugh to forget how shitty life can get. But I missed out on that, didn't I?"

Larson wasn't sure what Heather was planning to do. But the way her face lit up with a new intensity, a plan had been hatched in her defiled brain, and she was moments from enacting it.

"Please, Heather, we're trying to end your suffering. What do you know about Deborah Lindsey?"

"Her? You think you can trust Ted for anything? That he'll let you go if you put it all together? I'm not doing a fucking thing for that asshole. He watched me melt from the inside out. If there's anything I'd like to do, it's make it so he'll never ever know who killed his wife. Let him suffer for all eternity."

Threads of her skin melted in patches, like an acid rash that was spreading with wildfire speed. Larson could hear gurgling, bubbling and popping from within her body.

Heather struck a match.

Janet cried out.

"What the hell are you doing?"

"I'm going to set this place on fire!"

Heather tilted her head back and opened her mouth. Caustic fumes exited her mouth. Her breath was flammable.

Heather dropped the match into her mouth.

Larson covered up Janet with his body right before Heather combusted into a great ball of flames.

Chapter Forty-Nine

"Try this!"

Morty grabbed one of the wooden chairs inside the kitchen and threw it at the basement door. The chair shattered. The door wasn't even scratched.

"We have to save Cheyenne! I can't stand to think she's alone with that fucking psychotic!"

Bruce was as much in a panic as Morty. He pointed at the coffee table. "Grab one end, I'll grab the other. We'll use it as a battering ram. We're getting down there, don't you worry, Morty."

"I pray we will. *I pray!*"

Morty's hands couldn't steady themselves. He had to work through the nerves. It didn't help that his daughter's screams were filtering from down below. They were single shrieks, then begging, then long, drawn out peals of agony.

"You son of a bitch, I'll kill you!"

Morty and Bruce charged the basement door. The coffee table split down the middle and broke in two halves.

Bruce threw down the half he was holding.

"Goddamn it."

Morty struggled to focus beyond the fact Ted was having his way with his daughter. He heard the nails driven into her hands, and Cheyenne insisting she knew nothing about Deborah's killer. She was right. How could she? She didn't live here at the time. Neither did he. They were innocent people swept into a crazy man's purgatory. Morty's mother used to always say misery loves company. Ted Lindsey was one of the most miserable loathsome people to exist in human history to do this to honest, innocent people.

"Watch out, Morty! Coming through!"

Morty had to think fast. Bruce had located a bottle of bourbon in the kitchen cupboard. He stuffed a kitchen rag into the top and lit it with his cigarette lighter.

"Yeah, Bruce, fuck yeah! Do it! Burn this bitch down!"

Cheyenne's drawn out scream played out in the air: "*Pleeeeeeeeeease-gaaaaaaaaawd-noooooooooooooo!*"

Bruce braced his body and put all of his might into tossing the flammable concoction against the basement doorway. The second the bottle shattered, the doorway went ablaze with red. Those flames swallowed up the bottle and made it vanish. Then the door was as it was: no flames, no damage.

"It's not going to let us through," Morty shouted, stomping on the floor and bursting into tears. "This house is working against us. This fucking house. If you want us to solve your wife's murder, you might actually have to help us, Ted!"

Bruce did his best to calm Morty down.

"You can't expect rational thinking from a killer. The red lights, this house, the deaths, it's all insanity."

"Then how do I save Cheyenne? How do we get out of here?"

"I don't know, friend."

Morty saw the corpse standing in the kitchen. The refrigerator glowed a neon red on the inside, then the door came open, and out came a fat blue corpse. He introduced himself as Jimmy Loomis.

"You two boys need to relax a moment."

"How can I relax when my daughter is dying down there?"

"Oh, she's so dead. Sorry, pal. It is what it is. No use fighting it."

Bruce searched the floor for his rolling pin and quickly located it. "Who says I shouldn't bash you over the head with this?"

"Go ahead. I'm already dead. The problem is, I'm one of the few that still want to help you. The others who've died in the house are losing their patience. They're starting to think you can't solve Deborah's murder. If they believe that, they'll outright kill you. It won't be much longer before they come after you."

Morty searched the room for a weapon.

He grabbed a broken coffee table leg.

"So what can you do to help us?"

"One, I want to help you calm down."

Jimmy Loomis removed his shirt. He exposed a bulging belly. He opened up the front of his stomach like it was a cupboard door. Inside were two cold beers standing on a rack of deformed bones. Everything else in the man's body was hollow. The beers had frost on the outside. Ice cold.

"Drink up, fellas. Soothe those nerves. You've had a hard night."

"I'm not drinking anything that's been in your stomach," Bruce said in disgust. "What the fuck's wrong with you?"

"Everything's wrong in the red," Jimmy said. "One thing I do know that's right, you have to calm down and start thinking clearly. You're onto something here. The answer is on the tip of your tongue, but you don't quite have it yet."

"Then what do we do to get the answer?"

"As I see it, you have only one option. And that's to fight. Keep the bad people in the house occupied until your friends upstairs can put it together. *If* they can."

"You're asking us to throw ourselves into harm's way," Morty said. "Too late. We're in harm's way already."

"You think you're in harm's way right now? You've got a few things coming your way, pal. Well, you had a chance to drink a beer. I did what I could to help you collect your thoughts."

From upstairs, there was a sonic boom concussion. Morty and Bruce had to reposition their feet not to fall down from being jostled. The house was rocked on its foundation. A great ball of flames shot down the stairway and bathed Jimmy Loomis in fire. He was de-fleshed by the flames and turned to bone in seconds. Then he was ashes, burned so hot.

Morty and Bruce backed away, afraid to be cooked by the searing heat.

The stairway and the walls were on fire.

"What the hell is going on up there?"

Morty tried to get a better look upstairs. The flames were too thick and intense to battle through.

"Janet and the detective are up there! They're going to be burned alive."

Bruce pulled him back. Morty was coughing against the smoke. He couldn't breathe or see. Black smoke was choking the room.

Bruce was struggling to talk, losing himself to a fit of coughing. "We have to get out of here, and fast!"

Morty, sifting through the smoke, tried the living room door and beat against the windows. He had his eyes closed; it burned so bad to keep them open. Bruce had grabbed him by the arm in order not to lose track of him. All they had was each other at this point.

Unable to breathe, Morty was getting dizzy. Unable to see, he was completely blind.

The two men kept searching for a way out.
  They didn't *find* a way out.
  They *fell into* a way out.

Chapter Fifty

The upstairs hallway was ablaze one moment, then the next, it was raining—or so Larson thought. They were being pelted by something. Janet pointed through the thick of the flames at the bathroom door. There stood the dirt corpse woman. What remained of her exploded, and out of her body burst forth spinning clods of earth. So thick, so fast, so much, the dirt snuffed the flames. The detective could breathe again, but he was still shielding Janet from the dirt, because the pelting sheets kept coming harder and faster.

One moment, Larson was dodging dirt, the next, he was buried in it. Compacted by earth, he tried to swim against it. Eyes closed, mouth shut, head reeling from the confusion, Larson broke his fingernails, he fought so hard to free himself. How much longer before he suffocated? Where was he being buried?

Then he thought back to Morty and the tub full of dirt. Janet said he was forced into the dirt. Maybe Morty had been taken somewhere. Maybe they were being taken somewhere too.

What else did this house and these corpses have left for them?

How was this going to solve Deborah's murder, being buried in dirt?

Reaching, swimming against a thick current, he thought he heard Janet calling out to him. Everything was going fuzzy. He needed air. His lungs were burning. His head was aching. He wasn't sure how much more he could take before death set in.

"You're almost there! I need you, Detective. You can't die on me. Please don't die on me!"

Larson opened his eyes because he finally could. Air, precious air, he gulped it down, gasping sharply between intakes. He looked up to see a pitch black sky. Janet was dirty from top to bottom. She looked a wreck. He probably looked worse.

He was on his feet again with the help of Janet pulling him up. They held onto each other, steadying one another. Thrown from one extreme to the next, their bodies forced them to take pause.

A tall wooden fence surrounded them. They were in a backyard. There was no sound except for a woman's whistling.

It wasn't Janet.

It was Barbie.

Barbie was on her knees pulling flowers from her garden. She was leaving the dead weeds behind and ripping out the flowers. Every time she uprooted a colorful flower, Barbie said, "There. That's better. Those awful things keep popping up in my garden."

Janet gasped. "*My God.*"

The sound drew Larson's eyes to the plastic kiddie pool. Deborah's unborn baby, mere bones and a thin layer of leathery flesh, was swimming in muddy black water. The baby was eating from a dead German Shepherd's ribcage. The dog was chewing on the baby's foot like a rawhide, gnawing at it with delight.

"God is on the other side of the red," Barbie said, uprooting a tulip and crushing it in her hand. "God is certainly not here. Our savior is hosting parties elsewhere. This is Ted's meet-up, and the party's about to end. Sure, he'll invite new guests after you, interrogate them too, and this will just keep on going forever. A vicious cycle. We hoped you guys could bring this to an end. I liked you guys. You're innocent, like I was, before Ted got his hands on me. I only wanted to help Ted, and this is what I received. A lifetime of torment living in the red."

Barbie's words ebbed into sadness. She started ripping and smashing flowers at an accelerated speed.

"Everyone else has lost faith in you two. Forget Morty, that old dumbass, and his buddy, Bruce. Glenda had some juicy stories to tell, but as far as facts, she had very little to offer. Hannah's story was just as juicy, and she's as useful as a stuck pig. And Cheyenne Saggs was just a sniveling bitch. She got it *real* good. Worse than any of us. Ted got off on her suffering. He was inspired when he killed her.

"They were all relatively useless. Maybe they bought you two time. Perhaps that's why they were brought here. Only to buy you two time."

Barbie's sobs started anew.

Deborah's unborn baby paused from flensing the meat from the German Shepherd's ribs and considered crying, but started eating the dog's flesh with renewed verve instead.

"But you two, reporter and detective, I believed in you. I saw you two after you arrived here from the other side of the burning doorway, and I thought you were my ticket to Heaven. Surely together you guys would've come up with the answers to Deborah's death. Your failure hasn't changed how I feel about this place. I can't go anywhere else. I can't leave, I can only stay and *wither*. I would prefer to go to Hell. At least I could see new things and new people."

Barbie sobbed harder.

"No, no, no—I'm a good person! The red can't take that away from me. I'm going to Heaven. I will rest in peace. I have suffered enough. I can't wait on more people to attempt to solve Deborah's death. You were our best shot, because everybody else who's going to be sucked into this hell won't have a clue who that dead bitch is.

"I want out of here, and I'm not alone. There's so many out here in the red. It goes beyond this house. Can you hear their suffering?"

The black sky turned into a burning charcoal briquette. The sky was a smoldering cinder. A bright ember kissed by oxidation.

Tears fell down Larson and Janet's eyes. The red wasn't as bright, but it was intense. The red was the color of suffering. Red was the color of eternal damnation. And the two of them realized because they had failed, they kept the innocent in the red.

Larson couldn't accept it.

"How much time do we have left before our chance is up?"

Janet didn't understand why he was asking the question. She stayed quiet. Afraid, more like it.

Barbie beheld the burning sky. "You're almost down to nobody. There's very little time you have left."

"I want back in there," Larson said. Something in his gut said if he had another opportunity, he could find that detail, and link one clue with another and the answer would hit him. "I'm going in there. If you don't want to go, Janet, I understand, but I could use your help."

"But what did we miss? We searched, we put our heads together and we came up with nothing. What else is there?"

"I know Deborah's bedroom like the back of my hand. There was nothing new the second time I looked tonight. The same with the kitchen or living room; there's nothing new. The basement is Ted's workshop. You'd think if there were any clues, Ted would've stumbled upon them. He spent many nights down there."

"So where do we look?"

"The second bedroom's the only place."

"But we searched that room."

"We didn't get a chance to search every storage box. Those are their belongings. Maybe there's a clue in the boxes. We have to give it another shot. It's the only choice we have. Or would you rather wait for Ted to come after us and slaughter us? Think on that. We can't beat him. He's been shot by our guns, and it did nothing. This isn't a place where the rules of life and death apply. Our only way to fight back is to keep looking. Even down to the wire."

Barbie was standing up. She crept near them. Her rotting, disgusting body was bathed by the light of the red sky.

"We *are* down to the wire. I like your determination. The only problem is, everybody else counting on you has lost hope. They won't let you back into the house. They think you can't do a fucking thing for them. And they may be right."

Larson studied the house. The window shades were open. Huddles of dead corpses watched them with disdain. Hannah was among them, as were ten of the officers (mutilated, and many headless), and Ted's fourteen original victims, minus two, counting Barbie and Deborah's unborn child.

Barbie's eyes were heavy.

"We're not getting inside that house. They'll kill you."

Janet was hit hard by the words.

"She's right, Detective. There's too many of them. We'll be dead in seconds."

Larson checked his clip.

Four bullets remained.

"How many shots you have in that 9mm?"

Janet checked the clip.

"I'm down to two rounds."

Barbie's lips curled into a macabre smile. "You could have a thousand bullets, and it wouldn't matter."

"Hey, we only need to slow them down. If we can get them off of our asses, we can get back upstairs and search again. We have to try, damn it."

Larson didn't like the way Barbie had given them a death sentence. None of the people forced through the doorway asked to be sent here, nor did Ted's victims. Nobody had a right to give up. They had so much to fight for. Heaven, Hell, back to living life again, those options were all better than the red.

"So what if they kill us? We're dead anyway if we don't solve this case. Ted's not going to let us go. We're dead. Let's pretend we're goners. Fuck it. Fuck them, fuck the situation and fuck you, Barbie, for giving up on yourself. Yeah, go ahead, feel sorry for yourself. Cry into the red sky, weep for your lost life, let's all play host to the pity party. Fuck that. I'm getting in that house, and we're searching for clues. If they're going to stand in our way, if they're too stupid to help us, if they're so caught up in their own agonies that common sense has fled their minds, then I guess we're going to have to plow right through them."

Janet was taken aback by the detective's speech.

Then Janet went off on him.

"Plow right through them? Your macho talk solves nothing. We're fucking dead. I mean, look at them in the windows. They're chomping at the bit to rip us a new one. The second we step in there, whether we have an M-16, or sticks and stones, or courageous words, we're dead meat."

"She's right," Barbie said. "What can we do against them? I'm the only one who still believes in you, and I'm slipping. The longer you talk, the more hopeless it sounds."

The baby and the dog were done chewing on each other. The baby was paddling in the water and blowing bubbles at the surface. The dog had stepped out of the tub and started to dig a hole in the yard with both its front paws.

Larson was grateful for Barbie's flicker of hope in them, but the way she was talking, he had to sway this woman to their side again. Everything was about buying time. Enacting a plan. Saving themselves.

Larson had a wife and three kids. Their youngest had left the roost for college six months ago. They had the house to themselves, and it was like someone re-lit the candle of their romance. He was swooning over his wife. He fell in love with Angela all over again. Larson also knew Janet had a husband, and she was so young. Her life was ahead of her.

Ted's insanity was going to stop them from living their lives.

Ted's insanity wasn't going to force the dead from their peaceful slumber.

This had to end now, and he was the one to make it happen.

Barbie watched the dog dig happily into the hole until the dog buried itself. The dog was scared of what was to come. The baby stayed underwater in hiding.

"I'm this close to giving up on you," Barbie said. "Give me a reason to help you. That's all I want. I feel rage overtaking my soul. The red in the sky is changing me...*and it keeps changing me*. Make it good, and make it fast. Convince me not to kill you."

Larson and Janet were terrified. Barbie started gnawing on the tips of her fingers, eating off the leathery skin, and exposing tracks of pearl-white bone. Her teeth carved the tips of her bone fingers into daggers.

"I want to claw out your eyes. I want you to scoop out your brains. I want to drink your blood and feast on your insides. Curse you for damning me to the red forever! You were our only chance! GODDAMN YOU!"

"Stop it, would you, lady?" Larson stepped between Barbie and Janet in case the dead woman went off on them. "I investigated Ted Lindsey. I lived, breathed and shit Ted Lindsey to solve Deborah's murder case. I have an idea, if you'd stop chewing on your fucking fingers for a second and threatening to eat our insides."

Barbie's maniacal face didn't change.

She still wanted to eat their insides, but Barbie stopped chewing on her fingers for a moment.

"Ted Lindsey was a handyman. A fixer upper guy. There's something good in that shed behind you. It's a fine piece of work. I remember searching the shed during the investigation."

Janet grabbed him by the arm. "What's in the shed?"

Larson whispered to Janet, "I'll show you. But watch Barbie."

He spoke up again. "I'm going to the shed. I have a plan. I'm going to show you, okay, Barbie?"

Barbie snarled in response. She had her fingers together, considering the many possibilities on how to kill them.

The red painted wooden shed wasn't too far away, but the walk felt like it took forever to complete as the decayed woman stalked after them.

Larson used the butt of his pistol to bust the padlock.

The detective opened the door of the shed and showed them how they were going to get into the house.

Chapter Fifty-One

Morty's face was flat against cold concrete when he came to again. He didn't smell fire anymore, and he wasn't choking on smoke. Morty forced himself to stand. Bruce was already on his feet looking at something across the room. Bruce noticed Morty get up, and he rushed to his friend's side.

"You don't want to see this, Morty. Stand back."

The details of the room registered fast. The broken bricks scattered about the floor, the table covered in blood and nails, they were in the basement.

"Don't look. Ted's a monster. How could he do this?"

Morty's eyes searched the room. It was hard to see against the red of the light bulb. Everything was covered in the harsh color.

"Not over there, Morty. Spare yourself. It's horrible. She didn't deserve any of this. Nobody does."

"Cheyenne!"

Morty saw her on the floor with her back against the wall. Parts of her right hand were missing, it having been yanked free from the nail pinions on the tabletop. Ted had tortured her. He had desecrated his daughter.

"Bastard, where are you? Face me, Ted. I'll kill you myself!"

"Calm down, Morty. Please. I need you. If you break down, I can't do this by myself."

"I'm not calming down. LOOK WHAT HE DID TO MY PRECIOUS DAUGHTER."

The sight was so gruesome, Morty fell onto his knees several feet from his daughter's body. The life was deflated from him.

"I'm so, so sorry…"

Cheyenne's head was slumped down in a death pose. Between her legs, the shadows were merciful. The pool of blood oozing there painted the picture the shadows failed to produce. Morty thought Ted had raped her until he spotted a dildo with spikes jutting from both sides of it laying next to her body. As if she'd ripped it out of herself, then died.

Ted had used it on Cheyenne.

He desecrated Cheyenne's womanhood.

It was the worst thing for a father to see.

"...so...so sorry..."

Morty's weeping changed into fury. He got up, wanting nothing more than for Ted to materialize so Morty could beat the shit out of him. He had failed to protect Glenda, and now his daughter was dead too. As a father, as a husband, Morty was useless.

Bruce had been talking the whole time Morty mourned his daughter, giving condolences and commiserations with added promises of revenge. Morty didn't hear a single word. He could only apologize to his daughter. The corpse he couldn't stand to look at. Cheyenne, so defiled.

"My wife and daughter are dead. What's the point, Bruce? My family is gone. Who cares about Ted?"

Bruce was horrified.

"Are you giving up? I'm alive. You're alive. Wake up, Morty. Ted needs to be stopped. He'll only kill more people."

"Then what do we do? Search this house, look for clues to a murder we won't solve, and then wait for Ted to kill us anyway?"

Bruce steadied his breath. He had so much anger. He was also pale and weak. The night had been hard on his old friend.

Morty asked Bruce again, "Huh, what do we do, old pal?"

"We're not detectives. We could be standing on the evidence that points to the killer, and we wouldn't know it. I say let him come to us, Morty. We'll take him on together. He can't take us both on at once."

"Sure he can." Morty knew his friend was light in the head. Blood loss did that to people. Desperation did that to people. "You're forgetting he's dead. How can you kill someone who's deceased? What do we do? There's no way around this shit. We're dead. We're fucked. I failed my family."

Bruce took the blow of Morty's words. His friend agreed. They weren't going to survive.

The prolonged silence between friends was as painful as anything else the two had endured in the past twenty-four hours.

"I'm sorry I had to tell you those things about Glenda."

"It's not your fault. We're so desperate to solve this murder. I made you to tell me. It doesn't matter anymore. She's gone. You have no idea what it's done to me to see her, and Cheyenne, in the condition they're in. I loved them so much."

Bruce struggled to speak. He needed his fluids replenished. "What I wanted to say, the things I told you about Glenda, don't let it change the way you look at her. She's a wonderful, kind, decent person. Everything she did was in the name of the drugs. You were the best thing for Glenda. You saved her."

"No, she was the best thing for me. And if I would've known all of those things, I would've forgiven her. I wouldn't stop loving her. She gave me a beautiful child." Morty couldn't help but choke up. "It's been a tough life, but imagining it without either of them in my life, I probably would found myself in a very dark place. Worse than here even."

"I love you, Dad. This is the last time I can tell you that."

Cheyenne stirred from the floor. She stood up with a hunched gait. Blood trickled down from between her legs. With every ounce of red exiting her body, the flesh continued to grow pale. Her eyes were demented; her lips were bent into a lascivious smile.

What was his daughter thinking about, Morty wondered.

"Cheyenne, you—"

"Shhhhhhhh. Listen upstairs."

They listened.

A crowd of persons were taunting and challenging somebody who was outside to come on in. Feet stomped on the floor. Morty imagined twenty some-odd people. He knew they weren't people. They were corpses. Victims of Ted's.

"You guys have one more shot to come out of this alive."

From out of the shadows, Glenda appeared. She wasn't deformed by murder. She no longer had nails for teeth. Glenda came to Morty and hugged him close.

She whispered to Morty, "I heard every word you said. I love you so much. I'm sorry things turned out the way they did. There's no more time to say anything else."

They held onto each other for another moment, then Glenda broke away from Morty. When she did, her condition returned to its former state. Morty gasped at the nails that shined between the ripped-open lines in her cheeks. Half her head was smashed in. Morty did his best to withhold a reaction. It seemed like his family wanted to help them survive.

Glenda and Cheyenne stood together, the post-mortem pair. They faced the stairway, looking up.

Morty was afraid to ask, but he did. "What are you doing?"

Cheyenne spoke. "Being dead, you learn a few things. Ted's not the only one who can play the red to his favor."

"Forgive me, Morty," Glenda said, "for what's about to happen."

"I was born from my mother's womb," Cheyenne said. "A womb that'd been filled with the seeds of evil men. Together, we shall give birth to an ultimate evil! Stand back, Father!"

"What are you two doing?" Bruce asked. He went from befuddled to terror-filled in seconds. "What is happening? I'm so confused."

"The way I see it," Cheyenne said, "your detective and your reporter have one more shot at finding the right clues to Deborah's murder. We're going to use the red to busy the corpses upstairs."

Blood and birth fluids leaked out between both women's legs. They spattered against the concrete, infernal mixtures of water, blood and grease fat. Fluid sacks were breaking within their wombs. Their pelvises broke to facilitate the birth of inhuman creatures. Blood mushroomed from their mouths as their insides become a war zone; monsters from within battled to be unleashed. Acid oozed out of their nipples, burning through the tatters of their clothing and rendering flesh into smoke. Cheyenne and Glenda unleashed squeals of agony. Morty remembered when Glenda gave birth to Cheyenne, and this, THIS, was a thousand times worse to hear.

What slithered from their wombs, the things slashing and plowing forward up the stairway to attack, charging with speed and the integrity to pummel and destroy what crossed their path, Morty could only see details. These abominations defied logical classification.

A boy five years old with eyeballs the size of baseballs didn't have flesh. Instead, he had arms, legs and a head, but every inch of him was heart tissue. The boy had hundreds of aortas, ventricles and chambers furiously pumping piping hot blood. Livers, spleens and intestines were given fully functional arms and legs, crafted from warped bones, heaps of ripped up muscle tissue and hideous maws that could chew through steel. Misfires, should've-been abortions, slithered forth from the putrid stinking wombs. Siamese twins covered in glistening afterbirth smacked against the floor when they dropped free. One was inside out, so the other twin ripped off its own skin to match its sister. Together, they tromped up the stairway. Up the stairs, the anatomical army marched.

The doorway upstairs blazed that burning red.

"Do we follow after them?" Bruce asked over the roaring, growling and stomping of the beasts. "Tell us what to do."

Cheyenne and Glenda's bodies had shriveled, shrinking from being so depleted. Papier-mâché flesh hugged their brittle bones. The two bodies were dry kindling about to snap and break into so many pieces.

Cheyenne said it right before daughter and mother crumbled.

"Keep Ted busy. He's right behind you."

Chapter Fifty-Two

Larson searched the inside of the shed for weapons. What he found were bags of potting soil, vermiculite, weed killer, grass seed, insect spray, a rolled up garden hose, a stack of concrete cinder blocks and most shocking of all, a Raptor Heavy Duty 5000 riding lawn mower.

Janet pushed through him, spotting a rusty hatchet and a shovel and holding onto each one in opposite hands.

"I got what I need. How about you, Detective?'

Larson studied the riding lawn mower. "Maybe we can set this thing to blow up."

"And burn down the house?"

"What do you mean? That's impossible. Don't you remember Heather swallowing a lit match and almost blowing us to kingdom come? The house is still there. Something will put the fire out, but the fire will still happen for a short period of time. I say we rig the gas tank to blow and drive it right into the house. It'll give everybody blocking the way inside a distraction. I can shoot whatever ammo we got left at them, run up the stairs, and then we lock ourselves in that second bedroom. Something's in there we missed. I just know it. I've searched Deborah's room enough. The clue is in the other room. *I pray*."

Barbie entered the shed.

"Depending on prayers will get you killed."

Barbie was different than earlier. Her disposition was eager. Barbie was ready to fight on their behalf again. Whatever shred of hope was lost moments ago was regained by breaking into the shed.

Larson pointed at the dented-up gas can under a shelf. "I'm going to fill the mower up with gas."

"You don't need gas to run the motor. You need blood. My blood. It'll give the engine that certain kick it needs to get the job done."

Barbie stole the hatchet from Janet's grasp and dragged the sharp end down her arm. A wide trench was created. Blood trickled down to her hand, which she kept over the gas tank hole. Red trickled into the engine.

"What's blood going to do?" Larson honestly asked the question.

"You just worry about how you two are getting upstairs. I'll go in first. You two have to work together to do the rest."

Barbie handed back the hatchet to Janet. "I suggest you ditch the shovel. Use the hatchet. Go for the face. Don't chop down over the head. You'll get it stuck in someone's skull, and you won't be able to rip the hatchet back out. So go for the face."

"*Oh.*" Janet furrowed her brow. "Okay."

"Detective, I want you to go in there guns blazing. Don't pull the trigger unless you intend to hit somebody. Shoot out their eyes if you can. If they don't have eyes, or a head for that matter, they can't see to attack you. Otherwise, aim for the kneecaps. They'll have to crawl after you. It'll slow them down."

Larson wasn't sure how to take the advice. Just moments ago, the woman was considering murdering them. But this was good, he thought. Barbie believed they still had a purpose. They could still solve Deborah's murder and free the dead to enter whatever afterlife they belonged in.

He recapped what Barbie had said. "Eyes first, then the kneecaps. Got it. Anything else we should keep in mind?"

"Don't waste time once I'm in the house. Go right for the stairs. You have so very little time. If they're right behind you, barricade yourselves in the best room you see fit to search. This is your last shot. If you fail, even I can't keep you alive. Everybody in that house will want to kill you, including me. We can't help it. You take away our hope, we have no reason to keep you alive."

"Then we won't fail," Larson said. "So what are you going to do, Barbie?"

Barbie hopped onto the Raptor 5000 Heavy Duty riding lawn mower.

"I got ideas."

In every window facing the backyard, the ugly, nasty corpses watched them with eager eyes. Their roar increased. They were welcomed to enter the death house.

Janet clutched the hatchet tighter in her hands.

Detective Larson squeezed the handles of both his .28 revolver and the 9mm.

Barbie revved up the mower's engine. Pink mist shot out the exhaust. Blood turned vapor surrounded them like a red cloud of gangrene death fumes.

Barbie shifted from park to fifth gear. "GET READY! MY BLOOD GIVES THIS BITCH AN EXTRA KICK OF POWER!!!"

Barbie popped a wheelie and bounded forward across the yard at fifty miles an hour.

Chapter Fifty-Three

"Bruce—WATCH OUT!"

Too late.

Bruce quarter-turned right when the claw end of the hammer caught him in the left eye. Ted's swift strike dragged across Bruce's face, tearing out both his eyes. Morty watched both squashed orbs fly across the room and detonate against the wall. Bruce stood in place for five seconds as blood cascaded down his face and painted his lower half in crimson. Then Bruce tumbled forward, dead in every fashion.

Morty almost tripped over Cheyenne and Glenda's bodies in his haste to avoid the killer. The corpses of his wife and daughter were shriveled up like dried-out roots. Used up and degrading to dust.

Ted studied the chunk of pink orbital meat stuck on the hammer and grinned big.

"Your friend had nothing new to tell me. He would've been a waste of nails."

"Fuck you, psycho."

"You went a bit crazy too when you couldn't find Glenda, didn't you, Morty?"

"That was you making me that way. That burning doorway. It wasn't me. You were toying with me. You wanted me to draw in as many people as possible. It's been you the entire time, you fucking monster."

"I had to have you to bring in the right people. You were what brought them here. I needed you to go a little...*mad*."

"And what did it get you? A bunch of people, good people, dead. And your wife is still gone. She's gone forever. None of this has fixed anything."

"I only want her to rest in peace. Deborah deserves the sweetness of Heaven."

"She'd go to Heaven, and you'd go to Hell. Even if you both went to Heaven, she wouldn't want anything to do with you."

"What about you and Glenda? You don't love her anymore. You've seen a different side of her. Her truth."

Morty spat in his direction.

"I still love her. You're wrong. People are a collection of their experiences. Look, life is too short to judge people so harshly. If you love someone, you love them forever. No matter what happens."

"What a wonderful husband you are. A man who loves his wife, even if she's a whore."

"It was the drugs. She couldn't help it."

"Oh, you're wrong. Glenda fucking loved it. She would've let any bum stick it in her if it meant getting high and wasted."

"I don't care what you say, or what you think. You're nothing to me but a murderer. The worst kind. You're no better than the person who ended Deborah's life. And while you talk to me, whatever those things were that went up the stairs are going to kill what's in Janet and the detective's way. You might've lost hope in them, but I haven't."

Ted flicked a piece of meat off of his hammer.

"That's where you're wrong. There is no hope for you. Those two won't find a damn thing upstairs. I gave them a chance. They failed. And your wife and daughter have conspired against you. They lied, Morty. Those monsters are just as eager to kill your two friends as the rest of the corpses trapped in this house."

Morty turned his eyes down to the two bodies of his daughter and wife. Their faces were ruined by their mischievous grins. Ted was telling the truth.

He was confused, because the bodies of his wife and daughter were gaining back their flesh, although it was decaying and dead tissue replacing dust. The two women were soon up the stairs, launching themselves through the red burning door to join the battle.

"We'll be back for you, Morty," Glenda said.

"It's time to kill again, Daddy," Cheyenne said.

Once his wife and daughter were through the doorway, the burning doorway stopped burning. The basement door was a normal door again. But the light bulb in the basement burned an evil red. Morty had no time to process what happened. He was grabbed from behind, forced into a seated position at the table covered in various people's blood. A nail was hammered into his right hand, pinning him into place.

Morty unleashed a yawp of pain.

Ted lingered over him, his hammer ready to drive another nail into his bleeding hand.

"Sit with me, Morty. Get comfortable. I have some questions I want to ask you."

Chapter Fifty-Four

This is insane!

Larson watched with gaping eyes as Barbie drove the speeding riding lawn mower through the back door. She crashed into the house, ripping the sides of the doorway into chunks of flying, detonating wood. He couldn't see what was happening inside, but he could sure as shit hear it. The mower's engine raged. Gasoline, blood and oil compelled the killing machine to destroy. The machine was plowing through bodies. Barbie popped another wheelie in the kitchen, raising the mower up from the floor and smashing it back down. The sets of blades crushed those under the machine, shearing bodies and hacking victims into wet pieces.

Janet hadn't moved since the riding mower's entry.

Larson grabbed her arm and pushed her forward.

"Last chance, lady! You want to die being scared, or do you want to be brave and save your own skin?"

Janet answered the detective by raising the hatchet and charging towards the house like it was towards a fleet of opposing soldiers.

The closer they drew to the house, the brighter the sky burned red. Things were coming to a head, the detective thought, and they were coming to a head fast. In the house, every light on the first floor was blood red. Larson imagined they were on the very boundary of Hell.

Shooting through the broken-up doorway, Larson shot twice left, then once right. What he hit was something indescribable. A woman made of blood vessels and raw meat reached out to throttle him. He shot out both of her eyes. The other shot missed the corpse, the dead man with a sizzling scalp named Chris Neilson. Janet stabbed three other corpses dead center in the face, driving the weapon down like a crushing sledgehammer.

"I'll back you up! Up the stairs. NOW, JANET! MOVE!"

Larson ducked, dodging a flying hunk of a thing's head that reminded him of a man wrapped in a bubble-wrap version of meat. Janet was slashing away with the hatchet as she reached the detective's position. The horrible creatures rampaging about the room were anatomical nightmares. Up the stairs Janet ran, and Larson emptied both guns fending off the collection of enemies coming after them. Larson was mid-stairway when Barbie plowed through the wave of corpses and monsters. She popped another wheelie, and the blades landed hard on five enemies at once, squashing, slicing and reducing them.

"GO-GO-GO!!!"

Janet was far ahead of Larson. The riding lawn mower's engine shook the house, rumbling on to destroy whatever cavorted in the living room and kitchen areas. Most of the second floor hallway was blackened from the fire earlier. Piles of dirt covered the floor: what had put out the fire from earlier. They passed Deborah's bedroom.

"In there now! They'll be right behind us."

Janet did as she was told and entered the second bedroom. Larson was fast behind her. They barricaded the entrance with a large drawer and a desk.

"What do we do now?"

Larson studied the stacks of unopened boxes meant for storage.

"Rip open these boxes. You see anything interesting, say something."

Together, detective and reporter turned the boxes inside out.

It wasn't long before they heard things stomp after them up the stairs.

Chapter Fifty-Five

The red light bulb glowed an ultraviolet red.

Two nails Ted had driven into Morty's hands.

The questions kept coming in unrelenting fashion.

"Who do you know could've killed Deborah?"

"Name more of your wife's friends."

"Neighbors, relatives, anybody!"

"Spit it out, Morty!"

Morty threw out names of Glenda's friends. Nobody who could've murdered a woman ten years ago. Not Deborah.

Ted took practice swings with the hammer into his palm to coax Morty into spilling more names and information. A small box of nails sat at Ted's end of the table. How many would Ted use on him? All of them?

"Is it time for another nail? The more blood they spill, the looser their lips become."

"You son of a bitch! What if nobody you dragged through that doorway knows who killed Deborah? What if you never find out who killed her?"

"Then I'm in the red forever. I can suffer in purgatory, but poor Deborah, I won't allow it! Give me more names. People you know. Anybody. *Now*."

Morty stammered, then clenched his teeth as a new jolt of pain spread from his hand to the rest of the body. Any slight movement of his hand was pain city.

"Why aren't you questioning the detective and the reporter?"

"Because I'm giving them every last chance to discover Deborah's killer. But you, you haven't uncovered anything. You're useless to me."

"I have uncovered things, Ted. Goddamn you. You're so upset your wife was taken away from you, have you considered how you took away both my daughter and my wife? You tarnished their memory. And for what? For your sadistic pleasure?

"Yeah, okay, *Ted*, I'll tell you what I know. Forgive me, Glenda. Forgive me, God.

You see, I was a quarterback for the high school football team, and—"

Fingers clasped onto a single nail, then the hammer swung down hard right below the knuckle of his pointer finger.

"YOU'RE STALLING."

A gushing steam of blood spurted from the nail's point of entry and hit Morty's eye. So piping hot, then so ice cold, it gave Morty a jolt, a solid reminder that this was his life on the line and nobody was going to save him.

Morty became a wordsmith.

"I'm not stalling. During one of my football games, I threw away a pass into the crowd. The football hit Glenda in the face. When I found out it was her, and that I'd broken her nose, I was secretly happy. I owed her an apology. I would ask her out to the prom, and I'd get laid. It wasn't until later that I fell in love with her. But I did fall in love with her. We rushed into marriage because I got Glenda pregnant. Later, I doubted my feelings for her, and questioned my life—"

Ted grabbed another nail from the pile and gave Morty a menacing stare.

"No, not another nail! Hear me out! You owe me that much. Ted, you lunatic, I'm trying to tell you something important. I thought you were insane—fuck it, you are insane!—but the things I've learned today reminded me of something."

Ted hovered next to him with the hammer raised.

"*Look, look!* I finally remember something. You're right. A few fucking nails, and shit, my memory's crystal fucking clear, isn't it? Listen, I wasn't sure if I loved my wife, and I was in a really dark place about my life, all of it, and, and, and you see, I read her diary one day. The passages were normal woman stuff. I was flipping randomly through it and would stop to read a few sentences. One passage bothered me so much I couldn't read it all. It talked about being high. Glenda had taken several pills she couldn't identify. Glenda questioned her perception of what happened, or if it even happened at all. She was hanging out with friends in an abandoned house. At one point, it was so late, everybody had either fallen asleep or passed out. But Glenda woke to somebody standing over her. They were taking Polaroid pictures of her asleep. The flash of the camera woke her. She said she knew who was taking the pictures, but she didn't know his name. He wasn't invited to the party. He was just a kid who lived in the neighborhood who was socially awkward. Glenda told the guy to fuck off, but she said the way he ogled the Polaroid picture afterwards and talked to it instead of her, it gave Glenda the creeps."

"Who was this man?"

"Like I told you, she didn't know his name. I don't know his name! Please, look, we can narrow it down. I'll help you. Just stop the killing. I can tell Detective Larson about this guy, and he can go to the station and find out who this guy is."

"Why didn't you tell him about this person sooner?"

"Because it was a diary entry. I'm only telling you what jumps out at me about Glenda. And the nails through my goddamn hand are making me really scour my memories for something to make you stop hurting me. I still don't know what it has to do with Deborah's death. I'm reaching for anything. I'm trying to help you. I'm cooperating, even if you are a psycho."

Ted's face bent into a snarl.

"You have more you can tell me. I'm going to dig a little deeper. *Another nail for you!*"

Chapter Fifty-Six

Larson was tearing through boxes, and Janet was searching their contents. Most of the boxes had baby items and old clothing. The two worked in a fury to uncover anything. They doubled their efforts when the hands pounded against the doorway. The wall on the left side of the bedroom was taking a beating from the other side. They were coming at them from all angles. The corpses and monsters were bemoaning their failure to save them from the red. The collective mob was releasing their anger by shattering wooden panels and punching holes into the second bedroom's door. So little time, and they were getting nowhere, Larson realized. He had to stall the monsters as long as he could.

He scanned the room and located an aluminum baseball bat. Any arm, hand and head that poked through the holes would get walloped. He was horrified to slam the meat of the bat across Hannah's gangrene melting face. Officer Wright's jaw. Jimmy Loomis's skull cap. The rest of them were so rotted and afflicted by damage, he was simply fighting masses of moving bones and flesh. Buying time. Swinging the bat. Calling out to Janet to hurry the fuck up.

"I've got nothing here! There's only shit in these boxes. They're not telling me anything. We shouldn't have gone in this room. This was a mistake!"

"Keep looking!"

Larson struck the bat against an eyeball. The pressure caused a rat to shoot free from the corpse's empty other eye socket. The detective stomped the rat dead with his heel.

Items were spread out across the floor. Janet kept rummaging through them to the point her fingertips were bleeding.

"*Nothing. There's nothing here!*"

"Don't stop looking. Think. Take everything you know about Deborah's death, and, and THINK."

Three swings of the bat. He was playing a desperate game of whack-a-mole. The prize: fetid chunks of meat and rancid blood.

Larson knew he had to encourage her, or his only help would crumble to the pressure of the situation. He talked out loud as he bashed anything that dared to try to widen the holes created in the walls and the door.

"Deborah died alone in her bedroom. Somebody used a golf club to kill her. That says the person entering the house didn't necessarily plan on murdering somebody. They didn't steal anything. They went straight into her room. They wanted something from her. Maybe it's not about an object. Maybe it's about Deborah herself."

Janet stopped searching the room.

"Do you hear that?"

Larson listened.

He heard the great churning of a powerful motor.

Barbie was coming upstairs.

Chapter Fifty-Seven

Morty shouted in agony. How many nails could be driven into one hand? When would Ted start driving nails into his other hand? Or maybe something worse? The room was so intensely red, he couldn't see anything else in the basement but red. Was there another torture device waiting for Morty? He had to keep talking and stall, stall, stall this psycho. Even if he spared himself a few minutes, the time to die would come. The inevitability shattered Morty's reasoning to scour his brain for clues, answers and ideas that might busy Ted. He was going to die here in terrible pain. Why prolong the interrogation?

"I'm done, Ted. I've watched the people I love die, then come back again, and I've had to kill some of them, and they won't die. How fucked up is that? You've taken everything away from me, so you might as well finish what you set out to do. If I'm going to spend purgatory with you, in this red fucking hell, I'm going to make it miserable for you. *I swear to God I will!*"

Ted wasn't expecting Morty to give up so soon. The lumbering man stood there perplexed. Morty saw his chance. An opportunity.

Morty reached out with his free hand and stole the hammer from Ted's hand. Two strikes, one to the balls, and one the head. Ted bent forward in reaction. The crack of skull against hammer was so rewarding. Ted fell onto all fours, crouched down in pain.

Morty started working the claw end of the hammer to free the nails driven into his hand.

Larson backed up from the bedroom wall just in time before the riding lawn mower smashed into the room. He stumbled backwards, tripping over the boxes strewn about the area. Janet screamed in horror, recoiling into the farthest corner of the room. The blades of the mower were chopping through books, clothing and tatters of wood. Barbie's face was devious. She couldn't hold herself back any longer.

The woman was going to kill them.

On his back, Larson couldn't move. The lawn mower edged towards him. Barbie leaned back in the seat to lift the lawn mower to perform a death wheelie. He had a very troublesome view of the three spinning mower blades and the gory messes caught up in them.

Barbie was going to drop it down right on him.

Watching this happen across the way, Janet had new reasons to scream.

Morty worked two nails from his hands. He was near the point of passing out from the excruciating pain. Ted was stirring from the floor. The man would be up on his feet and coming at him in no time. Another nail Morty worked free. Morty had to turn his head, suck in a deep breath and concentrate when he saw a piece of bone stick up below his knuckle. One more nail he worked free. Then another nail. He dug the claw end deeper and worked the tip of the nail higher up from his hand, and jerked it back. The new dose of pain was rewarded with freedom from the table.

Morty dodged Ted just in time. The man crashed into the table, breaking it in half. Ted growled, desperate to get back up and wrap his hands around Morty's throat.

Morty tightened his grip on the hammer and met Ted's next attack.

Hot reeking fans of air whipped against Larson's body. The lawn mower was going to tip over and land on him any moment. How long would he feel the pain? Should he close his eyes when the blades tore him up into pieces? Would that make his death any easier?

No time to dwell on death. Larson reached out to Janet. Janet could pull him away. Save him.

The problem was, she wasn't looking at him.

"Janet, help me! Help meeeeeeeeee!"

Janet still didn't avert her eyes. She held a scrapbook in both her hands. It had been thrown in her direction by the speed of the wind created by the mower's blades. Janet's face scrunched up into a puzzled expression. Then something flashed in those eyes.

Realization.

Morty drove the hammer right in between Ted's eyes. The connection broke his plastic eye gear. The attack only infuriated Ted. Both juggernaut-sized fists squeezed Morty's neck.

"Aaaaaaaaaack!"

"You're no better than the others. I won't waste time torturing your ass. I'll skip right to killing you."

Morty was dizzy and blinking dots out of his eyes. His fight was weakening before it'd even started. He dropped the hammer. He wouldn't be able to guide it anywhere because he couldn't see straight.

That was wrong.

Morty could see.

Everything was red.

"Oh my God, it makes sense. Detective, *Detective!*"

Janet screamed when she looked up from the picture in the scrapbook of Deborah at around high school age. She recognized the picture. Janet had seen it before.

Tommy Ranscombe.

Tommy Ranscombe.

Tommy Ranscombe.

The name repeated in her head.

The bumper sticker with the middle finger. Tommy Ranscombe who lived in the town of Kirkwood. Tommy Ranscombe who was known to hang out with the Brundage kids. Tommy Ranscombe who finally moved out of his parents' basement and into his own house. Janet helped her second cousin, along with other family members, to move Tommy's things into the house. Janet had seen the picture by accident in Tommy's wallet when he dropped it. Janet remembered how he stared it, then whispered an apology at the Polaroid picture.

Tommy Ranscombe.

Her second cousin.

Tommy was the one who killed Deborah.

Much too late to matter, she realized.

The riding lawn mower dropped down on top of Detective Larson.

Morty's body went limp in Ted's hands. He hit the floor as dead weight. Did Ted think he was already dead?

I'll lay here. I won't move. I'll play dead. Ted will go away. I'll wake up from this dream. None of this will have happened. Nobody will be dead.

Morty floated between consciousness and unconsciousness. His view was tilted upside down. He could see Ted's boots and his legs move up the stairs. Morty was leaving the basement.

He's going to bury me in the backyard. Or he'll dump me in a vacant lot. No, he's taking me to another torture chamber. One darker, and more evil and more insane than this entire house altogether. This will never end. He won't stop subjecting me to this insanity until I've found the answer to his wife's death.

Ted opened the basement door. He stomped into the living room. Ted avoided the wide pools of blood, the cops and corpses slaughtered on the floor. Morty imaged if someone tipped over a giant display of butchered meats, what would fall on the ground would resemble what was in the living room.

Morty noticed the lights in the room weren't red anymore.

They burned yellow.

I'm dead. He killed me, and I'm somewhere else I shouldn't be.

Ted's still here.

That's all I need to know.

I'm not safe.

Not with Ted here with me.

The stairway leading to the second floor was a mess. The steps were in broken tatters. Chopped into pieces. Ted chose his footholds carefully.

The walls upstairs were singed black from a fire. The hallway walls were nearly see-through, with the amount of damage they'd taken.

Ted carried him into the second bedroom.

Morty came alive with a start. He saw a pair of human legs untouched. From the hips up, there was only red spatter and hunks of pureed meat. He saw a slice of Detective Larson's face floating in a pool of blood. On the other side of the room was another pile of gory mess. He saw Janet's hair tangled up in a human spine and part of her lips and nose attached to a lamp on the bedside table. A female corpse was laying limp over a riding lawn mower in the corner.

His eyes moved away from the death. It wasn't long before he found a special message. On the closet door, written about six inches off the ground, near where Janet's remains were located, were words written in blood: TOMMY RANSCOMBE.

Chapter Fifty-Eight

The basement was a sacred place. That's where he kept his women. They were there when he left the house, or when he was working, driving his rig across the country for Grober Trucking. A normal haul could take him away from home a week, maybe longer. But no need to worry. The women weren't going anywhere. They would be right where he left them. They were beautiful. Irreplaceable. His lovelies.

There he sat on his leather couch playing Credence Clearwater Revival on vinyl, sipping on a bottle of whiskey (it still took him liquid courage to be in the company of so many wonderful women). He slugged back a mouthful of twelve-dollar-a-bottle sour mash and steadied his nerves.

Guidance counselor Mrs. Greeves said he was a slow learner. He was socially maladjusted. He had a slight learning disability, but with hard work, he could overcome those limitations. "*They're only hurdles, Tommy. I know you're a good boy. As long as you keep trying, it's going to keep on getting better.*"

No matter how many years passed, his skin still burned when people talked to him. It was like a caught feeling. Blushing to the tenth power. He had short conversations, or cut them short, just for that uncomfortable sensation to end. He'd do anything to numb or erase that feeling altogether.

Alcohol helped. Drugs helped even more. Ryan Brundage, his next-door neighbor (though next-door was a mile's distance; his folks lived out in the middle of nowhere, Kirkwood, Virginia), invited him over to their special weekend parties. Louie Brundage gave Tommy drugs and booze at a higher price than Ryan's real friends. Tommy knew he was a charity case. A pity party pal. Tommy didn't care. As long as that feeling of unease went away, Tommy was happy. Charge him what they wanted. Fuck it.

The parties at Ryan Brundage's house, that's how Tommy got started collecting his ladies. It's how the basement became so full of his hot delicious babes. Years and years of work, and he was still building up his pieces of ass.

Ryan and Louie Brundage would buy hookers when they couldn't get their female friends to come over. Cheap hookers. Bottom of the barrel bitches. *They aren't pretty,* Louie Brundage often said, *but they always show you their parts. And they let you play with them too. You want to play with them, Tommy? I'll buy. On me. On the house. What do you say, Tommy? Let's get your dick wet. Huh, Tommy? How about it? Be a man. Give her the meat real good.*

Tommy said no. Drugs and booze couldn't quell that painful blush that was more than a blush. That awkward feeling made him feel like his insides were on fire and he could puke. No, he couldn't touch the girls. But he stood in the same room with Ryan and his friends and they'd take turns with the women. He could watch. That was safe. He could enjoy that just fine.

Then one day, while Louie was sitting on the couch with Glenda Saggs sitting on his dick, Louie said to Tommy, *Take a picture, it'll last longer.*

Take a picture.

It will last longer.

Those words were gold. Carve them into stone.

Tommy wasn't very sociable. His grades weren't high. He wasn't handsome. He wasn't going to marry a woman, fall in love or lose his virginity, but one thing you *could* say about Tommy, he was sneaky. Even with a bulky Polaroid camera, he could flash a picture, and sometimes, if he was real nice and careful, the women wouldn't notice.

The Polaroid camera allowed him to get a picture of a woman instantly. Sometimes it was a woman walking by him on the street. But most of the time, he snapped them through people's windows at night. Women eating dinner. Women on the toilet. Women who were changing their clothes, and their curtains weren't quite closed all the way. Other times, he'd pay hookers to pose and take pictures of them. He'd ask them to spread their legs wide. Smoke a cigarette for him. Finger themselves. He asked them to smile. That always confused the dumb fucking whores. *Don't ask me why I want you to smile! Just do it, bitch! Smile, you dumb whore. I'm paying you, so come on! Smile, bitch.*

Tommy became braver and bolder as he accumulated hundreds, *no, a thousand!* Polaroid photos. He taped them up to his basement wall and admired them. Tommy was working up the courage to take even bolder and wilder pictures. Ones that took risk to get. He could get caught. Someone could spot him, and he'd suffer those wicked painful flashes under his skin. *Oh, the pain! Don't see me! Don't talk to me! Just let me do what I want to and leave me alone!*

It was his first time trying this new tactic. The first night, Tommy drove at night and parked outside of a house when he noticed the husband driving up the street to the bar Side Pockets. The woman was all alone in the house. He could sneak into the house, take a picture of her without her even knowing he was inside with her, and he'd be out of there, nobody the wiser. He'd tape the lovely to his wall, fawn over her and honor her.

The moment Tommy stepped into the back door, he heard the shower running. The woman was taking a shower. She couldn't hear him. It was the perfect cover. He'd wait for her to go into her room, and he'd flash a picture, and run like hell.

No, no, no, that wouldn't work. She'd hear the camera click. She'd see the flash. And when she realized there was somebody in the house, she'd scream. The police would find him and take him away.

But if he knocked her out, that wouldn't be an issue. He wouldn't kill her. Only knock her out. He could take her clothes off, pose her any way he wanted, and he'd take his pictures (several, if he was going to work that hard for his lady!), and off he'd go free and clear.

That's exactly what he did. Tommy waited for the woman to leave the bathroom. She walked right into her room. By the time he got there, he realized he had nothing to knock her out with, so he grabbed a nine iron from the bag of golf clubs nearby. The woman had her back turned. She heard him move when the floor creaked. No worries. He whacked her a good one to the head. Not enough to kill her, no. She was unconscious, and sure, she was bleeding from the back of the head, but dead, no way. Of course not. He wouldn't kill her. Not for a picture. That would be stupid.

He wasn't a sicko. Once he saw that blood, he realized he couldn't use the pictures. Her head kept oozing red. It wasn't pretty at all. He was getting pissed because he was going to have to leave her house without a good picture. This had been a fucking waste of time.

Then Tommy looked to her bed. The scrapbook was open to a page. It was this woman's prom picture. There were dozens of them in the scrapbook. Who would miss the one? Tommy could cut out the bozo standing in the picture with her. It was his picture to own now. He walked out of the house a happy man. The woman would be okay. She'd wake up and clean her head wound and everything would be just fine. No big deal.

He wiped clean the nine iron of fingerprints before leaving. He didn't want anybody to know he was ever here. If they knew what Tommy did in his basement to burn the spare hours between work and free time, they would judge him. That burning feeling wouldn't end. The rest of his life, that shameful burning would continue on like a morbid eternal flame. Fuck that. A man's private life was his own business.

Now, Tommy got up from the couch to change out his vinyl records. He was now listening to Ted Nugent. He carried his sour mash bottle and scanned the wall of pictures of women. They literally covered the wall. Those he couldn't fit on the wall, he put in a scrapbook.

His eyes fell on one picture.

Deborah's.

Tommy only knew her name because it said *Deborah and Steve's Prom Night* on the back of the picture.

He had heard in the news way back when that Deborah had indeed died from massive head trauma. That was so many years ago. He didn't mean to kill her. It was an accident. Not murder. An accident, so stop thinking about it.

Tommy placed two fingers on Deborah's picture.

"*I'm so, so sorry.*"

Tommy swigged hard from the bottle.

"If it's any consolation, you are so beautiful."

The light bulb in the room flickered out.

"Shit."

Then it came back on.

"*Oh goddamn!*"

The room was blood red. Tommy was assaulted by the smell of burning things. The room was as hot as the inside of a furnace. Tommy dropped his bottle of sour mash and ran for the stairs leading up to the first floor. When he looked up, the doorway was burning red. Blinded by the heat, Tommy was forced back into the basement.

Somebody grabbed his arm.

Tommy was dragged across the room.

"*Who are you? What are you doing here? Wait, I can explain what's on the walls if you'd give me a second, please!*"

Two arms forced Tommy into a seated position. He reeled at the large table, not his table, because he'd never seen this table before! It was gouged with holes, scratches and mysterious faded orange-brown stains.

Before Tommy comprehended anything else, there it was, a nail hammered in the middle of his hand.

When Tommy looked up at the tall man doing this to him, his peals of horror reached ear-blasting peaks.

"Now, Tommy, let's talk about how you killed my wife."

–

Epilogue

Yes, this was his house again as it should be, but no, Morty would never sleep under its roof again. He wanted nothing to do with the property or the new memories created within its walls. Morty did one last thing before leaving his house for the very last time. He called the police. They didn't answer. The line was dead. He tried his cell phone, and he got no bars. That was impossible, being in town. He should've got a signal nice and clear. It didn't take Morty very long to understand why the phones didn't work.

The night sky owned shades of blood red. The streetlight shed crimson onto the street. He heard screams coming from down the block. From everywhere. Two fast-moving vehicles were racing after each other for unknown reasons. Both cars were firing guns at each other. Neighbors were standing outside of their houses asking each other what the hell was happening. People asked Morty if he was okay. Morty forgot he was covered in blood from top to bottom. His hand was leaking blood. He didn't feel the pain. He was numb. His body either accepted the sensation or didn't care one way or the other. Morty absorbed the pain like he was taking a punishment he deserved. Cheyenne and Glenda were dead. Bruce, his best friend, was also slain. Everything he lived for was gone.

Morty noticed rows of police cars were unmanned outside of his house. They were empty of officers or anybody that could help. Where they had gone, he didn't know, nor did he care to investigate. Morty wanted away from his house right now.

He approached one of the empty police cars on the block and noticed the keys were still in the ignition. Morty turned on the engine and drove.

He knew exactly where he was going.

Driving past Side Pockets, Morty saw there were people inside the bar barricaded in behind boarded up windows. He only saw a group of four persons through a small opening in the front window. He also noticed the corpse standing behind one of them with a knife pressed to her throat.

At Valley View Heights Church down the way, people were huddled together inside the property. The people inside, including Preacher Masterson, stared out onto the front lawn at the corpses standing around the property looking in at them.

The lights in the church suddenly flickered to red.

The people inside screamed.

The corpses approached the church.

Morty knew what they wanted.

There was nothing he could do for them.

Hitting the highway, Morty picked up speed fast. There was nobody in sight until he was approaching the exit he was going to take.

Two people, a man and woman, were running away from a Cadillac chasing after them. The headlights were deadly crimson beams. The driver, the cackling corpse of a mother and her two dead children in the back, were making fast progress after their victims.

There was nothing he could do.

Morty took the exit for Hillsdale Lake.

The dirt road leading to Hillsdale Lake was surrounded by dense woods. Those woods were active with moving flashlight beams the color of burning cherry. Morty distinguished people running or hiding throughout the woods, as he did corpses who taunted and appeared and reappeared out of thin air. The sounds of delight crashed headfirst against the screams of genuine terror.

Morty understood what was happening. He also knew where he was going, and he wasn't going to stop until he got there. That destination was the lake itself. He parked in front of it, turned off the headlights and eyed the pump action 12 gauge left in the passenger side window.

He picked the shotgun up and placed the firing end against his chin.

Apologies were all he had to offer the departed. He thought about Glenda. How he would've loved her no matter how dark or seedy her past was, or why she felt the need to keep secrets from him. Love was love, and his heart wouldn't change its mind. Poor Cheyenne, her children wouldn't have a mother. Her husband would be without a wife.

Morty rested his finger on the trigger. All he had to do was pull it back. He knew when he died, there would be no mystery. He killed himself. Nobody would have to solve a complicated murder if he came back to life to haunt the living. He could rest in peace. There would be no burning doorways, or red purgatories or access denied into Heaven or Hell. Morty would be going straight to where he belonged. He would haunt nobody in death. Death would be peace. Death would be permanent. Death would transpire as it should.

He closed his eyes and kept them shut.

Morty edged back the trigger.

Then he said goodbye to the world.

Red flashed. All he could see was the brilliant burst of neon red. Then he heard a long scream: "*Help me, please, help me! Oh my God!*" Morty opened his eyes and faced the lake. His eyes went small against the powerful glare of the red coming from the water's surface. Then two fists beat against the window of the police car. The woman screaming opened the car door and begged Morty to come and help her.

She didn't notice how he came so close to blowing off his own head. The woman was in her twenties with claw marks going down her shoulders to the meat of her forearms. The side of her blonde hair was thick with somebody else's blood. Those eyes had seen terror and death, and more was on its way.

"Please, sir, don't leave me alone. They killed my boyfriend, and they killed our friends. We were camping in the woods, and Jesus, I left my tent, and there was this dead guy who kept telling us how he was killed fifteen years ago. He wanted us, I, I don't know, I think he wanted us to solve his murder. But he's dead. He's dead!

"How can this be happening? It's weird. This dead man, he carried this lantern that burned red. I swear to God it was blood red! He's after me. He's coming. I can see the light from his lantern coming closer. You can't let him kill me. Please, don't leave me alone! Help me. I'm begging you. Drive me out of here. Save me."

Morty saw a moving light in the woods come closer to the lake. When the light moved closer, the lake burned an even brighter red.

"He died here," Morty said. "The man who's after you, I mean."

"Who cares? Please, just drive me out of here."

Morty held onto the shotgun and stepped out of the car.

"If you're going to survive this, we're going to have to solve his murder."

"What the hell are you saying? Drive me out of here now. It's not safe here."

"Listen, lady. I know things. I've been through this already. You've been chosen to solve this dead guy's murder. Whoever's after you won't leave you alone until you're either dead or his killer is revealed. It's insane, but so is a burning red lake and walking dead people."

The woman stared at Morty, dumbfounded.

The corpse carrying the lantern was close enough to be seen.

Morty had a lot of things to explain to this woman.

The night was far from over.

At least he had a shotgun.

About the Author

Alan Spencer has published nearly thirty books in the horror genre. His latest releases include *B-Movie War*, *Lampreys*, and *Demon Mansion*. He enjoys trash cinema. Some of his favorite movies are *Nail Gun Massacre*, *Sledgehammer*, *Day of the Dead*, *Night of the Zombies*, *Burial Ground*, and *Zombie 2*. *The Doorway* will be his sixth novel with Samhain Publishing. The author loves e-mails, so drop him a line at: alanspencer26@hotmail.com.

War is hell when the enemy is an army of B-movie monsters!

B-Movie War
© *2014 Alan Spencer*

A possessed movie reel is played at a theatre in New Jersey, releasing B-movie icon Mr. Ratchet into our world. Mr. Ratchet plans to play his film, *The Final Flesh*, at theaters across the planet with the help of villains dredged up from the most vile and offensive horror movies ever made. Movie monsters made real.

Once *The Final Flesh* makes its midnight premiere, it's the people vs. B-movie terror. Only a theatre manager, a man with a serious anger problem, and a B-movie aficionado can prevent full-scale war from annihilating everybody on earth. Can the rag tag team come up with a plan to save the world, or will everybody be sent packing straight to hell? Be warned, this war will be *epic*!

Enjoy the following excerpt for B-Movie War:

Plan B was real. The package arrived on Jules Baxter's desk only days after the previous monster attack in Chicago had ceased. This package would serve as the catalyst to a global scale war. Scrawled in red ink on the front were wild slash marks spelling out Jules's name and the business address for The Odyssey Theatre. Jules knew it wasn't a bill because there was no return address. Holding the package in his hands, judging by the weight and the way the object moved inside, Jules knew what it contained from prior experience. Film reels were shipped here by the batch regularly, but this package was much smaller. Tearing it open, he uncovered a single film reel. It wasn't enough for a complete film. That made the item all the more interesting.

Jules couldn't wait to view it.

The Odyssey Theatre would be permanently closed down in a matter of months, or whenever the bill collectors decided to spring their trap and take over his property. Since his wife, Darlene, died of breast cancer two years ago, the heart and soul of the place died with her. His ambition to run a quality establishment had been erased after eleven successful years of business. But all of his troubles were forgotten by this mysterious short reel.

What could be inside, Jules kept thinking. *Oh, I bet it's something so cool. Vintage cool.* Jules decided to give himself a special showing of the mystery reel after hours. The afternoon and evening went by agonizingly slow, but it was worth the wait. The staff had clocked out and were off the premises. Jules, a sixty year old overweight man, forgot about his financial failures and loneliness and enjoyed buttered popcorn and sat in the middle of Theatre 4 for his private showing. He had to set up the reel himself, having to hurry from the projection booth to find his seat so he wouldn't miss a single second. Watching in anticipation, a random scene from the film *Morgue Vampire Tramps Find Temptation at the Funeral Home* played out on the large screen. The footage was grainy. The print damaged by age. It didn't tarnish the experience. Jules watched with wide eyes and a big smile.

Footage of a graveyard surrounded in thick fog played out for five minutes. Nothing happened: no new scene, actors, or dialogue. Only the churning of fog. The soundtrack was creepy chamber music. The music got louder, and before the first scene panned out, a beam of bright white light streaked down the side aisle of the theatre. Where the beam stopped, the woman materialized. She was dressed in a red usher's uniform. She pointed her flashlight and held the beam on Jules.

In the sweetest voice she asked, "Why are you watching the movie all alone, honey?"

Jules lost his composure. Warm tears edged down his face. He rushed to touch her, to smell her hair, to reassure himself she was real. She was young again, in her twenties, with curvy hips, long black hair and a soft face. She was dolled up with ruby red lipstick and blue eye shadow. It was Darlene, or as Jules lovingly called her, "Darling."

It was Jules's wife.

"Darling," came a joyful gasp from Jules. "It's really you."

His wife drew him in for a long embrace. How Jules needed her touch. That one of a kind feeling. One he could never have again, he believed, until tonight.

Darlene drew him in for a kiss. They tore each other's clothes off in a wild display of passion. As they made love against one of the seats, the collection of vampire tramps, the naked black reptilian creatures with leathery wings, exited the theatre unseen. They flew high into the night. There was much work to be done.

The dead had failed to live up to their full potential in the previous attacks against the living in both Kansas and Chicago. Playing the ghost-possessed movie reels and unleashing B-movie villains on unsuspecting mankind wasn't enough. They needed a solid plan. Darlene, in the body of the vampire from *Morgue Vampire Tramps Find Temptation at the Funeral Hall*, stood in the kitchen of the Langley household. She left Jules at the theatre, after giving him the fucking of a lifetime. He was still passed out in the theatre, the sad, sad man. Jules would be hers to control. And how she'd use him in the coming months.

Darlene had ripped the heads off of Mr. and Mrs. Langley, a retired couple, and placed their bleeding heads on two stovetop coils in the kitchen. Decapitating calmed Darlene. Shedding blood reminded her their plan to kill every last living person in the universe would succeed this time. The other vampire tramps, the five of them, waited in the living room for Darlene's next instructions. The group craved to slaughter everybody in sight, but if they did that now, somebody would stop them again like the other two times.

So what to do this time?

They needed a plan for war.

Full-scale style.

Every living person would die and join the dead in their eternal suffering. But Darlene couldn't perpetrate this on her own. She clutched a set of reels in her hands. They were stolen from Jules's private collection from his house two blocks from the Langleys'. On the steel canister label, it read *Mr. Ratchet's Morbid Theatre of Death*. Darlene asked the vampires to set up the film projector in the living room, which was also stolen from Jules's house, and they played the first reel. If Mr. Ratchet couldn't help her, Darlene wasn't sure what to do. But if she was correct about this movie and its potential, the solution to her problems was Mr. Ratchet himself.

Five minutes into the feature, fog unrolled from the hallways of the Langley household. The foundation creaked, as if the whole house could collapse at any moment. Blood trickled down the walls, gushing in wicked torrents. The sound of screams echoed from beyond the afterlife from upstairs and down. Boiling water from cauldrons stirring poisons and curses, and on top of that, crypts being opened and closed, of dead feet pattering the floor, of infernal moans of pain and pleasure. The house was active with morbid emanations.

Then the walls stopped bleeding. The carpet tore in large sections. Chunks of wood exploded. From the floor sprouted movie projector after movie projector, spinning with movie reels. Twenty different projectors were going at once. From the hallway, out of the thick fog, arrived Mr. Ratchet. He was a white haired old man in a cheap silver suit, big red bow tie, fancy black shoes and the biggest smile.

Mr. Ratchet greeted the vampires. "Welcome to my morbid theatre of death, ladies."

SAMHAIN
PUBLISHING

It's all about the story...

Romance

HORROR

Retro
ROMANCE

www.samhainpublishing.com